In Heaven and In Earth

By David Foster

For James & Edward

Acknowledgements

Thanks to Cristina for her love and support as always, and Helen for her incisive comments.

Paris, May 1968

A blanket of grey had covered the city for days but had now been lifted away; sunlight pierced the clouds to reveal a sky of pale blue, painting her world in fresh colours.

She was leaning against the window, staring out through melancholy eyes, looking without really seeing. She ached to be outside, letting her face and body feel the heat of the sun, filling her lungs with reviving air. Closing her eyes, she could see herself running naked across the grass, could feel the warmth soothing her body, the breeze brushing her hair, each blade of grass caressing the soles of her feet.

She opened her eyes again and turned her gaze back into the room. The clock on the far wall seemed to have stopped, it was moving so slowly. The lecture would finish soon, thank God.

She saw for the first time that the room was full. These were troubled days in Paris, with students protesting every day and the authorities threatening to close down the university; right now students had other priorities than lectures.

Not only the students; the protests were escalating into a civil war; most of the workers of Paris were out, despite the intervention of President de Gaulle and the unions.

There was another demonstration planned for this evening. Monique thought that 1968 would turn out to be an interesting year.

London, January 2010

The stadium suddenly erupted, angry expletives bursting into the air above the crowd around him, like fireworks on the fourth of July.

Detective Inspector Sam Cooper leant back in his seat, closing his eyes and grimacing as a silent oath formed on his lips.

The opposition had just kicked the football into the back of the net for the fourth time that afternoon.

Not a good start to the New Year.

Cold, penetrating gusts of wind had been blowing a fine mist of rain into every corner of the packed stadium all afternoon, swirling about every seat, ensuring no-one escaped its attentions, but now the rain was growing into a steady downpour. As he breathed into his hands to relieve his fingers, numb with cold, he felt another drop of cold water run down his already sodden back. For him that was enough. He turned to look at his friend sitting next to him, huddled inside a heavy fleece against the cold and damp air, his face white and lips blue.

"I'm sorry Mark. I've seen enough of this shower for one day" he said. "Are you coming?"

"No, I'll see it through to the bitter end. I'll let you know this evening if you missed anything."

Cooper smiled.

"I don't think I'll miss anything I want to see. I'll see you later, then."

He stood up and stamped his feet to help the blood flow before making his way down several flights of stairs towards the exit, joining as he did so the steadily growing stream of supporters who had taken the same view and were heading for the various parts of London they called home.

Ten minutes and a little jostling later he was on his way home, standing in the centre of a crowded bus, narrowly avoiding an elbow in his eye as an overly tall man turned the pages of a newspaper. Inside it was hot; the clothing of those around him smelt damp, and the bus windows were misted over. Passengers squeezed their way past him at each stop as the bus edged its way through the packed streets.

He was never comfortable with crowds; at that moment he wondered why on earth he put himself through this week after week, but he knew he'd be back there soon, going through that again.

"Silly sod that I am" he muttered to himself.

He eventually managed to get a seat on the bus, next to a headphone wearing girl, clearly oblivious to the base sounding in his ear. Better than standing, he thought.

With the fading light outside he had some difficulty making out how far the bus had travelled along its route. He put his face to the window occasionally to make sure, like a child peering into a toy shop.

In the city centre the bus slowed to a crawl as shoppers hunting for New Year bargains overflowed into the road. The bus eventually escaped the crowds and Cooper recognised the streets closer to home.

Just a few stops away from his apartment his mobile phone vibrated; it was on silent as was his habit. He listened carefully, saying only "O.K." occasionally in a quiet voice, ending with "I'll be there as soon as I can."

Getting off the bus a few minutes later he walked the short distance to his apartment, his thoughts preoccupied with what he had just been told, oblivious to the rain now pouring from the sky.

"Is that you, Sam? I'm just getting ready" his girlfriend called from behind the bathroom door as he walked in.

"Sorry, Carol. Something's come up. I'm going straight out again. I'll need the car. Get a taxi there and I'll join you as soon as I can."

"Oh you're bloody joking, Sam, we're supposed to be having dinner with Mark and Tricia. They've invited another couple there as well, you know. I didn't plan to be alone on New Year's Day."

Her voice was raised enough to show her displeasure.

He made no comment; he had been expecting that. It wasn't the first time she had been frustrated with him. Saying nothing more he went into the larger of the two bedrooms of their small flat, hurriedly changed into some dry clothes and then picked up his wax jacket, wellingtons and a small bag he kept ready for such situations.

He thought of spending a minute or two trying to explain to Carol what he was going to do, but decided it would only make matters worse. The door banged shut behind him as he hurried down to his car at the front of the building. He edged the vehicle slowly along the crowded London streets, the queues of traffic always seeming longer in wet weather, towards the open spaces of Hampstead Heath.

Twenty minutes later his car was parked as close to the heath as he could get it, by two marked police cars, and he was standing under the shelter of his umbrella pulling on his wellingtons, squinting to protect his eyes from the rain blown everywhere by the squally wind. More drops found their way down his neck as he did so, and he cursed the weather again.

Looking up the path through the trees to the grassy slopes of the heath, he could see the bright yellow jackets of four uniformed constables standing out in the gathering gloom; his recently appointed assistant, Detective Constable Robinson, was waiting with them.

Cooper hadn't yet made up his mind about Mike Robinson. He had transferred to work for him two months earlier and had arrived with a health warning. "Competent, but with a reputation as a bully, especially towards women," the chief had commented, clearly not convinced Robinson had a long term career in front of him. He had already made a joke about one WPC that Cooper told him was out of order. Cooper also thought his private life was a disaster waiting to happen; he talked incessantly about his nights out clubbing, and at least once he'd been hung-over in the morning. On the other hand he did seem to be quick at working out priorities in a case and he asked intelligent questions.

Cooper thought it would be interesting to see how he would cope with a major investigation.

He cast his eye around the rapidly darkening heath as he strode up the track that was half path, half stream, wary of losing his footing on the stones, although his trusty old wellingtons usually held firm on slippery ground. The drops of rain were hammering against the large golf umbrella he held firmly in his hands, trying to stop it taking off in the wind.

The last time he had walked along that path it had been the height of summer. As far as he could recall it ran farther up the heath before re-joining the highway closer to the village. A picture came into his head; it had seemed so pleasant then, the hot, late summer afternoon when he and Carol had explored the area. They had been pleased to find some shade and he had fallen asleep, lying under a tree, listening to the call of the swallows, whilst Carol had been reading. The view of the London skyline from the top of the hill; how beautiful and impressive it had all looked.

He had only just moved to this role then; the challenges were great but he was excited at the prospect. Carol had been excited too; she had soon become less enthusiastic though. He sighed. Definitely not a good start to the New Year.

He ducked underneath a waist high line of blue police tape and scrambled off the path and up the grassy slope, the branches of the trees behind him creaking protests as they swayed in the wind.

He had to raise his voice to make himself heard above the weather.

"Move that tape farther down the path. Put it as close to the road as you can get it, near where I parked my car. We'll start having sightseers once word gets out that we're here, even in this weather, so the farther down the path, the better."

One of the constables started down the hill to move the tape, the others moving to guard the various paths through the area. He followed Robinson up the wet grassy bank in amongst the trees and bushes, his feet slipping several times as he did so.

"It's here, sir" Robinson said, as he shone his torch onto the saturated, leaf covered grass.

The beam of light fell onto what appeared at first glance to be a weathered, half-buried root or stick.

Cooper crouched down to take a closer look at the unmistakable white of bones protruding slightly from the muddy soil. He used his pen to carefully prod around them.

"Who found this, and when?"

"It was discovered by an elderly lady, a Mrs Diana Freedman, walking her dog about an hour ago. The constables here were dispatched straight after her call. After they had a look they rang in and were told to tape off the area until we got here. The lady then went back home, of course. She lives just across the road, apparently. They told me they offered to take her home but she insisted on walking home herself, although she seemed a bit shaken as you can imagine."

Cooper continued to examine the ground, heavy rain drops splattering the disturbed soil, small streams of water cascading down the slope. That there was a body underneath he was sure; how long had it been there, and who it was, was another question.

"Get onto the station, will you. Tell them to arrange for forensics to take a look at this first light tomorrow morning to see what's buried here. There isn't much we can do this evening; I'll go over the road and speak to the woman now, to hear what she says. Make sure someone's keeping watch over the site until the morning."

They started back down to the slope towards his car; one of the constables was sheltering under a tree as they approached. Cooper didn't blame him; he pretended not to notice.

"How was the football, sir?" Robinson asked him as they reached the road.

"Bloody awful. They were rubbish today. I got wet through as well."

It was now almost completely dark. Cooper left him to finalise the arrangements and drove the short distance to where Diana Freedman lived. He parked on the driveway of a large Edwardian house, set well back from the road in extensive gardens. He walked down the driveway, admiring the house as he did so. He wondered what you had to do to afford a house like this.

He half expected a butler to open the door as he rang the bell, but it opened to reveal a short, elderly lady with white hair, accompanied by a small dog whom she introduced as Buster. He showed her his ID card.

"I'm sorry to disturb you, ma'am, but I would like a word if I may about your phone call earlier this evening."

"Yes of course, inspector. I was expecting someone to call. Do come in out of the rain."

He stepped inside and she led him across a large hallway, past a magnificent, wide oak staircase and a tall, antique grandfather clock which was striking the half hour, through into the kitchen where she invited him to leave his dripping coat. He also pulled off his wellingtons, with a little difficulty, although she did not ask. She then showed him into her drawing room, the dog pattering along behind them all the while, his claws sounding on the parquet floor. Cooper could feel his feet slip slightly as his socks glided across the polished wood.

"You are not from London by your accent, inspector."

"No, ma'am, I'm from the North West originally."

"Where exactly?"

"A town close to Manchester"

"Ah, Manchester, my daughter went to university there. I used to love exploring the countryside in the area, especially over in Derbyshire. Please wait in here inspector whilst I make some tea. Make yourself at home."

She went back into the kitchen. Buster, a black spaniel whose greying hairs betrayed the fact he was no longer young, stayed with him. After being made a fuss of for a minute or so the dog was content and lay down on the rug in front of the warm fire of wooden logs, soon falling asleep.

Cooper found himself in a very comfortable if old-fashioned drawing room. He looked around as he waited, enjoying the warmth of the fire and the scent of the wood smoke filling the room. He looked closely at a collection of porcelain figures in a glass cabinet and various oil paintings, mainly of marine scenes, covering one wall. One was a harbour scene he particularly liked the look of; whether they were originals or not he didn't know, but he would have liked to have any one of them. He also liked a large carpet, covering most of the floor, and was pleased he had decided to leave his wellingtons in the kitchen. He had bought a considerably smaller carpet on a holiday to Istanbul once and it had not been cheap. Cooper then walked to a large, relatively modern walnut desk covered in papers to look through the window to the back. He could just make out the rear garden in the lights from the houses nearby, with its neatly trimmed grass, extensive borders of bushes and some kind of building, he suspected a summer house, underneath the trees at the rear. He thought of the weed-ridden flower box outside his flat window as he did so, with some guilt and more than a little envy.

Rain drops were running down the glass as he admired the garden although he could barely hear anything; only the sound of the slow, rhythmic tick of the grandfather clock from the hallway and the occasional crack from one of the burning wooden logs broke the silence.

The contrast between the scene he had left behind on the heath and the tranquillity of this home could not have been greater.

He turned away from the window as the lady returned with a tray of tea and biscuits.

"Do sit down, inspector" she insisted.

Cooper did as he was told. As he sat down he was looking at the plate of biscuits, wondering whether chocolate was safe but, deciding reluctantly that it would probably melt on his fingers, he chose a plain biscuit instead.

The dog, realising a possible treat was in store, trotted up to sit beside him. He rewarded him with a piece of the biscuit he had just taken.

"This is a lovely house."

Diana smiled at him.

"I'm glad you like it, inspector. I've lived here for almost fifty years and I have many happy memories here. My daughter Amanda was born here. Sadly I live alone now since my husband succumbed to cancer last year. Amanda left home some fifteen years ago when she married, and although she moved back to live here for a few months after she split from her husband, it was only until she found herself another apartment. It's too large for me now. I keep thinking I should sell and move to something smaller, but I have so many memories here, and so many things, including those paintings; my husband bought them when we were first married. I don't know how people downsize. I have walked all around the house, trying to imagine what I could get rid of to move to a smaller place, but how would I do without my things? And Buster here would miss the garden dreadfully. Do take another biscuit, inspector."

Cooper decided he may as well; he didn't suppose this would be a short conversation, and he was feeling hungry.

"I don't blame you for wanting to stay here. I certainly would. Would you mind telling me about your walk on the heath a little earlier, and how you came to make the phone call?"

"Of course; as Buster and I are here alone these days, I take him out for a walk twice a day, every day, unless Amanda is here. He isn't as young as he was, of course, but I still think he needs to get out and exercise. My husband used to do it until six months or so before he died when he wasn't able to walk well; since then it's been my job. In the mornings Buster and I often walk into the village and I usually pick up a few things from the shops. In the afternoons we walk across the Heath. We have our routine, the dog and I, and we normally walk the same route every day, which is up the path to Parliament Hill, and then back again. Buster is off the leash of course as he is fond of running off. He still likes to think he can scamper around as much as he did when he was young, but these days he tires easily. I think he would relish catching a rabbit, but he's never managed it yet, so I don't suppose he ever will."

Diana looked at Buster who had returned to his spot in front of the fire and was sleeping soundly.

"Poor old boy" she said quietly, "I do hope you'll be with me for a while yet."

Cooper let her be quiet for a moment.

"I'm sorry, inspector" she continued, "he means a lot to me now. Anyway, this morning the weather was absolutely dreadful, as you will know. We didn't take our usual morning walk, it was raining so heavily. By mid afternoon Buster was getting very fidgety and, as the weather was showing no signs of improvement, I donned my raincoat and scarf and we ventured out onto the heath. Because the weather was so foul, with dreadfully heavy rain, I decided to curtail our usual walk and take the shorter path. That one runs a little way into the heath but then leads back to the road after a short distance. Buster seemed to understand where I wanted to go so I let him off the leash as I usually do. He's fairly good, he normally comes to me as soon as I call. As I made my way up the path he scampered off up the slope in amongst the trees and bushes. After a few moments I heard him barking at something. I wondered if he had perhaps seen a rabbit, although I thought it unlikely he had actually caught one at last. I called to him several times and could just see where he was but he stood his ground, barking incessantly. He refused to budge, no matter how I called. I was getting wet so in the end I had little choice but to scramble as best I could up the slope to get him. I was jolly cross I can tell you. I intended to put the leash onto him and walk him home before we were too drenched."

Diana paused, taking a sip of tea. He nodded to encourage her to continue.

"He hadn't gone too far, thankfully. He was standing by a small bush, scratching and sniffing at the ground, and continuing to bark loudly. I always carry a small torch with me at this time of the year when we are on the heath. I wanted to see what all the fuss was about so I shone the torch down trying to see. I thought at first it was just the root of a tree, but then I looked closely and realised that it was a bone, protruding slightly from the mud. For a moment I thought it was a dead animal of some kind, but as I inspected it more closely I realised I could see the bones of a hand, a human hand. I was so shocked that I'm afraid I screamed out. Then I called the police."

* * * * *

Cooper arrived at his friends' dinner party later that evening, just as desert was being served.

"I apologise for being late" he said to the hosts and the other two guests who stood to greet him as he walked in; Carol looked at him briefly but stayed seated, saying nothing.

He decided to ignore her, although he thought she was being ridiculous in front of their friends.

"I had a call to go up to Hampstead Heath where some of my officers were waiting for me. Do please continue; don't let me interrupt what looks like a fantastic dessert."

"Anything you can tell us about?" Mark asked.

"Let's just say it was very wet and muddy, and we're going to have to have a better look at something tomorrow in daylight. I'd rather not say more at the moment."

Mark's wife Tricia looked at him sympathetically.

"I've saved some of the main course for you, if you're hungry."

"I'm starving, to be honest" he said, grinning at her.

As she went into the kitchen Mark introduced him to the other couple sitting at the dinner table.

"Sam's a brilliant detective" he said. "We met ten years ago when he was a mere constable, but now he's a lot more important."

The girl seated next to Cooper had long dark hair and dark eyes set in a pretty but pale face.

"You're a modern day Sherlock Holmes, then" she said to him, her eyes looking directly into his for a little too long; long enough for him to feel a slight shiver down his spine, forcing him to avert his eyes.

"Not exactly; my job is twenty percent intuition, eighty percent perspiration, as they say. It's often a case of just trying to tie up all the loose ends to make sure you don't miss anything, as well as attention to detail. I don't often say to people 'I see you came by train to Waterloo and then a taxi via Embankment' because of a ticket peeping out of a coat pocket, or whatever Sherlock Holmes would have said."

The girl burst out laughing which pleased him, but then Tricia set a dinner plate in front of him and, although he didn't want to ignore her, he was hungry so he turned his attention to that.

The girl carried on a conversation with Tricia; he thought she had pretty eyes but her voice was a bit high pitched. He wasn't sure he would have been able to cope with that too well, if he had to spend much time with her.

He glanced at Carol as he ate, who looked at him with a cold stare before turning away from him and speaking to the girl's partner, whose name he discovered later was Dominic. She spoke to him for most of the evening; Cooper was too tired to care too much, but he couldn't help noticing that she seemed to be flirting with him. The girl, who he assumed was his partner, didn't seem too worried, so Cooper focused on eating his dinner.

After dinner Carol drove them home, in silence, which was just as well as he fell asleep quickly.

TWO

Sunday morning dawned grey and uninspiring; Cooper spent the first part of it working at a cluttered table in the tiny spare bedroom of their apartment, reading through his notes, adding lines and thoughts as he went, at one point speaking to the chief on the phone, the handset tucked under his chin so that he could write as he listened.

Carol stayed in bed until late and was clearly avoiding him, so he let her be.

After a call to Robinson mid morning he picked up his coat and bag to walk down to his car; Carol was by now in the kitchen but she didn't respond to his few brief words to her, so he walked out of the apartment and down to his car, feeling down-hearted. He wasn't sure what else he could do.

On the drive to the heath he listened to classical music for inspiration. As always at the beginning of a case he was keen to make a start, although his stomach was churning. He had always been nervous of the unknown; the weight of responsibility felt heavier as he approached the crime scene.

A uniformed constable, controlling traffic entering the area, stopped him briefly before allowing him to continue down to the point where he had parked the evening before. As he climbed out of the car, adrenaline coursing through his veins, his mobile phone bleeped that a message had arrived. He checked the screen. It was from Carol.

'I hope you enjoy your day Sam, with all your friends. I'll be out until late.'

He pondered for a moment whether to send a reply. They had been together for a long time, and yet he didn't know what to say any more. She wanted him to change his job; he didn't want to do anything else. Perhaps they would never see eye to eye on that. For the first time, Cooper wondered if their relationship might be coming to an end. The realisation made him feel empty inside; he hadn't planned a life without her. With a sigh he put the phone back into his pocket.

A thin mist hung in the still air over the grassy slope where police and forensics had gathered at first light to begin the grim task he had set them. As he stepped along the path he shivered as he felt the cold, damp air on his face and neck.

Pulling his coat collar up around his neck and tightening his scarf a little more, he looked around at the area of ancient woodland close by where the little dog had made the gruesome discovery.

He had enjoyed exploring the same part of the heath last summer with Carol; they had only just moved to Camden and it had been their first visit to Hampstead. They had gone there several times over the summer; he had even taken an early morning swim in the pond in August, although it hadn't really been for him. He had been amazed how many people had been swimming there that morning. It made him shudder now to think about it, on such a cold day.

Cooper made his way up the still slippery slope to where they had been standing the previous evening; even with the police presence the tranquil scene, with the occasional bird singing in the trees, was so different now from the dark and stormy place he had visited last evening. He wondered how such a quiet and peaceful spot could hide such a dark secret.

Robinson was standing some way off, talking to a couple of uniformed constables, one of them laughing. Somehow he thought they should have been more sombre, but he knew it was pointless worrying about them. They were doing their job, that's all.

After a brief look around he stooped to enter the large white tent erected to protect the area as well as to keep out prying eyes. The scent of mouldy leaves and wet soil entered his nostrils as soon as he went in; as he stood surveying the scene he also became aware of taps on the roof of the tent, caused by drops still falling from the trees.

"Good morning Sam," beamed the head of the forensics team, vapour from his breath visible in the cold, damp air.

He was dressed from head to toe in a white overall, including a hood covering his head. Only his glasses, coloured bright blue, gave any hint of personality. Cooper knew him well and had never seen him unhappy; he obviously enjoyed his work.

"As you can see, we've nearly finished. It's a young woman. We've uncovered her full skeleton, albeit that a few small bones are missing, namely a couple of fingers."

Cooper stood quietly for a moment, looking down at the shallow grave in front of him, the full skeleton of the girl now exposed. Almost automatically he folded his hands together in front of him, as if he were about to start praying.

She was lying face down in the mud, her right arm pushed above her head as if protecting herself, the hand still partially above ground level, just as it had been when the lady discovered it. He shivered involuntarily; no-one should end their life in a place such as this, in an unmarked grave. It was especially wrong for a young girl, with a whole life unlived.

"Any idea how old she was?"

"We'll need to do some tests, of course, but I should think late teens or early twenties. Almost certainly not more than thirty years old."

"How long since she died?"

"A number of years, possibly as many as forty years."

"Forty? So long ago? It would have been around nineteen seventy then."

"Ever the mathematician. Yes."

Cooper smiled. "Any chance of being more accurate?"

"On what? Age or the date of death?"

"Both, naturally."

"I suspected so. We'll have to remove the body and take it to the mortuary to have a better idea."

"Do you know yet what killed her?"

"Difficult to say how, as there are no signs of fracture on the skeleton, so we don't have a lot to go off at the moment."

"Have you had a good look around the area outside?" Cooper asked.

"Yes, we have, but as you would expect given how long the body's been here, there is no visible evidence to tell us where or how she was actually killed. There was no sign of any disturbance near the grave either, apart from a few shoe and paw marks from yesterday evening. I think an animal must have been scratching around recently, allowing the rain to wash away sufficient soil to expose the bones for us to find."

"You say there are a couple of fingers missing. Could they have they been taken by animals?"

"I don't think so as they were missing from this hand, which was under the soil." He crouched down, pointing to the hand that was almost under her body. "It looks to me as if they have been cut off. I'll get a better idea when I'm able to examine them properly in the mortuary."

"Anything else needs to be done here?"

"No, we've pretty well done all we can at this stage."

"In that case we may as well remove the body."

Cooper was relieved to step outside of the tent and away from the musty smell; he had felt quite claustrophobic in there. He breathed in the cold air and stepped carefully back down the slope to the path, wary of slipping on the grass, looking up briefly when he became aware of the clatter of a helicopter hovering overhead. As he looked up he realised the mist was slowly clearing, the odd patch of blue showing through. The wind had disappeared too. The thought that the girl should have been enjoying the tranquillity here briefly came into his head.

Robinson was waiting for him on the path below.

"The press are gathering for a statement" he said. "There are a few TV cameras there as well."

"Let them know I'll make a statement in about twenty minutes, will you?"

Cooper walked down the path towards the police vehicles, entering the incident van and taking a seat at a table. He spent several minutes making notes before he called the chief at his home, updating him on the initial forensic findings, and his first thoughts.

"I'll need to talk to the press, sir. They're all gathered here now."

He read out the statement he had just prepared. The chief asked for a couple of small changes; Cooper knew he would do that, just to express his authority and to feel he had added some value.

"Are you happy with the statement now?"

"Yes sir, that's fine."

"Are you comfortable doing it alone? Do you want me to drive over and do it?" the chief asked him.

"No sir, I can handle it."

This was Cooper's first major case since his promotion last year; he hadn't made a statement to the press before. He was determined to handle this one alone. It was part of the job; he needed to show he was capable, and this was a very public way of doing it. This would be broadcast nationally; he couldn't think of a better way of showing his skills. Provided he got it right, of course.

"Good" the chief was saying, "let me know if there are further developments. In any case, call by my office tomorrow morning."

After mentally rehearsing what he was to say Cooper took a deep breath and walked several hundred yards down the lane towards where the press had been told to assemble. There were several TV cameras as well as a bank of reporters and photographers waiting expectantly; a hush descended on the group as he approached. He waited for a few moments while they got themselves into position, composing himself before reading out the brief statement in as clear a voice as he could muster, without being too monotonous. He then answered a few questions, but without adding much detail because at this stage it suited him not to reveal too much; he did however confirm it was a complete skeleton of a female that seemed to have been buried some years ago. He was sure that the other details would leak out over the hours and days ahead, but for now that was all he wished to reveal. He came away quietly satisfied. He wondered if his mother had been watching the broadcast; he doubted whether Carol had.

* * * * *

After he had finished there and spoken again to DC Robinson he headed to a favourite cafe near Camden before going home. The flat was quiet. Carol was going to be as good as her word; she would not be back until late in the evening. He sent her a text message to let her know he was home, just in case she changed her mind. He didn't expect a reply, and he didn't get one.

He rang his mother late afternoon. Cooper, as she usually reminded him, went to see her only infrequently, so he tried to call when he remembered.

Today she sounded unwell, complaining of feeling dizzy. She told him she hadn't seen his statement on television; she had been to one of her sisters for lunch and she spent most of the call complaining about her.

"When are you going to come and see me? I worry that you're always so busy. And Carol too. You haven't mentioned her. How is she?"

"Carol's fine, mum. We had a bit of a dispute the other day, but she'll get over it."

"What were you arguing about?"

"Oh, the usual. I got a call out to go to a new case, and we were due to go out that evening, so she got upset again. You know how it is."

"Well, try to make it up to her. Be nice to her. You should try to work less."

"I can't do that mum, you know that. This is what I am. I'm a detective police officer; we don't have resources and people coming out of our ears. If something crops up it has to be dealt with. I can't leave it for a few days, and I can't get someone else to go and have a look. It's never going to be a nine to five job. I don't know why you aren't able to understand that. You and Carol are just the same."

"I know, but you should try anyway. Think about Carol. Be nice to her."

"Ok, mum. I'll try."

"I know you're ambitious, Sam, but you have to try to get a balance between work and home. It can't be all work. I know you work hard, and it's a demanding job, but what's the point in achieving something if you've no-one to share it with?"

He was in bed when he heard the door open; he glanced at the clock. It was close to midnight. As he had expected, Carol let him know what she thought of him as soon as she walked in.

"You need to decide what your priorities are, Sam" she began, in a calmer tone than he had expected. "There has to be a time when we can be together, as a couple. We both work hard, and I work late in the evenings and weekends as much as you do, but the fact is you don't care. You drop everything as soon as there is an issue; you don't care where I am or what I am doing, you only think about your job. It wouldn't matter if it was only occasionally Sam, but it happens too often. It's no use telling me what happened the other evening; you decided you needed to be there, because you want to be seen to be the hero, the one who solves all the crimes. You aren't the only detective in London. It isn't good enough, Sam. You need to decide what you want in life; I can't cope with this any longer."

She didn't wait for an answer; he heard her go into the spare bedroom. He wondered if he should go to her, but then he drifted off to sleep.

* * * * *

Cooper was in his car, the radio on low. He was on his way to see the chief, anxious to have a clear plan in mind when he discussed the case with him.

Try as he might though he couldn't help thinking about Carol. They had been together since they were teenagers, some fifteen years now. They had never discussed marriage or children; they had always been together, and he knew he took her for granted. Perhaps his mother had a point. His job took a lot of his time, he knew he was often distracted at the weekends, but he couldn't imagine changing his job and he didn't know what else he could do.

He jumped slightly as the shrill sound of his phone ringing interrupted his thoughts. It was the pathologist.

"Hello Sam. I have some news on your body you might be interested in."

"Don't tell me, I'm overweight" Cooper said.

"Very funny. I mean the girl found on the heath. And if anything you're too skinny."

"Thanks. What can you tell me?"

"Female, aged early twenties, I estimate between twenty and twenty five. No signs of injury, so it's possible she could have been killed by any number of means; I can't be certain without further evidence. As I mentioned before, the second and third fingers of the left hand are missing; having examined the hand more closely my conclusion is that they were removed surgically, some time before death."

"So she had an accident, I assume?"

"That's the logical assumption. There is no evidence of disease at all. The final thing is to confirm that the body has been in the grave for approximately forty years, give or take five years, so let's say sometime between nineteen sixty five and nineteen seventy five."

"Anything else worthy of note?"

"She was buried face down, as you know. That suggests to me she was perhaps buried by someone who was in a great hurry; possibly he didn't want to look at her as he filled in the grave."

"Or she."

"Perhaps, but the grave would have been difficult to dig. The soil is full of roots so it would have taken a lot of effort. That is hard work for anyone, especially for a woman if she needed to carry the body there as well. But not impossible."

"May have been more than one person then."

"Quite possibly. It would have been easier and quicker if two were digging."

"Nothing else?"

"Not for now, Sam. I'll email the report to you shortly. Good luck with this one."

* * * * *

Cooper's office was neither large nor luxurious; he often called it his cupboard. He had no pictures or other small items some might use to personalise the space. Apart from the desk, usually covered in mounds of paper, there were two grey metal filing cabinets and a small wooden table one of his predecessors had brought in, just large enough for a small tray with a couple of mugs for coffee, and on which he usually threw odds and ends such as his car keys. On top of one filing cabinet was an electric fan to keep the heat down on summer days. Today it was silent; the weather outside was still bitterly cold. There was just about room for someone to enter and sit on the single visitor chair. This chair was reputed to be the most uncomfortable in the building; it was rumoured that Cooper had designed it specially to deter visitors from staying for too long. He denied this, even to himself.

"I've been through the missing persons file, looking for girls aged twenty to twenty five that have been reported missing across the UK, between nineteen sixty and nineteen seventy five, just to spread the range a bit wider."

Robinson was standing by his desk as he spoke; Cooper knew he had already learned to avoid sitting in that chair.

"That makes sense, but we may have to narrow it down later. How many are there?"

"Two hundred and fifty three, across the whole of the UK."

Cooper whistled.

"Hell's teeth."

"I've also put in a request to Europol for details of anyone they have on record as reported missing in the UK about that time, just in case they don't appear on our records for any reason, so the number may well go up."

"You'll need to keep chasing. With a case this old, it's not going to be a priority unless we push hard."

"This could take some time to solve, if we ever do solve it. To narrow down the search I've then broken the full list down by height, and by location when missing. I then eliminated a lot of names because they were too tall or too small, and from the remaining I've selected those reported as definitely missing from the London area; by doing that then we're down to forty five. Some of the others may have been in London at the time, but there's some uncertainty; that adds another fourteen, but I'm holding those in reserve for the moment. I've asked the relevant forces to check how certain it is the fourteen girls could have disappeared from the London area."

"So we still have forty five names, even on our core list."

"Yes; unfortunately none of the files mentioned a girl with a couple of missing fingers. None of the descriptions, circumstances or locations seems an obvious fit, so we need to keep looking."

* * * * *

Later that day Cooper picked up the phone to try to talk to Carol, but her mobile went to voice mail. Her work as a reporter took her around London, so he thought it possible she was interviewing someone.

"Or there again, maybe she's still mad with me" he said to himself.

He sent her a text telling her where he was, and then pressed send. Only then did he think he should have said 'sorry' as well. Too late now.

Carol wasn't at home when he finally arrived that evening, nor were there any messages. She often worked late, although she usually let him know when that was the case. Clearly not today.

He sent her a text asking her if she was ok, but had no response. Later he tried to call, but again she didn't answer her phone.

It did cross his mind that she might have had an accident, but Cooper decided it was far more likely she was still ignoring him.

It was almost midnight when he went to bed; Carol still hadn't appeared.

"She really has given up on me, this time" he said to himself.

February 2010

"Hello Mum, it's me. How are you? Graham sent me a message to say you've had a fall."

"Hello Sam. Oh, it's nothing really. I saw the doctor this morning. My leg is a bit swollen but nothing broken. My pride was hurt the most, I think. Your brother's just been; he's going to take me out for lunch on Sunday if the weather isn't too bad, so that'll be nice. How are you? Is Carol alright now? Are you two speaking to each other again?"

"She's coming round slowly. I'm not sure she'll ever fully accept my way of life, but we'll find a way of coping, I'm sure."

"Has she ever said where she was sleeping for those few nights she disappeared?"

"She just said she stayed with a friend, but she didn't want to talk about it too much so I stopped asking. Better to let sleeping dogs lie."

"It was a girlfriend, I suppose?"

"I assumed so. She didn't say it was a man."

"Let's hope you're right. Will you be able to come up this weekend at all? It would be nice to see you. You could have lunch with us."

"I'm not sure, mum. I tell you what; I'll ask Carol if she's got plans for the weekend. Perhaps it'll do us both good to get away. I'll see what she says."

"It would be nice to see you both."

"Well, I don't promise. I'm working on a case but it'll probably be a long haul."

"Is that the one you mentioned, the girl whose body was found on that heath?"

"Hampstead Heath, yes."

"I don't imagine it's much of a heath, being in the middle of London."

"Well, it isn't the size of the Yorkshire Dales, but it's bigger than most of the parks. It's a natural area, an ancient place that's never been developed. It isn't like a park at all. It's big enough to get lost in."

"Perhaps you could show it to me some time. It's a long time since I went to London."

"Well, you need to let your leg heal first. I have to go Mum. I'll speak to Carol and let you know."

"Alright Sam, you take care."

* * * * *

Diana Freedman and her dog Buster had continued to take their walks on the heath as usual since making their discovery, if only because she knew the dog would not let her get away with anything less. They stuck to their more usual route however, avoiding the spot amongst the trees where Buster had made his dreadful find.

It was a cold, crisp day, and Diana had allowed Buster more time than usual to run around as she sat on a bench in the sunshine. As soon as they were home however she went into the kitchen to begin to prepare dinner for her guests; she was expecting her daughter Amanda and her new partner, Simon, for dinner.

After preparing everything for the meal, and after a long soak in the bath, Diana spent some time in her bedroom choosing a suitable outfit that was elegant without being too formal. After several changes of clothes she was satisfied and went down to make sure the house was presentable and to complete the preparations for dinner.

At just a few minutes after the agreed time the doorbell rang; for a moment Diana was surprised as she had given Amanda a key. Then she realised that her daughter would probably not want to walk unannounced into the house with her new partner. She went to the door and opened it, greeting her daughter with a hug and a kiss on both cheeks and Simon with a more formal handshake.

As they closed the door Amanda picked up an envelope from the floor.

"There's a letter for you here, mummy" she said, handing it to Diana.

"How odd. I collected the post when I came back with Buster" Diana said, looking at the envelope. "There's no stamp on it so it must have been pushed through the letterbox, probably when I was upstairs taking a bath. Most unusual. I'm used to getting leaflets, but not hand written letters these days."

"Aren't you going to open it?"

"I'm sure it will wait until after dinner. Let's go through to the living room. Would you care for a drink, Simon?"

* * * * *

That afternoon had been quiet; Robinson had taken a day's leave and Cooper knew the chief was away at a training seminar, so he decided to work from home. He wanted to be home before Carol, for a change.

He found a parking space for his car in the street and walked up to the flat. As he approached he noticed the lights were on in the apartment; Carol must be at home early after all. She had been working late a lot recently; sometimes she hadn't been home much before midnight.

He was about to put the key in the front door lock when a voice he didn't recognise made him pause. It was a man's voice. Cooper listened for a moment, but then realised he could hear Carol laughing. It wasn't a burglar, then.

He opened the door and went in. He took off his coat and hung it by the door, as was his habit, dropping his keys into an ashtray on a small table as he did so.

He walked towards the living room, but realised he could hear voices from the bedroom. He frowned; what was going on? He walked to the doorway and looked in. He froze as he tried to take in the scene in front of him.

"Oh shit!"

It was Carol's voice. The man, who was lying naked on top of her, jumped off the bed, covering his penis with his hands as he did so.

"I think you'd better leave. Now."

Cooper wanted to sound demanding, even angry, but his voice almost pleaded with the man just to go. His face was burning, his throat tight and dry, his head buzzing.

"Ok, I'm going now. I'm going" the man was saying, holding one hand towards him in a defensive way.

He didn't want to see or say more. He felt a knot in his stomach as the adrenaline flowed and his breathing rate increased. Carol was sitting up in the bed, the sheet pulled up to her eyes; he knew she was naked. She held her head in her hands and started to sob quietly, her body heaving as she breathed.

He wanted to punch the man, who by now was hurriedly dressing himself, but his training told him to walk away, sit down, remain calm.

He turned and walked quickly into the living room, closing the door behind him. He sat on one of the chairs, leaning forward with his head in his hands. He felt dizzy. He could hear a whispered conversation and the hurried sounds of movement.

Cooper sat still, breathing deeply. He realised he was trembling. It was shock; he knew that much from first aid training. He wanted to get a drink of water from the kitchen, but he didn't want to see the two of them again. He suddenly remembered who the man was; he had been at Mark's that evening on New Year's Day. He tried to remember his name. It came to him after a moment; Dominic.

There was a bang as the external door closed; he must have gone.

Cooper didn't move. The ensuing silence was broken only by the faint sound of Carol weeping in the bedroom.

After he had regained his composure he went into the kitchen to take a drink and then went out into the hallway to put on his coat. There was little to say now. Any changes to his lifestyle, any plans for the future had now evaporated.

He walked once again to the door of the bedroom; Carol was now half dressed, sitting on the bed, dark streaks under her eyes from the tears on her face.

"I'll stay somewhere else tonight; then I'll find another flat to rent" he said. "You'll need to pay the rent on this place if you want to stay, or give the landlord notice if you want to move out. I'll let you know when I want to come for my stuff."

"I'm really sorry it had to end like this, Sam. I was going to tell you soon."

Cooper said nothing; there was nothing to say. The years they had spent together meant nothing at that moment. He picked up his keys and walked out of the flat.

Back in the street he sat in the car, wondering what to do. He picked up his mobile phone.

"Hello Mark, it's Sam. Look buddy, I've just split up with Carol, and I need a bed for the night. Do you mind if I kip on your couch, just for a night or two while I sort myself out?"

* * * * *

On the Monday morning Diana Freedman was writing at her late husband's desk in the library, as was increasingly her habit these days. Over the years she had written a few short stories, as a hobby, although as a busy mother and wife she had not had much time to dedicate to writing. Now that she had more time for herself she wanted something to focus on, rather than just to vegetate, as she put it to her friends, so of late she had spent a lot of time writing the beginnings of a novel at this desk.

She opened one of the drawers looking for a pencil and saw an envelope; she realised it was the one pushed through the letterbox, found behind the door by Amanda on Friday. She had forgotten about it. She tore the envelope open and looked at the contents with curiosity.

Her thoughts were interrupted when she heard the dog bark as the front door opened; her daughter Amanda shouted a greeting.

"I'm in here darling" Diana shouted.

Amanda walked into the library, which overlooked the front of the house, to greet her.

"Hello mummy, I just wanted to thank you for the lovely dinner on Friday; Simon and I had a good time."

"Well it was nice to see you too darling, and it was nice to meet Simon too, after I've heard so much about him."

"I wondered what you thought of him."

"He's really very nice; he has a pleasant manner about him, he seems very kind, and he was dressed elegantly as well, which I appreciate. He's welcome here again at any time. You're very fond of him, aren't you?"

"Yes, I am; he really has helped me to get my life together again in the last few months, and to start thinking about the future rather than the past. You have been a tremendous support and help as well of course, but you know what I mean."

"Of course I do darling. You need to get your life together, and find someone to share it with. If that's going to be Simon then that's fine with me."

"That's lovely to hear, because I think I'm falling in love with him."

"Does he love you?"

"Yes, I think so. He's told me he does. He's a lovely man, and I think he means it."

"I think you may trust him, but in any case you should of course take time to see how things work out."

"I'm glad you like him anyway, because I want you to be happy for me. We hit it off right from the start really, and we have a lot in common. I think we may have children together if it works out; I was principally interested in my career before, but now I've started to think it would be nice to have a family."

"Have you discussed this with Simon?"

"Yes, in fact he raised it. We were in the park one day and there was a toddler running around near us. Simon just came out with it; he said he would like a child one day."

"Has he been married before?"

"No; he lived with a girl until last year when they split up. They didn't have children either."

"Well, grandchildren would be nice. I haven't quite given up on that."

"Actually talking of children, you've reminded me of something I wanted to ask you. You remember we were talking a couple of months ago about our family history and I said I wanted to work on our family tree?"

"Yes, I do remember. Did you manage to do anything on it?"

"Well I haven't dedicated a lot of time to it, so there are still a lot of gaps; it's a time consuming process. I was telling Simon the other evening that I remember granny once telling us a story about one of our ancestors who travelled from England to France and fought in the French Revolution. Is that really true?"

"Well it's a story that runs in the family dear, but how true it is I wouldn't care to say."

"What were you told?"

"You know that my maternal grandfather was French. He once told me, many years ago when I was quite small, that one of his ancestors was English. Apparently this ancestor went to France and ended up being a hero for taking part in the revolution in Paris. I assume it is true at least in part, but what his name was, or how he ended up there I have no idea."

"Do we have any family documents that go back that far?"

"I don't have any darling, but it is possible the French side of my family have something. I could ask my cousin Marie if you would like me to; we keep in touch from time to time, although I haven't seen her for years. Perhaps you could go over there if she has anything worth seeing."

"It would be wonderful if she has, as I really want to complete the family tree as far as I can. Anything I can get from Marie would be really interesting."

"Well, I'll get in touch with Marie and see what she comes back with."

"That'd be super, thank you."

"By the way, that envelope you found behind my door that evening contained something rather curious."

Diana took the envelope from the desk and handed it to Amanda, who opened it and looked at the contents. There was a drawing and a newspaper cutting; she looked at both carefully.

"Have you told the police about these? I think you should."

* * * * *

The desk phone rang. As Robinson was standing by Cooper's desk he answered it before handing the receiver to him.

"It's Diana Freedman. The woman from Hampstead."

Cooper took the handset from him.

"Yes Mrs. Freedman, how are you? How do you feel after your ordeal?" he asked.

"I've been tolerably well, thank you inspector. Things are more or less back to normal now. After news of the discovery came out I did receive a few telephone calls from newspaper reporters but, as I really couldn't add much to what they already knew, interest in me soon waned and the calls stopped, thank goodness. For a little while a few photographers could be seen hanging around the village, and I think I've had my photograph taken a few more times than I would have liked, but now they too seem to have packed up and moved away, so all has gone quiet. I'm sorry to disturb you this morning inspector, but I rang you because I've received a letter, or at least an envelope with something inside that might be of interest to you."

"Oh? What's that?"

"It must have been pushed through the door sometime on Friday afternoon. I had collected the post late morning as usual, but then Amanda arrived with her new partner and she found the envelope behind the door, although I admit I only opened it this morning. In the envelope there's a drawing, rather childlike I must say, of a person lying on the ground by a tree and another figure standing over her, I say her although it could be a man. The other figure seems to be holding a knife. There's also a page torn from a newspaper containing a report of the discovery of the body. I first thought that it was someone playing a rather macabre joke – indeed it may of course be just that – but I notice that whoever sent the article has written on the newspaper. It isn't clear as the writing is somewhat childish, but they appear to have written the name 'Monica' in the margin."

"Have they? Look, I'd like to see it. Could I pop over and collect it from you? Are you in all afternoon?"

"I had planned to do a little shopping later on, but I'll stay in if you wish. It will wait until tomorrow. Buster is asleep anyway after a longer walk than usual this morning."

"Thank you, Mrs. Freedman. That would be kind. I should be with you in a couple of hours or so. By the way, I meant to ask you the other evening; did you see anyone on the heath the other night? Did you see anyone on the way there, before you found the body, or immediately afterwards?"

"No, it was such foul weather that I doubt anyone was so foolish." She paused for a moment. "Although when I was on the path, just as Buster scampered off up the little hill, I thought I saw a figure amongst the trees, but then I almost lost my footing and I had to look down. When I looked up again I could see no-one, so I put it down to my imagination."

"I see. Did you see anyone other than that?"

"No, nothing at all. Have you made any progress at all? Do you have any idea who the poor girl was?" she asked.

"We're still working on it. We have a few possibilities but nothing definite as yet."

"It must be very difficult if she's been there for many years. I do hope you find out one day, for her sake, and for that of her family."

He thanked her and put down the receiver.

"There isn't a girl named 'Monica' anywhere on the core list, I don't suppose?"

Robinson checked.

"No, I'm afraid not" he replied. "There's a girl called Marjorie, but no Monica."

"Thought so. Perhaps it's a wild goose chase, but someone has sent Mrs Freedman a newspaper clipping with a report of the discovery of the body. He or she has written the name Monica on it. There's also a drawing which seems to be of a person lying under a tree. Seems macabre. Let's just finish this review. Then I'll drive over there and have a look."

* * * * *

Thirty minutes later Cooper stood to put on his coat to go out. He hesitated, then picked up the phone and dialled a number.

"Hello Mum, how are you today?"

"Hello Sam. The doctor's just been. My leg's still a bit bruised, but the cut is healing nicely, so he was quite pleased with it really."

"That's good. I have some bad news, I'm afraid. I've left Carol and moved out of the apartment."

"You've moved out? Whatever for?"

"I've split from Carol. She's found someone else, it seems."

"Oh dear, that's very sad. I'm sorry to hear that. Where are you living then?"

I've moved in with some friends for a few days, and I'm looking for a place to rent."

"She got fed up with your long hours, I suppose? Well, she's losing a good man, that's all I can say."

Yes, I guess you're right, but it's time to move on."

"Well that may be, but don't give up on her straight away. She might come round and want you back."

"I'm not sure I want her back, Mum."

"Were things so bad? I thought you two got along fine together."

"We used to get on, Mum, but not in this past twelve months since I got promoted. I think we're better apart."

"Well if that's how you feel, then perhaps you're right."

49

"I need to go now; I just wanted to let you know."

"Well thanks for ringing, Sam. It's nice to hear from you. Take care of yourself now."

"Bye Mum."

* * * * *

Today, in the sunshine, the house in Hampstead looked even more impressive than the evening he had first called there.

He rang the bell expecting Diana Freedman but the door opened to reveal an attractive woman, with shoulder length blonde hair and striking blue eyes; he guessed she was perhaps in her thirties. When he introduced himself she smiled and extended a hand.

"I'm Amanda, Diana's daughter" she explained.

She led him across the hallway and into the drawing room at the back of the house. Cooper couldn't help noticing the gardens at the rear of the property through the French doors; he caught sight of a man walking across the lawn with a rake, presumably the gardener.

Diana was seated at the small desk under the window as he walked in. She smiled and stood to greet him.

"Have you ever looked at your family tree, inspector? I find it fascinating. We were just having a look at ours," she said. "Amanda has been working on it; she wants to find out about one particular ancestor, who we believe was English but somehow became caught up in the French Revolution. The family story is that he was involved in some trouble over here and sentenced to prison, but escaped and fled to France, so at least one ancestor was adventurous. Amanda is planning to go to Paris to meet a French cousin of mine to see what she can tell us."

"That sounds interesting" Cooper said, turning to Amanda. "I'm reading about that period of history at the moment. There were a lot of problems across England at the start of the industrial revolution. It changed the lives of tens of thousands of people working in the countryside, not just due to people moving to the towns to find work, but because of the mechanisation of agriculture. The introduction of machinery, such as threshing machines, led to people losing jobs and lower wages. There were serious riots in some areas. There were gangs going around the countryside smashing machinery, and a few people got killed. Perhaps he was caught up in that and ran away to Paris."

"Well, maybe you're right. It'll be fascinating to find out. We'll let you know what I discover" Amanda replied.

"I'll look forward to hearing all about it."

He then turned to her mother.

"You said you'd received something you thought I should see."

"Yes, of course, I'll get it."

She left for a moment to go the library. Cooper smiled at Amanda.

"My mother tells me you're from Manchester," she said. "I went to university there; I enjoyed the city very much."

"Actually I'm from a town a few miles outside. But yes, it's a nice city. I went to Manchester University as well."

"Did you read history there?"

"No, perhaps I should have done as I find it fascinating, but in fact I read sociology."

"Have you been down in this part of the world for long?"

"I moved down when my girlfriend, or should I say former girlfriend, got a job down here. That was in nineteen ninety eight. Still haven't lost my accent, have I?" Cooper smiled as he said this.

"Not exactly."

He thought Amanda was a good looking woman, and a similar age to him, but well above his pay grade. He knew he would never afford to pay for a lifestyle she would have been used to.

Diana reappeared, carrying the envelope, and handed it to him. He took out the contents, looking at the drawing first. He thought it was crudely drawn, and could have been done by a child. It showed a tree with someone, possibly a woman, lying on the floor. Another figure stood with what appeared to be a knife. There was nothing else to give a clue as to who drew it, or what it meant.

He opened the newspaper cutting; it had been cut from the local newspaper, and was a report from a month earlier of the discovery of the body on the heath. As Mrs Freedman had told him, someone had written the word 'Monica' on the margin of the newspaper. The writing was spidery; again it could have been written by a child.

Cooper put the papers back into the envelope.

"I'd like to keep these, if I may."

"Of course. Do you think it may be connected to the murder, or is it just a hoax? If it is a hoax, it's a horrible one."

"No, I don't think it is a hoax. I don't think that at all."

FOUR

"I have some good news for you."

"I could do with some good news."

Cooper was speaking on the phone to Mark.

"That flat we mentioned to you the other evening is definitely available. The owner's a good friend of ours, and he's happy for you to move in straight away if you want it. No need for references and all that. He's happy to sort out a contract with you, but he says he doesn't need that before you move in, as we can vouch for you. Tricia's been over to take a look at the flat with him this afternoon. She says it's very nice. He's just redecorated it, and so it's clean and tidy. It has a separate kitchen, although it's too small to eat in, and the bathroom was done a couple of years ago, so that's nearly new. She thinks you'll like it. Do you want to see it? I suggest you do it soon, because he's just about to put it with an agent to let it out. He'll give you first shout, if you want it."

"That's great. If Tricia likes it, then that's good enough for me. Will you tell him I'll have it? Do you know when I can move in?"

"It's free now, so I guess if you and he are both happy, then no reason you can't move in right away. I'll call him now to confirm. I guess you'll be on your way here soon so we can make arrangements then. If you want to move in this weekend, then I'll give you a hand with your stuff."

"I'm really grateful, Mark. You're a star."

The flat was even better than he hoped. It was Saturday morning before he saw it when he and Mark arrived with the clothes plus a few books, papers and DVDs he'd already taken from the flat he had shared with Carol. It was smaller than their old flat, with only one bedroom, but it suited him perfectly.

They dropped the boxes on the floor and then made their way back to the car. Mark climbed into the passenger seat at the side of him, and they drove the short distance to Cooper's old flat. He still had his key, but he pressed the intercom button by the door on the ground floor. Carol answered.

"It's me" he said. "I need to collect the rest of my things."

She didn't say anything, but the door clicked open.

"Do you want me to wait here for a few minutes?" Mark asked.

"Might be better, in case she wants to talk. I'll bring the first stuff down when it's all clear."

Cooper walked up the familiar stairway to the second floor. He opened the door with his key, dropping it into the ashtray by habit. Carol was standing in the doorway of the living room.

"Do you want a coffee?" she asked.

"No, thanks. Mark's downstairs. I said I'd bring some stuff down in a minute or two. He was kind enough to suggest we might want a minute alone."

Carol looked away, and walked into the living room, sitting on the sofa. He followed her in, but declined to sit.

"You've found another flat?"

"Yes, I've just agreed to take it for a year. It's a bit smaller than this, but it's nice and clean."

She looked down at the floor.

"We were together a long time, Sam. Perhaps we took each other for granted. I'll always love you, and I miss you a lot. The other evening with Dominic was a fling. He isn't really my type, but I know I hurt you badly, and I'm sorry. I was really at the end of my tether. You're not easy to live with. You need to decide whether you want a relationship or your career, because I can't see you having both, Sam. Right now, you've chosen your career. If you change your mind, then you know where I am. But I won't be here forever."

"I've given it a lot of thought too. I think we've started to grow apart over the past couple of years. I do think it possible to have a career and a relationship, but maybe not between us. I'm sorry but for me it's already over; we had some good times together, but it's better if we part company and start new lives, rather than trying to make the best of something which isn't working."

Cooper picked up some books.

"I have some boxes in the car. I'll go down and bring them up. I'll ask Mark to come up as well."

"As you wish."

An hour later he and Mark had taken everything down to the car. Carol was standing by the window.

"I've got everything now. I'm leaving" he said.

She looked at him.

"Good luck, Sam. I hope you get what you wish for."

As he was leaving he went to pick up his door key, but then pulled his hand away. He left it in the ashtray and closed the door behind him. He wouldn't need it again.

* * * * *

The next Monday morning dawned cold; to the east the fine wisps of cloud in the pale blue sky were tinged with a faint hint of pale orange.

WPC Catherine Harper was on her police issue bicycle patrolling the Hampstead area, making her way slowly up the steep slopes of the narrow streets close by the Heath. She heard a radio call asking for a response to an emergency call; she stopped and responded that she was close by, then pedalled back down the slopes, arriving at the house from where someone had called within a couple of minutes.

A group of men were standing outside the door as she approached; she quickly realised that most of them were mentally disabled. One of them, who was standing apart and was clearly in charge, introduced himself as Andy Jones, the manager of the building.

He led her inside; the others followed without saying anything. He asked them if they would go to sit in the lounge while he took the constable upstairs. Without a word they did as he asked. He then turned and walked up the stairs; WPC Harper followed him.

"As you've probably gathered, this is a home for mentally disabled people. I called the police because I think we have a suicide here," he said as they walked up. "I think one of the residents has hung himself."

"Let me take a look, sir."

He opened the door with a key and pushed the door partially open before standing back. The WPC pushed the door fully open to see a pair of legs; she looked up. The man was hanging from a short rope, tied to a hook in the ceiling. She stepped into the room, pulled a chair closer and stood on it to try to lift the man free.

"Let me help you" the manager said, getting hold of the legs and lifting the weight.

The WPC touched the face of the man but the cold flesh told her that he was beyond hope. The rope was wrapped around the hook and it took her a few seconds to undo the knot. They then gently laid the body on the floor. He stepped back whilst she felt for a pulse, although they were both sure that there was none. The WPC gently undid the rope from around his neck and laid it to one side.

The sound of sirens announced the arrival of a police car closely followed by an ambulance; the manager went down the stairs to open the door, greeting two police constables and an ambulance crew then leading them up to the room where WPC Harper was examining the body.

After the ambulance had taken the dead man away, the other police officers took another call and left. WPC Harper went downstairs to speak to the other residents, who were still waiting in the living room. Andy Jones was present as they were all somewhat nervous and agitated.

The name of the deceased was Angus Forsyth. They had all last seen him on Saturday, and one of the residents had heard the door bang shut early evening but didn't know who it was.

"If Angus went out on Saturday evening, where would he normally go?" she asked them.

"He liked to go to the cinema" replied one of the residents, who had been introduced as George.

"Which cinema, George? The one near Belsize underground station?" Andy Jones asked him.

"Yes, I saw him go in there a few times."

After another five minutes WPC Harper concluded that the residents were unlikely to add any more. She then went with Andy Jones back up to the room, and looked around for anything that might shed light on why Angus Forsyth would have hanged himself.

The room had a single bed, a small wardrobe and a small desk with a couple of drawers. They looked carefully on the desk and amongst the books, magazines and assorted papers on the floor, but there was no note or any obvious clue that either of them could see. She opened the drawers of the desk and took out the contents which seemed to be drawings and some leaflets, as well as a couple of newspapers.

The drawings were child-like, but one of them caught her eye; it was a drawing of a tree, with a man standing underneath it, holding something which appeared to be a spade; a crudely drawn figure lay on the ground. She put it to one side and then looked at the other pieces of paper, which were mainly other drawings.

She picked up the newspaper; it was the free newspaper which could be picked up anywhere in

London. The headline was of the discovery of the body of the girl on the Heath a few weeks earlier.

"I think we shouldn't touch anything else just now; I need to report to my inspector and see what he says."

* * * * *

Cooper had woken early that morning, still unused to sleeping alone in strange surroundings, hearing unfamiliar sounds of neighbours moving around. He had forced himself to climb out of bed, feeling the air cold and making a mental note to reset the timing on the heating.

After a simple breakfast he went out to scrape a thin layer of ice from his car windscreen, shivering despite a heavy coat and gloves. He rang Mark's mobile phone as he drove to the police station.

"I just wanted to thank you and Tricia for finding the flat for me, and wanted to let you know that I really like it," Cooper told him after the usual greeting.

"That's great. I'm glad you like it, Sam. Did you manage to fit all your stuff in?"

"I must admit I didn't realise I had so many books, and some of them are stacked against a wall, but I'll get sorted out soon. It's really comfortable; it's quiet as well. I haven't heard any neighbours yet, but maybe they're away or something. I was wondering if you and Tricia would like to join me at a nice restaurant for dinner tonight. My treat, as a thank you for helping me out like this."

"That'd be great Sam, thanks. I'll give Tricia a call to check, but we aren't doing anything as far as I know. Where do you want to go?"

"I'll book something, and send you a message. Speak later."

There was a knock at his office door almost as soon as he sat at his desk, and Robinson walked in.

"Good morning, sir. How are you this morning?"

"I moved into my new apartment over the weekend, which is good. I couldn't have slept on my friend's sofa much longer. I felt surprisingly content yesterday evening; I think I might enjoy living on my own. For a while, anyway."

"I think independence is underrated, personally. Anyhow, sir, there's someone in the interview room downstairs I think you should have a word with."

"Who?"

"A French man. Name of Pierre Bertrand. He thinks our girl on the heath might be his sister."

"Does he? Well, let's talk to him then."

As they walked down the corridor to the interview room they passed a young woman PC; he glanced at her and caught sight of a scowl on her face. She was looking at Robinson. Cooper glanced at him, but his face betrayed nothing. Either he hadn't seen the look, or his skin was thicker than he thought.

"Mr Bertrand?"

"Yes"

Cooper shook hands with the man and they sat down opposite him in the interview room.

"I'm detective inspector Cooper. How can we help you?"

"As I was saying to the detective constable, I saw in the newspaper a few weeks ago that you have found a body near here. Then on French TV they said that it was the body of a young woman, suspected of being in her early twenties, and that she could have died forty years ago. As I was scheduled to visit London this week, I arranged to fly out a day early so that I could speak to you this morning about my sister, to ask if it might be her."

"I see; what can you tell me about your sister?"

"She came to London in nineteen sixty eight and then disappeared after just a few months, in February nineteen sixty nine. She hasn't been seen since. I have spent many weekends over many years here in London just walking, talking to people, looking for her, or at least for clues as to what might have happened to her."

"What was she here for, sir?"

"She came here to study. You may be too young to remember, but nineteen sixty eight in Paris was a very difficult year. There were a lot of protests, and people were very divided. It all began as a student demonstration, but then the trouble rapidly escalated to include workers calling for the resignation of the government. The protests became full scale riots. Things became so bad that President de Gaulle and the Prime Minister Pompidou eventually sent the army onto the streets of Paris. There were even tanks at one stage. It was a very dangerous time."

At that point the door opened and a uniformed constable brought in some tea and biscuits, setting them on the table. Cooper took a biscuit from the plate in front of them. Robinson looked up from taking notes.

"What was your sister's name, sir?" Robinson asked.

"Her name was Monique. Monique Bertrand."

As Robinson started to write the name he stopped, looking at Mr Bertrand.

"Could you spell that for me, sir?" Robinson asked him, suddenly sounding interested in the story.

He spelled it out, and Robinson duly noted the name. He wrote 'Monica?' on the sheet and showed it to Cooper, who nodded.

"Please continue sir" Cooper said, still chewing his biscuit.

"Monique was at the university in Nanterre where the rioting started. The university closed after a while, and our mother wanted her to quit the course and find some work, but Monique decided to follow her English boyfriend to London. For a while she wrote to my mother regularly, but then after a few months the letters suddenly stopped. My mother became frantic. I was too young to help as I was only eleven at the time, and my mother did not speak English at all. She complained to the local police in our district in Paris, but they shrugged her concerns off. My mother was Algerian, and there were a lot of prejudices in those days, so that probably didn't help. The police told my mother that Monique had probably gone travelling somewhere with her boyfriend. After several months of complaining, the police finally agreed to contact the English police, but we never heard any more. My mother became very sick and I had to go and live with an aunt. My mother never really recovered and we never heard from Monique again."

"Where was your sister staying when she was in England?"

"I'm afraid I don't know. I have found no note of an address in my mother's papers. I have the letters from my sister to my mother, but they are almost all short informal notes, without any address on them. I have one envelope which has a London postmark on it, and I do remember Monique talking to me about London once, but of course I was a young boy and I didn't know anything about London then, so if she had told me it would have meant nothing to me."

"How old was Monique at the time?"

"When she went to England she was twenty two."

"Did she have any distinguishing features? Do you have a photograph at all?"

"Yes, I have a photograph here."

Cooper looked at the black and white photograph of an extremely pretty young girl, dressed in fashions of the sixties with a very short skirt and what seemed to be white boots.

"May I keep this?"

"Yes, I have a copy of it."

"Is there anything else that might identify her?"

"She had lost two fingers from one of her hands, in an accident, some while before."

Cooper glanced at Robinson, who had raised his eyebrows, his eyes wide open.

"What accident was that, sir?"

"One evening in Paris, during the height of the riots, she and her boyfriend were in a car with another couple. There was a bad accident. I think they were all drunk, I'm afraid. One of the boys was killed, and Monique lost two fingers from her left hand."

"Which fingers?"

"These two."

He held up the second and third fingers of his left hand. Again the two policemen exchanged glances.

"Do you think it may be my sister you have found?" the Frenchman asked, seeing the exchange of looks.

"Well it isn't possible to say right now sir, we would need to do some DNA testing to be certain, but I can confirm that some parts of the description you have given us do appear to match the description of the person we have found" Cooper told him.

He looked at them both, his eyes filling with tears. When he spoke his voice had changed.

"That would be an immense relief to me if it is my sister, inspector" he said, swallowing with some difficulty before continuing, "I have spent years hoping I would be able to bring her home and bury her properly."

"You said she was coming over here to see her boyfriend at the time. What can you tell me about him, sir?"

"He was English and his name was Charles. They were at university together. He was also in the car when the accident happened, although he wasn't injured."

"Do you know his surname, sir?"

"No, I'm afraid not. I never met him; he was always simply referred to as Charles. My mother might have known, but I have never found reference to his surname in Monique's letters, she only ever referred to Charles. My mother always refused to discuss it with me after she gave up hope. She became ill, as I said, and I'm afraid she had a complete breakdown. She died ten years ago. She ended her days in a mental hospital."

* * * * *

Robinson was standing leaning on the filing cabinet in Cooper's office as they reviewed progress, having placed his papers on the visitor chair. Cooper was pleased it was useful for something.

"So we know the girl was killed sometime in the late sixties or early seventies," Cooper began, "and we have a possible, let's say probable identification; a French girl called Monique Bertrand. Supposing that it is her, all we have to go on at the moment to determine who killed her is the name of the boyfriend, Charles, no surname. We're no nearer a cause of death, however let's assume it was murder. We know that this Monique went to Nanterre University, and we think that Charles went there as well. We also know that Monique was involved in a fatal car accident, and we believe that Charles was also involved. So let's start by finding out if the Paris police have records of anyone called Charles, involved in a car accident in the second half of nineteen sixty eight, who was a student at Nanterre, and where one of the other occupants of the car was called Monique."

As he was speaking the duty sergeant knocked on Cooper's door.

"Sorry to disturb you sir. Now you're back in your office I wanted to report that we took a call just half an hour ago from young WPC Harper. She was asked to attend a house in Hampstead this morning, where a man appears to have taken his own life. She's had a look around and she seems to have found something she

66

thinks you might want to see. Some kind of drawings, I believe. Do you want me to tell her to just bring them in?"

Cooper looked at Robinson with eyebrows raised. "Drawings? Where is she now?"

"She's still at the property. She has the key to the room in her hand, and is waiting for instructions."

"Well, tell her to go back inside and wait for me there. I'd like to see these drawings and have a look around."

The duty sergeant looked a little surprised but confirmed he would relay the message and went back down the stairs.

"Catherine Harper's a bit bloody thick in my book, so don't expect too much." Robinson said, as soon as the sergeant had gone.

Cooper said nothing; she had once made a formal complaint against Robinson, claiming he had made suggestive remarks to her. Robinson was clearly not going to sing the girl's praises. He left him to start sending out enquiries to the French police and went down to his car.

Some twenty minutes later he was outside the Hampstead property where WPC Harper was waiting for him.

"Why aren't you inside?"

WPC Harper blushed.

"I was just told to wait here, sir. The room is locked, and I have the key. The manager of the building is inside with the residents, and he felt they would be calmer if I wasn't inside. I also thought that I needed to be here to make sure no-one entered or left in case you wanted to speak to them."

"What kind of residents do you mean?"

"This house provides accommodation for several mentally disabled people, sir. They live here as they are capable of looking after themselves, but the manager comes most days to make sure that they are managing properly."

"I see. Well, let's go and take a look at the room."

"Do you want to speak to the manager first, sir?"

"Not yet, I'll take a look at the room first. His name?"

"Andy Jones, sir."

WPC Harper led him up the stairs, unlocked the door and stood back to allow him in. Cooper went in and looked around.

"Tell me what happened."

"Yes, sir. I heard a call at nine thirty five, and told them I would respond as I was on my bicycle patrolling the area. I came straight here. The manager had reported that he had found someone dead, which he confirmed when I arrived. When I opened the door into this room, the body of the resident, Angus Forsyth, was hanging from that hook in the ceiling."

He looked up.

"Why is the hook there?"

"Mr Jones told me it would have been for an old Victorian light fitting, sir."

"And you think it was suicide?"

"According to the manager, this door was locked. The chair by the desk was on the floor when I came in. It looks to me as if Angus stood on it, kicking the chair away once he had the rope round his neck. He was still hanging there when I came in; the manager helped me to get him down, but he was obviously dead. A patrol car arrived at the same time as the ambulance, and the two officers had a look around as well, but there are no signs of a disturbance, nothing to suggest anything other than suicide."

"I see. What was it that you thought I needed to see?"

"After the ambulance took the body away, I was looking for any form of a suicide note. When I looked in the drawer of that little desk, it was full of pieces of paper, most of them drawings and some notes, plus a couple of newspaper clippings. I looked through them for signs of a suicide note, even if I thought he would have been unlikely to leave one in the drawer rather than in full view. When I looked at the drawings I noticed there was one which seemed a little odd; it's of a tree, with someone lying on the ground, and a figure that seems to be holding a spade. Then I looked at the newspaper clippings. One is of an article on the recent discovery of the body on the heath. It might be a complete red herring, but it struck me as odd that we should find that in the room of someone who has committed suicide, so I decided to report it."

"Have you spoken to the other people here?"

"Yes, sir. I have spoken to them all as a group. A couple of them have some difficulties expressing themselves, but they all say they have no idea why Angus would commit suicide. The manager was with me when I interviewed them. He knows nothing either."

Cooper was looking slowly through each of the pieces of paper in the drawer as she spoke. As the WPC had said, there were a number of childish drawings, but the others were pictures of animals or groups of people. The one with the tree looked odd; it seemed similar to the one Diana Freedman had given him earlier. That drawing was on his desk; he regretted not picking it up to bring here.

He put all of the papers into a plastic bag and spent another ten minutes searching the room. He opened the wardrobe, examining the clothes, and looking inside a cotton bag. He tipped the bag out onto the floor. There was nothing remarkable, except that a shirt and a pair of jeans in the bag were covered in mud. The comment Diana made about seeing someone on the heath that night came to his mind.

"I wonder if this is from the heath. Is it likely that the ground there is still muddy?"

"No, sir, the ground has been fairly frozen for the past few days. I have a little dog that I take out for a walk on a regular basis, and I know he hasn't been muddy. He has white fur, and it's a nightmare when it's been raining."

Cooper thought for a moment.

"It's probably nothing, but get onto the station, will you, and ask them to send forensics here. I want them to have a good look at the place, and take away these clothes and any other evidence this person – what did you say his name was?"

"Forsyth, Angus Forsyth, sir."

"I want to see if there is any evidence he might have known something about the body on the heath, if indeed he did. Let's talk to the manager now."

They went back down to the living room where Andy Jones was waiting. He looked pale; Cooper asked

WPC Harper to get a glass of water for him, which he accepted gratefully.

"Can you tell me what exactly you do here, and what happened this morning?" Cooper asked.

"Of course. The people that I normally work with are those who are mentally disabled but who have been assessed as able to live in the community, and who don't need daily medical supervision, but who do need some help to manage their affairs. I make sure that they eat properly and that they are looking after themselves, keeping the house tidy and themselves clean. This building houses ten men who share a communal living room and kitchen. I help them to organise sharing the chores of washing and cleaning, although each tends to cook for himself. Most of the time it works, although Angus, who had Down's syndrome, had a habit of being a bit lazy and letting the others do his share if he could get away with it. Nonetheless I liked him as he had a great sense of fun, although sometimes I was concerned that he could be a bit reckless."

He paused for a drink of water.

"This morning I walked up the hill from Hampstead Heath station, arriving here at just before nine. I went into the kitchen at the back where I usually leave my rucksack and coat before I chat to each of the residents. I often visit them in their rooms. That gives each of them some privacy, but also gives me the opportunity to see how they are living, without being intrusive. As soon as I walked into the kitchen I noticed there were unwashed dishes in the sink; it wasn't unusual to see a few cups, but there were plates and cutlery as well which meant someone had missed doing the washing up yesterday evening. I also noticed one of the kitchen knives was missing from the knife block; I checked the washing in the sink but it wasn't there. As I was looking around the kitchen the door opened and George came in. George is the eldest resident at sixty, and seems to have taken it on himself to try to look after the others, which on the whole he does reasonably well, although one or two resent it sometimes."

He paused again.

"Take your time" Cooper said, gently.

"I asked George to tell me who was supposed to have washed the dishes; he told me it was meant to be Angus, but he hadn't been here in the evening and he hadn't seen him since. I then asked George when he'd last seen him. He said Angus had been watching the rugby on television with them on Saturday after which he'd gone for a walk. He'd returned later than usual and he hadn't seen him since then. I was quite concerned at this, so I walked up to Angus's room and knocked on the door a couple of times, but I got no response. The door was locked but I have a key to all the rooms. I unlocked the door and opened it slightly, knocking again. There was still no response, so I pushed the door fully open. I was confronted by a pair of legs, and looked up to see Angus's body held in the air by a rope. Angus had hanged himself. I had to walk out. I couldn't look at him, hanging in the air like that."

"You're certain the door was locked?"

"Positive."

"Does anyone else have a key?"

"No, we only allow each resident to have his own key. Any spares are kept by us."

"Who do you mean by we, sir?"

"I mean the managers employed by Camden. I'm the only one looking after this property, so no one else would have access to that room other than Angus and myself."

"Thank you for allowing us to talk to you, sir" Cooper said. "By the way, did you find that knife?"

"No, I didn't. It seems to have disappeared."

* * * * *

"I can't believe what Carol did to you," Tricia said.

She was sitting at the table of the restaurant with Mark and Cooper.

"I know she was mad at you, but that was just ridiculous. She must have known you would walk out as soon as you found out, even if she didn't expect you home that afternoon. You were bound to find out, sooner or later. If she thought it would make you change the way she wanted, then it was an odd way to behave. No, she wanted out, whatever she thinks now."

"Well, whatever she had in mind, she only expressed what we were both thinking. I'd already decided I wasn't going to give up my career, so I think the break up was inevitable."

"According to Dominic's face book page, he's in a relationship and he's posted a photo of himself with her."

"She told me it was a fling. Obviously it wasn't. Anyhow I thought he had a girlfriend."

"The girl at the New Year dinner? We didn't know her; we invited him on his own because he said he didn't have a partner, but then he rang to ask if he could bring someone, and he brought that girl. That clearly was a fling as well."

Cooper smiled.

"Well, it seems to have been just a short term relationship according to Carol. Whether he thinks it was, I guess we'll see in due course. Frankly I don't give a damn; I need to move on with my life."

FIVE

Since she and Buster had discovered the girl's lonely grave on the heath, Diana Freedman had been troubled with dreams in the night. Last night was no exception; her only consolation was that as she lay awake a few ideas had come to her that she could use in her novel.

She climbed out of bed as dawn broke to write the ideas down before she forgot them, switching on her laptop before going into the kitchen to make herself her morning coffee. She had never enjoyed tea first thing in the morning; a good strong coffee was much better, she thought. She rarely ate much breakfast; just the occasional biscuit with her coffee was usually enough for her.

She returned to her laptop in time to hear a sound telling her an email had arrived. She did not get many, so she looked to see who was writing to her. It was her cousin Marie in Paris. Diana had asked if she had any knowledge of their common English ancestor who was rumoured to have taken part in the French revolution.

She read the reply with increasing interest, which took several minutes because Diana's French was a little rusty, and the email quite long. She then forwarded it to Amanda, suggesting she call her when she received it so they could chat about it.

Diana was surprised when the telephone rang only ten minutes or so later. Amanda wasn't normally an early bird, and she hadn't expected a call for at least another hour, if not two.

Diana picked up the receiver.

The caller wasn't Amanda at all.

It was a man.

* * * * *

WPC Catherine Harper was doing her usual route through the streets of Hampstead when she cycled past someone who waved at her. She recognised him and stopped.

"Hello there Mister Jones, how are you?"

"I'm fine thanks, constable. My name's Andy, by the way. You're Catherine as I remember, may I call you Catherine?"

"You can call me that as long as I'm not with any other police officers."

"Fair enough."

"How are you now and how are things at the house?"

"I'm fine now, thanks. It was a shock to us all at the time, and I miss Angus's practical jokes, but life has to go on. I just keep busy. Everyone else is pretty well settled down now that the funeral is out of the way. You might remember George; he was the one who did most of the talking. He has been a bit out of sorts recently, but I hope he'll sort himself out soon. The others seem to have settled down more quickly than I could have hoped."

"That's good. It must have been a real trauma for them, as for anyone, but they seem like a family so it must be hard."

"Yes, it is hard for them; we can only try to get them to focus on today really. May I ask you one thing?"

"Yes of course, what's that?"

"Can I buy you a drink, after you have finished your duties of course?"

Catherine was taken aback, but she was flattered as well. She needed to think about this.

"Well I'm not sure."

"Well please think about it and let me know if you decide you would like to. I have a card here with my mobile phone number on. Give me a call anytime you like."

"OK, I shall. Thank you."

She smiled at him and took the card.

"Oh, before you go can I ask you one other thing? Strictly business of course?"

"Go on."

"There is a very old lady I've seen walking around here. She is almost bent double, and walks with a stick. She usually has her head covered with a headscarf. Do you know who I mean?"

"I think I do. Why do you ask?"

"Well, I saw her the other morning talking to George, and then I remembered that I saw the same lady talking to Angus as well, just before Christmas. None of the residents has ever spoken about her to me, and I have no idea how they should know her. I once asked Angus who she was but he wasn't keen to talk about her. The reason I mention it is that I don't like mysteries, especially when it comes to the residents. When I saw George talking to her this morning it looked to me as if he gave her something; it looked like an envelope, and that set my curiosity off."

Whilst he was speaking he looked at his watch.

"Oops, I need to run to get my train. Look, I'll be at Dingwalls bar at Camden Lock this evening after seven with a small group of friends."

He started to walk towards the station.

"If you like we can continue this conversation over a drink" he said over his shoulder.

Catherine watched him walk away. She couldn't help smiling to herself. He was quite attractive really.

* * * * *

Later that day DC Robinson was sitting on the chair in Cooper's office; he looked distinctly uncomfortable, as if he regretted his decision not to stand.

"So what do you think, sir, was the drawing pushed through Mrs Freedman's door done by this Angus Forsyth?"

"Well, to my eye all the drawings are by the same person. And the subjects are similar" Cooper surmised.

"So could Angus Forsyth have known something? Are Monica and Monique the same person?"

"He would only have been a child at the time she was killed, so it's unlikely he was involved, but he may have found something out about this murder relatively recently."

"But if all these drawings are his, and if he pushed the drawing through Mrs Freedman's door, then he must have been trying to tell her something before he committed suicide. I assume it was definitely suicide?"

"Forensics have found nothing to make us think otherwise, although we don't know why he did kill himself. There were some muddy clothes in his room, which tell us he'd been on the heath some weeks earlier, but nothing else was found to give us any clues as to what made him kill himself."

"So what do we know about him?"

"I'm told he had Down's syndrome; apparently he could neither read nor write very well. If you remember it was difficult to make out the name written on the piece of newspaper in the envelope pushed through Mrs Freedman's door. However I also know that Down's children weren't always given a full education so that doesn't necessarily indicate his capabilities."

"So the question is what drove him to commit suicide?"

"Good question. You've reminded me; I wanted to clarify a few things with the manager of that place again. I'm going to ask him if he's ever come across a Monica as well."

Cooper dialled a number from his office phone.

"Hello Mr Jones, this is DI Cooper here, from Camden police. We spoke briefly the other day when you discovered the death of Angus Forsyth. How are you feeling today?"

"I'm fine, thanks. It was a shock because you get to know all of these people really well. In a way they're only children, you know. I enjoy my time with all of them. It's a real shock when something happens, as if it had happened to a close friend."

"Do you have a moment? I have a few questions about Angus if I may."

"No problem, fire away."

"I have Angus's full name as Angus Forsyth, born in Hampstead on the fifth of April 1961?"

"Correct."

"How long had Angus been at the home in Hampstead?"

"He'd been there for about eight years."

"Where was he before that?"

"He lived with his mother. His father left the family not long after his birth apparently; Angus told me he didn't remember him at all. His mother died eight years ago, and he was given a place in our little community."

"Did he live in Hampstead with his mother?"

"Yes, actually it was down near the hospital not far from where he lives, or rather lived until last week."

"So quite close to the heath, then?"

"Yes, he knew the area well. He often took walks over there."

"Did he have any other family at all? Or anyone that would have known him?"

"There isn't anyone that I'm aware of, but if you hold on I have his file in my drawer, and I can check to see if it mentions anyone. Give me a moment."

Cooper waited; he could hear a filing cabinet drawer open and close.

"OK, let me see. His next of kin is listed as a Mrs. Isabelle Edwards, who lives in Notting Hill. Apparently she is a cousin of his mother's. I'm just looking through the rest of the contact details. No, there is no mention of anyone other than her."

"I assume that Mrs. Edwards would have been told of Angus's death?"

"She should have been informed by the social services office in Camden."

"Did she ever visit him?"

"Not that I'm aware of. He never mentioned her."

"Does the name Monica mean anything to you sir?"

"Monica? No, no I can't say I know anyone called Monica."

"There's no-one Angus might have known, or come into contact with, with that name? A doctor or nurse, perhaps, or social services?"

"I can't think of anyone called Monica, inspector, in any area that Angus came into contact with."

"You were with WPC Harper when she found the drawings and the newspaper in his desk?"

"Yes, I was."

"Had you seen the drawings before?"

"I knew he liked to draw, but he was quite secretive in a way, so he never really showed them to me. I only saw them briefly and they looked childish to me."

"That's what I thought at first, but having looked at them more closely I think he had a bit of talent. You said that he often went on the heath?"

"Yes, he enjoyed walking on the heath, and used to go most days. He knew the place like the back of his hand. He took me on there once, and we went along all kinds of small paths through trees; I was completely lost. How he found his way through I have no idea, but he obviously knew every inch."

"You remember the drawing that WPC Harper found? It was of a tree and two figures, one of them lying on the ground."

"Yes, I remember it. I don't know why he drew that, although it may have just taken his fancy, but the man with a spade is a bit odd, I agree. Perhaps he read the story in the newspaper and it was just from his imagination."

"I would agree with you if it were not for the fact that someone recently pushed an envelope through the front door of the lady who discovered the body on the heath. The envelope contained a similar drawing plus a newspaper clipping about the discovery of the body; what is more somebody had written the name 'Monica' on the newspaper."

"And you think that was Angus?"

"The drawing looked very similar in style to the one found by WPC Harper; it was of a tree, and again two figures including a person lying underneath the tree who might have been asleep, but it could also have been a body."

"So do you think he knew something; was he not just using his imagination?"

"That may be, but it doesn't explain why he wrote a name on the newspaper clipping. If he did know something, would he have been likely to tell you?"

"Difficult to say. He generally kept himself to himself, but as with everyone there I tried to make sure he was given a little time with me in case anything was bothering him, so I would hope he would feel able to tell me."

"And you don't know where the name Monica might have come from?"

"I'm afraid I have no idea."

"Could you give me the name and address of his next of kin? You said she was called Mrs Isabelle Edwards?"

When Cooper finished the call he looked at Robinson, by now perched on the edge of the famously uncomfortable chair.

"I think we should pay a visit to Mrs Edwards later today, to see if she knows anything at all. Maybe nothing, but we don't have much else to go on right now."

* * * * *

It was about seven in the evening by the time Cooper and Robinson arrived at the Notting Hill address of Isabelle Edwards, flakes of snow blowing around in the freezing night air. Robinson was driving. They pulled up outside of a large Regency style house, trying to read the number on the door.

"This is the one. Is this building divided into apartments, or does she own all of it?" Robinson wondered.

"I'm not sure. Looks like one house."

The front gate was locked, so Cooper pressed the intercom button. As he did so, Robinson looked through the gate and whistled softly.

"Nice place."

The intercom crackled into life and a man's voice asked who was ringing.

"Is that Mr. Edwards?"

"Yes."

"I'm sorry to disturb you sir," Cooper said into the speaker. "I am DI Cooper from Camden police and I have DC Robinson with me. We would like to ask a few questions if we may."

The man sounded surprised, but not alarmed.

"Have we been misbehaving?"

"No, nothing like that, sir, we're just hoping you can help us with one of our enquiries."

"I see, do come in."

The gate buzzed and clicked open. They walked towards the front door which opened as they arrived at the step. They both showed their identity cards to the man standing in the doorway.

"We're just having dinner at the moment; do you mind waiting in the study for five minutes?"

"Of course" Cooper responded. "I am sorry to disturb you. It won't take more than a few minutes."

The man left them to wait, returning with a woman a short while later. They were both far more elegantly dressed than he would have been for eating dinner alone; there didn't appear to be anyone else in the house.

"This is my wife, Isabelle."

Cooper shook hands with her.

"And your name, sir?"

The man looked surprised he didn't know his name, and frowned.

"My name is Charles Edwards."

"I see." He turned to Isabelle. "I understand you have a cousin, by the name of Angus Forsyth."

She gasped slightly in surprise.

"Oh, yes. Angus is the son of a distant cousin to be precise. His grandmother was a cousin to my grandmother, as far as I recall. I assume this is about his death?"

"In a way, yes. Did you know Angus well?"

"No, barely at all. His mother knew my mother a little, and she visited my mother's home a few times, but I only recall seeing Angus once, soon after he was born. Sometime after that Angus's father left them and his mother became a bit of a recluse."

"I see. Did Angus or his mother have any other family at all?"

"Angus was an only child, as was his mother, so he had no other family on her side. I don't believe his mother kept in touch with anyone in her husband's family, so it's unlikely he knew of any family there either. I was the only family she had, which is, I suppose, how I ended up being the next of kin to Angus, although I barely knew him."

"And you don't know of anyone who he might have been in touch with on a regular basis?"

"I have no idea I'm afraid. I assume social services were looking after him, but other than a letter after his mother died and another one after he died last week I have heard nothing about him at all."

"Amongst his papers we found the mention of a name 'Monica'. Does that name mean anything to you?"

For a split second Cooper saw a startled look in Isabelle's eyes, but she recovered her composure in an instant.

"No, I'm afraid not."

Cooper looked at her husband.

"Does the name mean anything to you, sir? She isn't a relative or friend that could have had contact with Angus in any way?"

He looked very relaxed, and smiled.

"I'm afraid not."

Cooper thought he was either very good at telling lies, or genuinely knew nothing, but he had seen something in his wife's face for an instant which made him alert.

"Ok sir, madam, I'll leave you to your evening. Thank you for your help. If you do think of anything then please let me know."

"Can you tell us anything of what this is about?" the husband asked.

"I'm just following up on Angus Forsyth's death, sir. We are trying to establish a reason for him to kill himself, but as yet we have no idea why he did it."

Isabelle gasped.

"I didn't know he had killed himself. The poor man!"

"I'm sorry," Cooper apologised, "I assumed that you had been told all of the facts by social services. He hung himself."

"It isn't your fault, inspector, that we didn't know," her husband asserted, "but perhaps we might let you go now."

"Of course sir. As I said, please let me know if anything occurs to you. Goodnight."

Robinson looked at him as they drove away.

"What were they hiding? They seemed to be expecting us to ask something else."

"I thought so too. It's interesting that his name is Charles."

"That same thought occurred to me as soon as he said it, but then I thought it was just too good to be true. It couldn't be the same guy, surely?"

"I don't know. See what you can find out on those two. And chase the French for answers on that accident Monique was involved in."

* * * * *

Catherine Harper made her way to the bar in Camden that evening. At first she wondered if Andy Jones would in fact be there; she looked around the crowded bar but couldn't see him. She walked to the back of the room to take a seat in a corner to wait; she thought she would give him fifteen minutes, then go.

She had been there for less than five when he came in; he saw her, smiled and came straight over.

"Would you like to join me and my friends who are finding seats on the other side of the bar?"

"Yes, I'd like that very much."

Several hours later, after what was a very pleasant evening although the bar was too noisy for her, they left his friends and walked out of the pub together. They then walked slowly along the towpath of the canal; as they did so Andy gently took hold of Catherine's hand. She was pleased he had.

"You asked me about that old lady this morning" she said, looking at him with a curious glance. "Why were you interested in her?"

Andy hesitated.

"When she was with George this morning, there was something in the way he was behaving that made me watch them. He gave her something, and it looked to me like an envelope. I don't see any reason why George would have any dealings with anyone that I don't know. It might be nothing of course. I also saw the same woman talking to Angus a few weeks before he died. Again, it might be nothing and she may be someone who they've confided in from time to time, but I'm surprised that no-one has mentioned her to me at all."

"I think I know the lady. Her name is Elizabeth Marsh, and she's lived in Hampstead most of her life as far as I know. She was an actress at one point. I was told that she had some minor roles in a few big West End productions in the fifties and sixties. Then she married a local man and had a daughter so she gave up acting. It seems her daughter disappeared in the early seventies, and her husband died a few years after that, so she lives alone now. She is known as a little bit eccentric, but I once saw her going out of an evening very well dressed, and in a kind of way she is still glamorous. I think she was quite a beauty in her day. I often see her walking in the centre, always with a headscarf, whatever the weather. I'm not sure how old Mrs Marsh is, but she must be in her eighties."

"Then I wonder why she was talking to Angus and George?"

"Do you have any charities that raise money for the people you look after?"

"Not that I know of. I know it's an odd thing to say, but George looked a bit furtive when he was talking to her. I have absolutely no reason for saying this, but it crossed my mind that she might know something about Angus that we don't. She may even have some idea why he killed himself; I'm at a loss to understand that."

"I wouldn't mind talking to her anyway, to get to know her. I'll have a quick word with the DI tomorrow though, before I do. You never know it might be something he would find interesting."

They walked a little farther along the canal side, hand in hand, talking a little about themselves to discover more about each other. Catherine looked at her watch.

"I need to go home. I have to be up early tomorrow."

They took some steps up to the high street where Andy stopped a black cab for her. He seemed surprised when she kissed him on the lips just before she stepped inside the taxi and drove off into the night. As she arrived home her mobile phone bleeped. It was a message from Andy.

"Had a lovely evening. Are you free tomorrow evening?"

"So did I. I'll call you tomorrow," was her message back to him.

SIX

It was a lovely sunny but cold morning and the cherry trees were showing the first signs of blossom. As Catherine cycled down the hill past Hampstead hospital she thought this was one of her favourite times of the year. Spring was on the way.

As she turned towards Hampstead Heath station she saw an elderly lady walking with a bent back, dressed in a raincoat, her head covered with a scarf.

Catherine rode a little way past her, and then stopped her bike, getting off.

"Hello, Mrs Marsh, how are you today? It's a lovely day."

The old lady looked at Catherine for a moment in a bemused way, causing Catherine to wonder if she had startled her somehow. Then the old lady smiled.

"Hello, my dear. Yes it is lovely, but I'm afraid I still feel the cold very easily, so I am still very wrapped up. Still, you must keep warm with all that exercise on your bicycle. I've seen you riding around here a few times over the past several months. You obviously know your business, as you have taken the trouble to find out my name."

However frail she might seem, the old lady's mind was still very sharp.

"Yes, I did ask someone as I had seen you and I wanted to know if you needed any help at all."

"Well that's very kind of you, but I cope on my own very well indeed. I take a walk over the heath every day if I can manage it. I've been doing it every day since my daughter disappeared all those years ago, in the hope of finding her. I presume you know about my daughter?"

"I had heard that your daughter ran away."

"Well, that was the police supposition, but I never believed it."

"What makes you say that?"

"Because Tina, my daughter, was known to be mixed up with a group of people who were using drugs, and the police thought she had gone way with one of them as they both disappeared at the same time. However he turned up some weeks later, denying that he had seen my daughter. Tina was never seen again. Because Tina and I had had a difficult time, they thought she had moved away, you see, but I never believed she would have gone away without telling me. Even if she had spoken to me after the event, she would have found a way to tell me."

"When did you last see your daughter?"

"On the sixteenth of June, nineteen seventy."

"How old was she?"

"She was born in May nineteen fifty, so she was not quite twenty."

"You said you walked on the heath to try to find her. Do you think you'll see her there one day?"

The old lady looked at her.

"Not walking around dear. I'm looking for her body. She is dead, I am sure. When that girl's body was found the other day I thought it might turn out to be Tina, but it wasn't her, as we know."

"You think she was murdered?" Catherine asked.

"I'm sure she was. If it had been an accident somewhere then someone would have told me. And she was murdered right here, in London, because if Tina had gone away then she would have sent me a message somehow. I saw a fortune teller some time later who told me to look for her in an open space. I've been coming here ever since."

Catherine was taken aback by the comment.

"Do you mind if I ask you another question?"

"That's fine dear, but perhaps we could start to walk towards the heath as I am getting cold standing here."

"Oh of course, I'm sorry."

They began to walk, Catherine wheeling her bicycle as they did so.

"I saw you speaking with a mentally disabled man the other day. Do you mind if I ask how you know him?"

"You must mean George. Well, I knew his friend Angus better, until he died. I only knew George through him, really. I met Angus regularly on the heath, as he used to like to walk around there. He however was on there every day, even in inclement weather and in the midst of winter. I once asked him why he went so often, and he said that, like me, he was looking for someone."

Catherine looked at her.

"What do you think he meant by that?"

"I'm not sure really. At first we used to just say hello, but after a while we used to stop and have a little chat, about the weather or something. Despite his condition – you know he had Down's syndrome?"

"Yes, I was aware of that."

"Well, despite that, he was actually very funny, and liked to tell me stories. After a while I told him about my daughter, and he started to cry. I was upset for him, but he then told me a story about seeing a woman's body being carried away. He told me he'd overheard someone later say that she'd been buried on the heath. I thought this was just another of his stories and that he was trying to make me feel better about making him cry, so I didn't ask any more. After that we tended to walk together if we met, and he often used to say he was looking out for my daughter when he walked around. He never mentioned the story about that woman again."

"And how did you meet George?"

"It was just a few weeks before Angus died. I met Angus on the heath, and George was with him, so we walked together for a while. I didn't meet him again after that until after Angus died. Then George met me as I was walking back from the heath. I think he had been waiting for me, because he had something for me."

"Do you mind if I ask what that was?"

"Not at all. Angus was a talented artist, and had shown me some of his work in the past. I had always encouraged him to paint, as I could see he was really rather good. George had some of his paintings, and gave them to me as he thought I would like them."

"What were the paintings of?"

"They were all paintings of the heath. All except one, that is. That was a painting of a woman."

"Mrs. Marsh, you have been very helpful. Would it be possible for me to see the pictures?"

"Well I would love to show them to you, but the detective has them."

Catherine looked at her.

"May I ask the detective's name?"

"His name was Renard. He's from the French police. He's working with the English police because of the investigation into the death of the French lady."

"What did this detective look like?"

"He is quite tall, well over six feet I would say, and quite thin, almost too thin. He is probably about sixty, perhaps a little older."

Catherine made a note.

"And was there anything else about him? His hair, for example?"

"He had quite untidy hair, quite grey."

"I see. When did you speak to him?"

"It was just three evenings ago."

"How did he know about the pictures from Angus?"

"I have no idea, he didn't say. Do you not know him?"

"Well I'm not aware, but it might be he's working with some of our detectives. I'm sure it's nothing to worry about."

Catherine was now not sure what to think, and decided to ask no more without talking to Cooper. She should have spoken to Mike Robinson rather than the inspector really, but she didn't trust him.

* * * * *

During the morning there was a knock at Cooper's office door. It was Robinson.

"You asked me to look into Charles and Isabelle Edwards, boss. I have some details."

He waved to his chair as an invitation to sit, but Robinson declined. Despite himself Cooper smiled at his preference to stand.

"O.K., go ahead."

"Charles Edwards has worked in the City for about twenty five years. He was born in nineteen forty six, went to school at Harrow after which he went to Oxford. He graduated with a first in modern languages in nineteen sixty seven. After that he spent a year in Paris with his uncle's family, where he was on a postgraduate course in business administration at Nanterre University. That was in nineteen sixty eight, the year there were serious riots in Paris."

"Yes, I've read about that. In fact from what I have read it came close to being a revolution; the army were on the streets with tanks at one point" Cooper said.

"Maybe, but Edwards is on record as saying that for him it had all been fun; it had been a diversion from this business course that his father wanted him to take before joining the family business. He says he never wanted to get involved in the business at all. Apparently his great-great grandfather started the business somewhere in the north making cotton making machines in the nineteenth century; the company ended up making aeroplane components in the nineteen thirties and grew rapidly during the Second World War. By this time his grandfather was running the business, and apparently he made a lot of money during the war years. By the end of the war he was a wealthy man, well connected in government, and the business was employing over a thousand people. Edwards' father became managing director of the business during the nineteen fifties. It had been expected that Edwards would join the company and take over from his father at some point, but he wasn't interested and did everything to avoid going there. Fortunately for Edwards his younger brothers were much keener on the family business and his father then encouraged them to join him in running it. One of his brothers is today still the chairman, although it is now a quoted company and the family only has a minority stake."

"So what did Edwards do?"

"He spent about a year in the family firm but then left to qualify as a barrister, when he spent several years in a law firm in Hong Kong, from nineteen seventy to nineteen eighty, before returning to the UK. He then went into politics; he was elected as an MP in nineteen eighty two; he was once tipped to become a minister, however a newspaper reporter saw him on a number of occasions in a nightclub with a woman who was not his wife, and he was apparently told by senior figures in the party that he was not likely to make it to the very top."

"That rings a bell; I do remember that now."

"Yes, there were a lot of press comments at the time. At that point it seems he decided to use some of his contacts to join a merchant bank, which he did late in nineteen eighty eight. He now works for a large American Bank, as chairman of corporate finance for Europe. He travels extensively between London and New York, and visits Paris, Frankfurt and Zurich regularly. He still sees his uncle's family whenever he is in Paris, and is fond of spending time at a family villa down in Provence; he usually spends a week or two there every year if he can."

"That's very comprehensive."

"It wasn't difficult. He likes publicity, and I lifted that from various newspaper reports and some glossy lifestyle magazines which he's appeared in from time to time. He isn't exactly keeping a low profile. That may be why he seemed a bit put out when we had no idea who he was."

"Well it's a pretty good summary, anyway."

"There's just one other thing on him I thought you might be interested in. I printed it from the internet; it's one of those glossy lifestyle magazines."

Cooper looked at the print of a magazine article about Charles Edwards' wife, written during he was an MP. The headline in particular caught his eye.

We talk to the wife of high flying MP from Hampstead

"Hampstead?" he said. "I didn't realise they used to live in Hampstead. They told us they didn't know Angus, but they lived close by. A coincidence?"

"I don't know, sir. I just thought it was interesting they used to live there."

"Can you find out exactly when they lived in Hampstead, and the address?"

"Will do, sir."

*＊＊＊＊

"Come in" Cooper said, hearing a knock on his door later in the day.

It opened and WPC Catherine Harper looked in.

"I'm sorry to disturb you sir, but I wonder if you have some time?"

"Yes, come in."

She walked in, looked at his visitor chair but then continued to stand. He was surprised its reputation was so widespread; he thought to himself he really ought to get the chair changed.

"You may remember, sir, that when you came to Hampstead to see where that poor man had hanged himself, you spoke briefly to the manager, Andy Jones?"

"Yes, I remember. I also called him a couple of days ago."

"I wanted to let you know I met him yesterday evening for a drink; he asked me out with some friends of his so I accepted."

She frowned as she spoke, as if she was worried she might have done something wrong. Cooper assured her that it was fine by him.

"We were discussing an old lady from Hampstead, who seemed to have some connection with Angus Forsyth that we don't understand. This morning I saw the lady and had a chat to her. I thought some of what she said might be of interest, sir."

"Do you always talk about old ladies on first dates?"

She looked confused for a moment, and then smiled as she realised he was joking.

"Not usually, sir. But this was a very interesting old lady."

"I'm glad to hear it."

"The lady is called Elizabeth Marsh; she's lived in Hampstead most of her life as far as I know. She was an actress at one point; she is known locally as a little bit eccentric. You should also be aware, sir, that her daughter went missing many years ago, and was never seen again. The investigation at the time concluded she had run away from home."

Catherine then repeated the conversation she had had with Mrs Marsh.

"So she's convinced her daughter was murdered, although we didn't think so?" Cooper asked.

"She told me she was sure her daughter had been murdered. If it had been an accident somewhere then someone would have told her. And she was murdered right here, in London, because if her daughter had gone away then she would have sent her a message somehow."

"What was her daughter's name, and when did she disappear?"

As Cooper asked the question he was looking at the spreadsheet of missing girls from Mike Robinson.

"Her daughter's name was Tina, Tina Marsh. She disappeared in June, nineteen seventy, at about the same time as the girl on the heath, which struck me as a strange co-incidence. When she told me she knew Angus well and that she'd spoken to him about her daughter, it occurred to me he may have been imagining her on the heath when he made the drawing."

"Possibly. She had some drawings but gave them to this so-called detective called Renard, you said?"

"Yes, it seems so."

"I'd like to know who he is. I wonder why her daughter's name isn't on our list of missing people. When did she speak to this Renard?"

"It was just three evenings ago."

"And how did she meet Angus?"

"She met him walking on the heath. He was often there. She said she had once asked him why he went so often, and he said that, like her, he was looking for someone."

"Looking for someone?"

"He told her he had once seen a woman being carried away from where he used to live, when he was a child. He told her he had overheard someone later say that she'd been buried on the heath."

"He told her he saw someone carried away when he was a child? She used the words 'carried away'?"

"Yes, sir" said Catherine, referring to her notes.

"And he'd heard this woman had been buried on the heath?"

"Yes, sir."

"Have you reported this yet?"

"Not yet sir. I have of course written it all down here in my notebook, but I haven't filed my report yet. I wanted to tell you first."

"I think I'd like to know a bit more about her daughter. Would you talk to this Mrs Marsh again, and get a description of her, a photograph, and anything that might help to find where she went to, who she was seeing."

"Of course, sir."

She left his office. Cooper looked at the door as she closed it, sitting back in his chair, looking very thoughtful.

* * * * *

It was early evening. Cooper was jogging along the deserted canal bank, the ground beneath his feet glowing orange where there was a lit section, slowly darkening where the lights didn't penetrate the gloom.

He was red-faced and hot from his efforts at keeping to his target pace, despite the cold February air. He had, for reasons that now seemed foolish, agreed with a couple of friends to enter a half marathon in April, and he needed to be able to keep up a decent pace so that he wouldn't embarrass himself too much on the day. He had resigned himself to some embarrassment; it was merely a question of damage limitation now. He had been timing himself carefully for each all too infrequent run, but the improvement was minimal.

As he reached his usual turning point, which was the tunnel before Little Venice, he stopped to check his watch and to get his breath back for a moment before jogging along the path back to Camden.

He was leaning forwards with his hands on his knees, giving himself a few moments to recover his breath before the run back, when he felt a stinging blow to the back of his head which made him cry out. This was swiftly followed by a punch into his ribs which sent him onto his knees, gasping for breath. A kick in the back sent him forward, his head hitting the floor with a crack. He felt another kick into his ribs as he lay there, making him cry out in pain again; his self defence training had taught him to avoid going down if at all possible, but he was on the floor before he could react at all. He realised he could feel someone pulling his rucksack; his wallet, phone and keys were in there. He tried to turn over to grab at the arm that he could see, but for his trouble he received another kick in the ribs, followed by one to the head moments later which stunned him.

His rucksack was gone and his assailant was running away.

He lay on the path by the canal for a moment, the cold floor seeming to move around underneath him like the deck of a ship, trying to breathe despite the pain in his ribs.

He heard someone running towards him and, fearing his attacker had returned, he moved to try to get up, gritting his teeth against the pain. He looked in the direction of the sound of footsteps and was relieved to see two young women running along the path towards him.

Cooper lay back onto his side; he tried to sit up as they came to him, but one of the girls bent down and pressed his shoulder back down gently to dissuade him from trying; she then helped him to lie on his back, putting something under his head to make him more comfortable.

"Is that better?" she asked.

"I think so," he said, coughing in pain, "I think I've just been mugged."

"We saw a young guy running away from us down the path just a few seconds ago" the second girl said, "was it him?"

"I really don't know, I didn't see him at all," he gasped. "Did you get a look at him?"

"No, I'm afraid we didn't see his face at all. He had a hood pulled up."

Cooper tried to lie still. He felt increasing pain in his chest, and his head hurt. There was no point worrying about his aggressor right now.

The first girl knelt down beside him.

"Let me have a look at you. I'm a nurse. Where do you have pain?"

"Right now, everywhere, but especially here."

He pointed to his ribs. As she felt gently at his ribs he felt a sharp pain.

"Ouch!"

"Caroline, will you wait here with him? I'm going to call for an ambulance."

She stood up besides Cooper, who was still lying on the floor, trying not to move.

"Stay still for a minute. I think you may have broken ribs. I want to get you to a hospital so that they can have a good look at you. I'll be back in a minute."

As she walked away she turned back to look at him. Despite his shock and pain, he looked at her and thought she was very pretty; right then she was very definitely his angel of mercy.

The ambulance arrived quickly, by which point Cooper had managed to get himself partially sitting up onto his elbows, which was more comfortable than lying on the cold pathway, despite the advice of the pretty nurse and the pain stabbing at his chest, whichever position he adopted. As the ambulance men came up and took charge, the two girls wished him luck and made to go.

"Will you at least let me have your name and phone number so that I can call you and thank you later?" he pleaded, gasping with the pain as he spoke.

The pretty nurse smiled at her friend, and she took a piece of paper and a pencil from her handbag, writing on it before handing it to him.

"Take care of yourself first" she said to him with a smile.

The two girls walked away as the ambulance men checked him over for what seemed a long time. Placing him carefully onto a stretcher, Cooper still clutching the piece of paper, they carried him up the steps by the bridge and into the waiting ambulance, blue lights flashing in the night sky as it drove away.

* * * * *

It was evening of the same day when a man was driving across some of his land to his sprawling manor house. He glanced at the landmark visible for several miles around; a surviving cotton mill chimney from the many that had once dominated the landscape of that part of Lancashire. It was always a reminder of his ancestors' route to prosperity.

The car went between the gateposts and swept down the long driveway towards the manor, past trees planted over a hundred years ago to conceal the house from visitors until the final moment of the approach. Even though he had seen it thousands of times during his almost seventy years of living there, he never failed to appreciate the beauty of the house whenever he drove up to it.

He stopped the car on the semi-circular driveway in front of the house, jumped out and walked up the couple of steps to open the heavy wooden door which was as usual unlocked, a habit developed after many years of having servants around the house. These days, doors were locked at night as the family now had only a couple of gardeners and a housekeeper but in his parents' day they were never locked.

He wasn't sure he could really afford even the few staff he had these days. The price of sheep was at an all time low, and the dairy herds were not doing much more than breaking even. The accounts he had just reviewed at one of his farms had not made him feel any better about his finances, and he knew that work to the roof of the house was going to become desperately needed within the next eighteen months.

He walked through the hallway past its paintings of family going back to the late eighteenth century when the family had become prosperous, into the library overlooking the gardens to the west of the house where he kept his accounts and papers; he took the papers from the briefcase he was carrying and dropped them onto his desk. He then walked through the house to the kitchen, where his wife was with the housekeeper; they were sitting at the table eating a light supper. The housekeeper stood up when he walked in and went to the fridge to take out a plate she had prepared for him; he bent down to kiss his wife on the cheek as she did so, and he sat down as the housekeeper put the plate in front of him.

For him it still seemed a little odd to eat in the kitchen, but they had stopped using the dining room except for formal occasions after the last of the children had moved out of the house; for the housekeeper to carry food halfway across the sprawling house for the two of them to eat in the dining room seemed preposterous these days. He felt slightly guilty however, conscious of lowering the standards that his parents and grandparents had been very proud of. He could hear his grandfather speaking to him now. "Everyone has their place my boy" he had often said, "including the landed classes. We need to follow the rules as much as the working classes do. That is how the world works."

"How are things down on Bob's farm?" his wife asked, bringing him back to the present from his daydreaming. "Did you see Joan? She was going to see her mother the other day, did she mention that?"

"No, she didn't. Bob and I were pretty busy going through the books and sorting out the next visit from the vet, but she seemed cheerful enough so I presume her mother was ok when she saw her."

"She's always cheerful. Her mother is deteriorating rapidly though, poor soul."

The housekeeper had been sitting quietly while they chatted, but as they began to eat she took the opportunity to speak.

"There was a telephone call for you this afternoon, Mr Clarke. I wrote down the message and left it on your desk, if you haven't already seen it."

"Can you remember who called, Dorothy?"

"It was Doctor Portman."

Richard Clarke looked at his wife then continued to eat without saying anything. They both knew that the call would be about his brother Marcus.

SEVEN

Cooper was not asleep, but his eyes were closed from sheer exhaustion. Every part of his upper body was aching or in pain, every move was a torture. The nurses had him on a raised bed so he was not lying flat, surrounded by pillows, nonetheless he had yet to find a comfortable position.

His chest was bandaged to restrict his movement so that when he heard the door open he could barely move his head to see Robinson walk in.

"What, no chocolates?"

His voice was quiet; he was taking short breaths as he spoke.

Robinson grinned. "I thought of flowers, but then decided you'd think I was taking the piss so I decided against it."

"Good decision."

Robinson sat down on a chair at the bedside.

"How do you feel?"

The smile on Robinson's face disappeared, his voice sombre, as he leant forward to look at him.

"Sore all over," Cooper replied.

"You look pretty beaten up. Did you see anything of who did this?"

"No, not a thing. It was pitch dark; the guy hit me from behind. He ran off after he'd taken my rucksack with my wallet and my phone, then two women came along and helped me."

He was speaking slowly to avoid breathing deeply.

"One of them called an ambulance. They told me they had seen the guy as he was running away down the canal path but he had a hood up so they didn't see his face. I don't think you'll get far if you investigate. Probably best to stick to our murder enquiry."

"Well, I could have a quick word with the two women. At least make sure they haven't remembered anything useful before we forget about it. I'll also check to see if anyone else has been mugged by some guy around there in the past few months, because it strikes me that this bastard could well have done this before."

"One of the girls gave me her phone number. It's in there" he said, trying to point to the bedside cupboard without turning.

Robinson opened the small drawer in the cupboard at the bedside, taking out a handwritten note, but as soon as he did so Cooper regretted telling him about the phone number. He wasn't sure why, but he felt jealous that Robinson would call the pretty nurse before he did.

Robinson looked at the paper and copied the number into his note book.

"Melanie" he said, looking at Cooper with a smile on his face. "Didn't waste any time, did you guv?"

"She was a witness. Treat her properly."

Robinson shrugged and closed his notebook. He reached into a battered canvas sports bag and pulled out a file of papers on the case they were working on.

"Are you feeling up to an update on the Hampstead case?"

"Fire away."

"After we spoke to Mr Bertrand, I thought it odd that if the French police had reported her missing there was nothing on our file. I looked through the files again, including files withdrawn for any reason, and eventually found a reference to her disappearance. For reasons I don't yet understand, the file has been removed from our archive and sent to Scotland Yard. I couldn't see any details at all. It just said 'SB'."

"Special Branch? So it was a Special Branch case?"

"So it seems."

"This case gets more interesting. We have a missing girl. She is found forty years after being buried. It's less than a mile from where" Cooper paused for breath "from where a former junior minister used to live. The former minister is called Charles Edwards. We know the girl had a boyfriend called Charles. Shortly after the girl is found, Edwards' nephew commits suicide. We find the nephew made a drawing, which seems to be of someone being buried. The same guy possibly wrote 'Monica' onto a newspaper clipping. Edwards says he doesn't know of a girl called Monica, but the girl buried on the heath is called Monique. And now the case is with Special Branch."

"Maybe someone's buried the case as well as the body."

Cooper stopped and winced, holding his chest as a stab of pain went through his body.

"Are you ok, sir?

He nodded but said nothing. The pain was excruciating.

"Look sir," Robinson said quietly, "you're not fit to worry about this. Can I suggest that I talk to the Chief Superintendent about this and see what he says?"

Cooper nodded in agreement, taking shallow breaths to avoid his ribs moving too much, unable to speak.

"I've also spoken to the pathologist and arranged to get a DNA sample from Mr Bertrand, to see if we can get a positive match for our girl. I'm hoping we should know in a week or so."

Robinson then put his folder back in the sports bag and went to door of the room.

"Get some rest, sir, and I'll keep looking into this. I'll report back in a couple of days."

He nodded and closed his eyes. He suddenly felt extremely tired. He heard the door shut and his eyes closed. He didn't have the energy to open them again. He drifted off to sleep almost immediately.

* * * * *

WPC Catherine Harper was getting ready to go on duty that morning when her mobile phone rang.

"Hi Andy."

"Do you want to go out with me and my friends again this evening, or would you prefer somewhere quieter?"

"Somewhere quieter would be nice. I like your friends but it would be nice to have time together."

No problem. I know a nice quiet pub in Belsize Park. They do nice food as well. I'll text you the details."

"How are things at the house in Hampstead now?"

"Everyone is more or less back into the old routine. Angus's room has been emptied and cleaned now. We have a new resident called Sean. He's beginning to be accepted by the other residents. He seems to keep himself to himself, which really means he hasn't tried to give George any orders, but seems willing to let the others lead, which makes my life easier. George likes to be in charge."

"That's good."

"Yes it is, but after the story of Angus and Mrs Marsh, I'm beginning to wonder what else happens there that they don't tell me about. Yesterday I arrived at the house and had a look at the kitchen, as usual. All seemed clean and tidy, probably more so than usual, so I went into the lounge to see who was there. Sean was sitting watching television, alone. I asked him how he was and said I was glad he was settling in well. I then asked him if he was making friends with the others, because I was a bit concerned he was on his own. He told me he was getting on fine with them all, but then he told me he had a new friend as well. I said I was pleased, but who was the new friend? He said to keep it a secret, but his name is Marcus. I said I don't know anyone called Marcus, and asked where he lived. He told me he wasn't sure but he often saw him on the heath when he went walking there. He then told me this Marcus used to see Angus a lot, too."

"And you don't know who this Marcus is?"

"No. It seems Angus was speaking to more people than I knew about. When I said I didn't know him, Sean looked a little agitated. He told me Marcus was Angus's secret friend, and that he was now his secret friend too. He asked me to promise not to tell anyone."

* * * * *

Some time later, he had no idea how much time, Cooper found himself drifting between sleep and consciousness, neither able to rouse himself nor focus his mind on what was happening close by him. He slowly became aware of whispered voices nearby, but he was unable to make sense of them or force open his eyes to see who was speaking.

For a fleeting moment he wondered if this was how death felt; floating in the air, seeing and hearing but unable to speak. Slowly he managed to rouse himself and to open his eyes; he could see two women in the corner of his room. They were both nurses. One had her back to him, the other was wearing a coat as if she was ready to go out; he recognised her from somewhere, but from where he couldn't remember. He lay still, looking at her, trying to focus his thoughts.

The nurse he vaguely recognised noticed he was awake; she said something to the other nurse, who turned around and came to him straight away, taking his wrist in her hand and looking at her watch as she checked his pulse. Her skin felt cool and smooth to the touch. He was sorry when she let go of his wrist, it was comforting somehow.

"How are you feeling now? You were in some pain last night and the doctor gave you something to make you sleep."

So that's why he had struggled to wake up. It was coming back to him now. He had been speaking to Mike Robinson but then felt unwell. Later he had been trying to eat and had choked on something; he had felt as if his ribs were on fire with each cough. He remembered taking some tablets; they must have been powerful painkillers.

"I'm a bit groggy, but much better."

"Good. You have a visitor. I'll leave you two together."

She went out, and the other nurse approached the bed. As she sat down, Cooper remembered where he had seen her before.

"You're my guardian angel" he said. "Thank you for looking after me and calling for an ambulance."

She smiled; it was a very pretty smile.

"You don't need to thank me. My friend and I were walking past the canal when we heard a shout. Then we looked down to see a man running along the path and you lying on the floor. We came down to see if you were injured. When it was obvious you were then I called for an ambulance. I'm not sure that qualifies me to be your guardian angel."

"In my book it does. I'm Sam, by the way."

She smiled again; Cooper liked seeing her smile.

"And I'm Melanie. Yes I know you're Sam, and I know you're an important man. I'm glad to see you're in good hands here."

"Important? Hardly that. I may have moved up the ladder a couple of rungs, but I'm not exactly the commissioner at the Met. But I'm pleased you took the trouble to come here to see me. You've cheered me up. Anyway, you're a nurse, so that makes you pretty special as well."

She stood up as if to go.

"You aren't leaving already? You've only just arrived."

"I was just passing by here. I knew where you were because your colleague told me yesterday when we spoke, and I thought I'd call in. He said you needed cheering up."

"You mean Mike Robinson, I presume. I hope he behaved himself when he spoke to you?"

"Oh yes, he was very proper, don't worry about that. He was very concerned for you."

"I'm glad to hear it. Will you be calling by again, soon?"

"If you'd like that, then I will."

"I'd like it very much."

"Then I'll call tomorrow then. They tell me you'll be here for a few days yet."

"Do you work in this hospital?"

"No, I don't. But I can still pass by here."

"I look forward to tomorrow then."

She made her way to the door, and then looked back at him.

"So do I."

With that she left. Cooper put his head back on the pillow and smiled. He felt at peace with the world.

* * * * *

WPC Catherine Harper knocked on the door of the small house. She was in her police uniform, with her cycle helmet tucked underneath her arm. The door opened and Mrs. Marsh greeted her with a smile.

"Hello dear, how nice to see you again. Would you like to come in?"

Catherine followed her into a small sitting room at the front of the house, which Catherine suspected was only used for the occasional visitor. She had caught a glimpse of a tiny kitchen at the back, which she guessed were the only two rooms on the ground floor. A friend of Catherine's had bought a similar house a few years ago, but like many houses in the area it had been extended both upstairs and down. Catherine thought this house hadn't been updated for years, although Mrs Marsh kept it very clean and tidy.

"Do sit down, dear"

Catherine looked around the room as she did so, and noticed a number of photographs of Mrs Marsh, obviously as a young woman, and another girl who she assumed was her daughter. Catherine noticed there were no photographs of her late husband.

After a few pleasantries, Catherine asked about her daughter.

"Tina was a lovely child, very bright." Mrs Marsh responded. "She began to change once she got to her early teens, as all children do, but she became more and more withdrawn. By the time she was fourteen or fifteen she used to go and stay with friends quite often, but as I said to you last time, she would always call me to let me know where she was going. One day she came home and

117

she had had a small tattoo made, on her arm. She was only sixteen. We had a frightful argument, I'm afraid. I was very angry. I had always said to her there were things she might do and regret, but as long as they were not things that she would have to live with for the rest of her life then she would get over them. When I had said that I had been talking about her getting herself pregnant of course, I hadn't imagined for one moment that she would get herself tattooed."

"How did she react?"

"Oh, she just got angry but then went off in a sulk. After a while she told me she was sorry, but it was a few weeks later. After that she seemed to become more withdrawn than ever."

"How was her relationship with her father?"

"As she got older she became colder and colder to him. She used to adore him when she was a little girl, but once she got into her early teens she seemed to avoid having anything to do with him."

"Was he very upset by that?"

"He didn't say anything to me about it."

Something about Mrs Marsh's demeanour whilst she was talking about her husband bothered Catherine. There was something she wasn't telling her.

"Was there anything else that might have upset Tina?"

Mrs Marsh looked at Catherine, and then looked at the window for a few moments. Catherine let her compose her thoughts.

"After my husband died, I found a box hidden at the back of his wardrobe. It was full of photographs."

Catherine waited for a moment.

"What were the photographs of, Mrs Marsh?"

"Of children. Girls mainly, but some were boys too."

"What were the children doing?"

Mrs Marsh hesitated.

"I didn't look at them very much. They were too disgusting. I took them and burned them all."

Catherine didn't want to ask the next question, but she had to do.

"Were any of the photographs of Tina?"

"I don't know. I didn't want to know. It wasn't going to bring her back, and my husband was dead. I just burned them."

"Did Tina ever tell you anything? About your husband, I mean?"

"No, she didn't ever speak of him, not in that way. She just became withdrawn."

"Do you think that's why Tina drew away from your husband as she got older?"

"I don't know. I don't know."

"Did your husband see Tina after she left home?"

"No. No, I am sure he did not. He would have told me if he did. And Tina would have told me."

"When did your husband die, Mrs Marsh?"

"He died in nineteen eighty; September the third."

Catherine decided that the old lady was not going to tell her anything more on this subject, and decided to leave it. She wanted to remain on friendly terms. If more questions had to be asked, she would leave that to the DI to decide.

119

"You said Tina had a group of friends. Can you remember any of their names?"

"I still have Tina's things here, and one is her address book, so they will be in there I am sure. I think though that the police spoke to some of them at the time."

"Could I borrow the address book? I'll let you have it back as soon as possible."

"Does this mean you are going to look into her disappearance?"

"I've spoken to the Inspector and he asked me to speak to you to find out more about Tina. We don't know if there is any connection with the discovery of the girl's body on the heath, but of course if there is any new evidence about your daughter then we will investigate it. Do you have a photograph of your daughter that I could borrow as well?"

Mrs Marsh took a photograph from a drawer and Catherine put it into her pocket. She thanked Mrs Marsh and left on her bicycle to make her way to the police station. As she pedalled up the hill she had a lot to think about, so she didn't notice the tall, thin man watching her through the window of a coffee shop as she passed by.

* * * * *

"Hello Mum."

"Hello Sam. How are you? How's the new flat? Have you settled in? I'm assuming you haven't got back with Carol?"

"No, I haven't gone back to Carol, mum. I'm in hospital."

"In hospital? Whatever's the matter?"

"I've been mugged. I was jogging the other evening, and someone pushed me to the ground and snatched my bag. I've cracked a couple of ribs, apparently. Nothing too bad, so don't worry, but I need to be in here for a couple of days to get some rest."

"Oh dear, Sam, whatever next? Are you sure you're fine there? Do you need anything?"

"I'm fine mum. I was lucky because there was a very nice nurse who helped me after I'd been robbed. In fact she's just called by to cheer me up. She's a nice girl, you'd like her."

"So how long will you be there?"

"Just for two or three days, then I'll be fighting fit."

"It must be painful. I had a friend whose husband broke a rib; he was in agony for days."

"Well, my chest is painful, but they're giving me painkillers. Trouble is, they make me feel sleepy. I've also got a bit of a headache where my head banged on the floor when I fell."

"It sounds worse than you're telling me."

"No, honestly, mum, I'm alright. I'll be here for a few days. I'd rather be working, that's true, than lying here."

"Has anyone been to see you other than a nurse?"

"My detective constable, Mike Robinson, came this morning and my friend Mark called on his way to work. Anyway I'll give you a call in a few days when I'm home."

"There's nothing you need?"

"No, I'm fine. I'll call you when I'm out."

"You take care now. I'll let your brother know."

"Ok mum."

* * * * *

WPC Catherine Harper knocked on the door of Cooper's hospital room, her cycle helmet tucked underneath her arm.

"Come in Catherine" he said. "Do you enjoy cycling in Hampstead?"

"Yes sir, with all the hills it's extremely good exercise; it saves on expensive gym fees to keep my weight down."

He smiled.

"I'm sure it does. Did you speak to Mrs Marsh again?"

"Yes sir, I've come to tell you about it. I asked about Tina. She said she was a lovely child, very bright, but she began to change by her early teens. Tina became more and more withdrawn. I asked if they used to argue, if there might have been any reason for her to run away. She said they had had the odd row about things, but nothing serious, and they'd been very close right up to her disappearance. She's adamant that if Tina had decided to go away she would have told her. Whilst we were talking we were sitting in her living room; there were a number of photographs of Mrs Marsh and her daughter, but no photographs of her late husband. I thought that was a bit odd, so I asked how Tina had got on with her father. Mrs Marsh's demeanour changed as soon as I mentioned him. She said that Tina had loved him dearly as a child, but then as she got older she became colder and colder to him. I felt at this point there was something Mrs Marsh wasn't telling me. I pressed her as to whether she had any idea why Tina might have left home, whether there was anything else that might have upset her. Mrs Marsh sat looking out of the window for a while, saying nothing. Then it came out. She told me that after her husband died she found a box hidden at the back of his wardrobe. It was full of photographs. I asked what the photographs were of. She said they were of children. Girls mainly, but some were boys too. I asked what the children were doing, and she said that she didn't look at them very much, they were too disgusting."

"Oh God, the poor woman. What did she do?"

"She took them and burned them all. I asked her if any of them were of Tina. She said she didn't know, she didn't want to know. It wasn't going to bring Tina back, and her husband was dead. I asked if Tina had said anything to her, anything at all about her husband. She said no, she didn't ever speak of him, not in that way. She just became withdrawn. I decided then that Mrs Marsh was becoming upset and wasn't likely to tell me more, so I told her I was very sorry and thanked her for her help. I did warn her that you might want to ask her a few more questions, but it would only be to help find out what happened to Tina. She seemed pleased at that. I then asked if she could remember the names of any of Tina's friends, and she gave me Tina's address book. She also gave me a photograph of her."

"Well done Catherine. So we have a possible motive for leaving home. But where did she end up? Have a good look through that address book and see if you can track down any of her friends, will you? I'd also like you to check what we know about Mr Marsh, if he has a record at all."

"I've already done that, sir, and he doesn't have a criminal record at all."

"Well there's not much we can do about him, anyway, but let's bear in mind the possibility that she left home because of him. Have a good look through that address book. See what you can turn up; you'll need to check any girl's names against any missing persons. I want to know that there isn't a bigger issue here than we think."

* * * * *

Early evening saw Cooper propped up in his hospital bed, reading a book, getting increasingly bored and feeling that he wanted to get up and do something, anything, rather than just lie still as he had been told. He sat up and swung his legs over the edge of the bed. He could do that with only a little pain, and he decided to try to stand up without assistance for the first time in a few days. He did so, gingerly, feeling a pain in his chest as his muscles worked to pull his body upright into a standing position. He stood still for a moment before taking a gentle, small step forward. Again, the pain in his chest, but not so much that he couldn't tolerate it.

As he stood the door to his room opened and DC Robinson walked in.

"Hello sir, feeling better?"

"A little bit thanks. Still very stiff and sore, but definitely on the mend."

"Well, don't overdo it. Broken ribs can be nasty."

He turned and tried to sit down on the chair at the side of the bed; that was probably a step too far, he quickly decided, as trying to control his muscles whilst bending to sit in a low chair sent a spasm of pain through his chest, and he winced.

Robinson frowned. "Are you ok, sir?"

"Yes, don't worry."

Cooper gave up, and sat cautiously back onto the edge of the bed. He looked at the DC.

"Any news?"

"I have several things to update you on. First I had Mrs. Freedman on the phone this morning. She told me she'd received a call from someone claiming to be a detective from France."

Cooper started slightly as he said it, but regretted it as a stab of pain went across his chest. Robinson looked at him, frowning again in concern.

"A detective from France? Did she say what he wanted?"

"He asked to look at the drawing she received in the post. It seems she told him that we'd taken it. She clearly didn't believe him; she said she thought he was a reporter so she rang to let us know."

"And did she ask this so-called detective for his name?"

"Yes sir, she did. He said he was from Paris, and his name was Renard."

He paused while he thought.

"Might be worth asking our friends in Paris if they know anyone of that name, just in case."

"I've already asked Paris, sir. They have no-one of that name and certainly no-one operating out of London. They were quite indignant I even asked."

"I'm pleased to hear it. Interesting though. I wonder who he is, and how he knows about the drawing."

"Why don't you ask our other French friend, Mister Bertrand, if he has heard of anyone called Renard?"

"Assuming it wasn't him, sir."

"Do you think it might be him?"

"I don't know what to think, sir. I've no reason to think it is him, but I don't know who else it might be."

"I think it unlikely. After all, he came to us in the first place. I'm not sure how he would know about the drawings, but even if he did and wanted to see them, which I doubt, then why didn't he just ask us?"

"Good point, sir."

"Find out where he is and where he has been for the past few days of course, but I doubt if he has anything to do with this. I think we have another Frenchman that we know nothing about just yet. Anything else?"

"We have a definite match of the DNA sample from Mister Bertrand. The body is definitely that of his sister Monique."

"Good. So that's another positive development. Have you spoken to Mr Bertrand yet?"

"Not yet, sir, I only found out just as I was about to leave to come here."

"Well, let him know as soon as you can. All we have to do now is establish who killed her, and why."

"One other thing, sir. After we spoke to Mr Bertrand the first time, you asked me to find out if the Paris police have records of anyone called Charles, involved in a car accident in nineteen sixty eight, who was a student at Nanterre, and where one of the other occupants of the car was called Monique."

"Yes, have they got back to you?"

"Yes, I've had some information from Paris this morning. They confirm they have a report on file of a car accident involving four people, on the twenty ninth of May nineteen sixty eight, although they only have three names. Two of the names involved were Charles Edwards and Monique Bertrand, the third was a boy called Jean Paul Dufaure, who died in the accident. They gave me Edwards' address at the time of the accident, which was his parents' address in the UK, here in London. I've done a lot of cross checking; it is the Charles Edwards we know."

"So he was the boyfriend. Now that is interesting. So what part did he play in her death? I can't wait to talk to him."

EIGHT

He had taken a while to get dressed, but in the late afternoon Cooper picked up the small overnight bag with his clothes, and went to the door of the small room in the hospital that had been home for the past three days. It seemed to him that he'd been here a good deal longer than that. He still felt some pain in his chest, and the doctor advised him he would feel sore for a few days, but he was certainly feeling a good deal better. He briefly saw one of the nurses on duty and she wished him well, after which he went outside and took a taxi home.

After unpacking his little bag his first act was to pick up the telephone; no one answered the number he dialled, and so he left a message.

"Hello Melanie" he said, "I wanted to let you know that I'm home from the hospital. Thanks for calling by again yesterday as you promised. I was hoping to see you again, and wondered if you are free this evening. Please let me know if you can make it. You have my mobile number. I'd love to see you again. Bye for now."

It wasn't much later when his mobile phone rang.

"Hello sir, WPC Catherine Harper here. I hear you're out of hospital."

"Good news travels fast. Did you manage to track down any of Tina's friends?"

"I've been through the address book and noted the names, but there are addresses all over the country which were friends from college probably."

"A needle in a haystack, then."

"Well, I also saw a name and address in Camden. That's where Mrs Marsh said Tina used to go to see friends that were into drugs. I thought that might be a good place to start."

"That was forty years ago. Why don't you start by having a look at the electoral register to see who lives there now?"

"I already have, sir. It's a different name entirely, but it might be worth going anyway; you never know."

"Yes, I agree, go there tomorrow and talk to whoever lives in the flat now. As you say, you never know what you might find out."

He made a note of the name and address, and went to make himself a coffee.

* * * * *

Diana heard the front door open; she knew from the way Buster ran towards the door with his tail wagging that it must be Amanda. She left the library immediately and walked into the hallway. Amanda was taking off her coat before bending down to greet Buster who was desperately trying to get her attention. Satisfied that he had been noticed, he gave a small bark of appreciation and returned to his basket in the kitchen. He was too old to do anything much more energetic these days.

After the usual greetings and kisses, Diana and her daughter sat down together in the drawing room.

"So it seems from the email from Marie that the old family rumour about one of our ancestors being in the French revolution was out by a few years." Amanda said. "He travelled to France to fight, but not in the revolution in seventeen eighty nine. He ended up being in Paris during the uprising in eighteen thirty, although he went there in about eighteen fifteen."

"Yes, I was astonished to read that, although I didn't follow everything. Still, your French is better than mine. Have you managed to find out any more?"

"A little bit. The company I contacted found a record of his birth in the Parish records in Salisbury, from a now demolished church in a small village nearby. He was born in June seventeen ninety nine, so he would only have been sixteen when he ended up in France. They also found a record of a warrant issued for his arrest for murder."

"For murder?"

"So it seems. I assume that, rather than face a trial and almost certainly be hanged, he ran away to France and ended up in Paris."

"Do we know what he did?"

"I'm not sure. I've read up a bit about the period. If you remember, the detective told us that there were riots about that time after the introduction of machinery led to the loss of jobs in agriculture, and some people were killed. There was also a lot of resentment about the taking of what had been common land for grazing by the landed gentry. There was a lot of trouble, but it may or may not be because of that."

"Eighteen fifteen was the Battle of Waterloo, although that's in Belgium of course. Did he fight in that battle I wonder?"

"He may have done, but whether he went to France with the English army and then deserted to Paris, or whether he was on the side of the French of course I don't know."

"But he became a hero in Paris?"

"Well apparently he is cited within some records from the time of the uprising in eighteen thirty as being a hero in defending the people, but what exactly he did we may never know."

"So what else can we find out?"

"I want to discover more about how life was back in the late eighteenth century when he was born, and try to find out a bit more about what might have caused him to kill someone – assuming of course that he was guilty. And I'd like to see what other records Marie has."

* * * * *

Cooper felt very self conscious. It had been a long time since he had been on a first date. He and Carol had been together since they were teenagers, so starting a new relationship was not something he'd had lots of practice at.

He arrived at the restaurant early, taking a seat at the table to wait for Melanie, rather than sit at the bar, as he didn't want to drink. The pain killers he'd been given by the hospital should not be taken with alcohol, they had said, so it was strictly water for him.

He looked at his watch after waiting ten minutes; it was only now the time they had agreed, so don't panic yet, he told himself. As he looked over towards the door for the twentieth time, he saw an elderly couple walking in. Melanie was behind them. Not for the first time Cooper thought just how beautiful she was. He found himself thinking it was strange she was single, and available. He stood up and waved. She saw him, smiled and walked over to greet him. She kissed him on the cheek, sweeping her long dark hair with one hand as she sat down, revealing large circular gold earrings which made her look very different from the nurse he had seen on her visits to him in hospital.

"This is the first time I've seen you stand up" she said, with a smile on her face. "You've been lying down on every occasion until now."

"Hush, don't tell everyone, they'll wonder what I do for a living" Cooper teased her, and she blushed slightly as she laughed.

"How do you feel?"

"Still sore in the chest, but I'm planning to go to the station tomorrow. I'm working on a couple of cases, and I need to catch up on what's happening."

"The body on the heath?"

"Ah, I guess Mike told you that."

"Yes, but he didn't go into detail at all, so don't worry."

"Not really a subject for dinner, but yes I'm working on that, and on another missing girl case going back a long way that may or may not be connected."

Melanie looked at him.

"It must be difficult, dealing with death like that."

132

"Well, I tend to look at it that we are trying to prevent the next crime, by solving this one. In this case of course the crimes are in the distant past, but that's unusual. Anyway, you know something about me, but I know very little about you other than name and phone number, and the fact that you're a nurse. And my guardian angel, of course."

She blushed again.

"Not really that. But yes I'm a nurse. I work mainly with children, and have been at Great Ormond Street for about seven years now, which I love. I'm twenty nine and single, because I was with someone for four years but we split up about four months ago. That still hurts a bit, but more importantly I have a baby, a little girl called Lilly, who is fourteen months old now. I lived with my mother for a while after we split, but I've just moved into a small rented flat nearby. Mum helps me to look after Lilly, which suits us both, because my Dad died just after Lilly was born so she is glad of the company. I'm sure that's enough to put you off, but thank you for not walking out when I mentioned the word baby."

Cooper smiled.

"You're honest, I like that. Is Lilly as beautiful as you?"

Melanie looked at him; he thought her brown eyes were stunning.

"She's beautiful of course, but has blond hair. Her father has red hair so she gets that from him. But she has my smile."

As she spoke the waiter arrived to see if they were ready to order; they asked for a few minutes more but Cooper ordered his water; Melanie said she was happy to avoid wine as well.

"Have you always lived in London?" he asked.

"I was born in Essex, which is where my grandparents live and my mother was raised. Dad was born in Stepney, he was a real Londoner. We moved closer to London when I was six, and ended up in Ilford. When I moved in with John, my former partner, he had a flat in North London, but to be honest I never enjoyed living there. At some point I want to try to buy something, but I don't think I can afford it where my mother lives. What about you? You're obviously not born and bred in London."

"No, is it so obvious?" Cooper laughed, suddenly very conscious of his strong northern accent. "I'm thirty four; I was born in a town near Manchester and lived there until I moved south about twelve years ago. Before moving south I had moved out of my parents' house and started to live with a girl I'd been going out with for some time. We'd been living together for a couple of years when she was offered a job in London, with a national newspaper. She's a journalist, and it was a huge opportunity for her. I was then a constable on the beat in a small town, so I applied for a move to the metropolitan police, and was offered a move to the south of London. I managed to pass various exams but I really wanted to do detective work, so when the opportunity came up, I took it. That's when my problems started, because Carol couldn't live with the uncertainty of my hours. Sometimes I have to drop everything and just go. On the beat that is a lot less likely. I made sergeant fairly quickly, and last year I was promoted to inspector. I split up with Carol just a few weeks ago. Thinking about it, perhaps she was my mugger."

Melanie smiled, not quite sure what to make of that.

"Sorry, just my sense of humour. No, it wasn't her, of course. Anyway she chose to leave me, not the other way round. Just in case you're wondering, it is a permanent split. I can assure you there is no chance that we would ever get back together again. She found someone else, and I discovered about it when I found them in bed together."

Melanie's eyes opened wide and her hands went to her mouth as she gasped.

"Oh you poor thing. That must have been quite a shock."

"It was, but I neglected her a lot, I know that. Even when I was at home I was wrapped up in the cases I worked on. It's very difficult to go home and forget. I don't blame her for finding someone else, really. No children by the way, but not because I don't like kids. Just never been the right time. My poor mother has given up on me."

"Do you have any other family?"

"I have a brother. He still lives in the north; he isn't like me at all. He's happy where he is. I've always been ambitious. I never saw myself as living in the town I grew up in. I'm not sure we'll stay in touch if anything happens to Mum, we don't have a lot in common."

"That's a pity. You should try to see him sometimes. You'll regret it if you don't"

"Maybe you're right."

"What do you do to relax?"

"Oh I've been interested in history for a long time, and last year I decided to do an Open University degree, so I'm studying for that when I have time. Other than that I try to get to the gym and I have a bicycle, although

I must admit I only use it when the sun shines. What about you?"

"Oh I don't get much time for myself, and my life revolves around Lilly as you would imagine. But I read when I get the chance, and I enjoy music, mainly folk music."

The food then arrived, and they began to eat. Cooper was enjoying himself and felt more relaxed than he had done for months.

The evening went too quickly. At one point Melanie looked at her watch.

"I'm afraid I ought to be going. I don't like to be out too late while Lilly is so small."

"Of course."

They paid the bill and went outside.

"I enjoyed seeing you this evening," he said as they waited for a taxi. "Could I see you again tomorrow if you are free?"

"I enjoyed the evening as well but I have to look after Lilly of course. Perhaps we could see each other again on Saturday?"

Cooper saw a taxi and hailed it; as it stopped he opened the door for Melanie. She gave him a quick kiss and climbed in. As the taxi pulled away she smiled and waved through the window; he stood and watched as the taxi drove off, feeling once again like a young boy on his first date.

* * * * *

When Cooper entered the police station the following morning he tried to walk carefully without appearing like an invalid. He climbed the stairs without too much difficulty; several officers greeted him on the way who, somewhat to his surprise, seemed genuinely pleased to see him. He settled back in the chair at his desk, happy to be back and out of that hospital.

He began by reading some of his backlog of emails before turning his attention to his post which included a lot of get well messages amongst other things. One piece of post caught his attention, a hand written envelope with a post mark from France. He tore the envelope open.

"Dear Inspector" it began, "I am sorry to write anonymously, but I have heard you have found a body in Hampstead, and I wonder if it might be a good friend of mine, Paulette Dijon, who was seventeen when she went to live in London in nineteen seventy nine. She disappeared a year later. She was staying in a house owned by an English couple, a Mr and Mrs Terence Brown, in the west of London, in Richmond. If it is her then I would be sad, however I would at the same time be pleased to know that she has been found at last."

The letter was unsigned, but Cooper looked closely at the envelope; it was postmarked in Lille, France.

"Hell's teeth, how many disappearing girls do we have here?" he muttered to himself.

He searched the internet for Paulette Dijon without any success, before looking for Terence Brown. The voter register showed one match, a Terence Brown living in Richmond.

He telephoned Mike Robinson.

"Morning, sir, how are you feeling this morning?"

"Better, thanks. Listen, do we have any record of a missing girl by the name of Paulette Dijon, missing from about nineteen eighty?"

"Hold on."

Cooper could hear the tap of a computer keyboard.

"No, that's not a name I can find. Where did that name come from?"

"There was a letter waiting here for me, sent over from France. It just says a friend called Paulette Dijon had gone missing in about nineteen eighty. Apparently she was staying in Richmond."

"Does it tell us anything about her?"

"Nothing other than a name, and the fact she was seventeen. Would you talk to your friends in Paris yet again, and see if they can help with some details on this girl, if indeed she is missing? And get onto the Richmond police. Ask them to call on these people to see what they know about this girl."

* * * * *

WPC Catherine Harper walked up the steep steps and pressed one of the bells by the door of an address in Camden. The property was a tall, Victorian house divided into several apartments. The front door needed painting, and the front garden was a concrete patch where several dustbins were kept. Rubbish was blowing around the side of the building, which had clearly not been cleaned for quite some time.

"Hello?"

It was a woman's voice from the intercom.

"I'm a police officer" Catherine replied. "I would like to ask you a couple of questions please. It isn't anything to worry about, and won't take long."

"We are on the top floor" came the reply.

There was a sound of a buzzer and a click as the door opened. Catherine went inside and climbed the stairs to the top, looking at the doors of the apartments as she did so. The stairwell was clean but in need of decoration; there were no sounds from any of the other apartments. She knocked on the door of the top apartment at which it opened and a young woman stood looking at her, slightly worried.

"Good morning" Catherine smiled at her. "I'm sorry to bother you, but I am trying to trace someone who used to live at this address, and I called on the chance that you might know the person I am interested in."

The girl looked slightly confused for a moment. "I am sorry, but my English is not so good. I am from Poland. Who are you looking for?"

"I'm looking for a man called Clarke, James Clarke."

"No, I'm sorry I don't know of anyone called Clarke."

"How long have you lived here?"

"I have been here with my boyfriend for a year now. We rent the flat from an agent in Camden. Maybe he can help."

"May I come in to see the apartment? Would you mind? It might be helpful."

The girl seemed reluctant but turned and walked inside, Catherine following her into a tiny, one bedroomed apartment, a small kitchen in the corner of the living room. She looked out of the window to the rear of the building, and could see there was a flat roofed extension on the ground floor. The rear garden had very little to commend it; it didn't appear to be used. A lot of it had been concreted over at some point, presumably to make some kind of a patio.

"Do you know any of the other people in the building?"

"Not really, no. Everyone keep themselves to themselves. My English is not so good."

"I understand. Are the other people here all English?"

"I think the man on the ground floor is English, but I don't like him. The other people are not, they are from different countries."

"Why don't you like the English man?"

"He stares at me. He doesn't seem very nice. I stay away from him."

"What is his name?"

"Mister Fox."

"I see. You've been very helpful. Thank you for showing me the apartment."

NINE

Cooper suddenly remembered he hadn't called his mother and cursed himself. He dialled the number, but there was no answer. He waited another few minutes before trying again, but still she didn't answer the phone. He looked at his watch; it was six in the evening. She rarely went out of an evening, so he started to feel anxious as to why she didn't answer. He wanted to let her know he was out of the hospital.

"I should have called her last night" he muttered to himself.

He decided to call his brother.

"Hello Graham. I've been trying to call mum, but she doesn't answer. She isn't with you, I don't suppose?"

"Hello Sam, are you out of the hospital? No, she isn't here. I called by this morning on my way to work. She seemed fine then. Let me give her a call just now. If she doesn't answer I'll nip down there to make sure she's alright. She's probably got the television on so loud she can't hear the phone. Let me try, and I'll give you a call back. How are you anyway?"

"I'm fine, back on my feet even if still a bit sore. Let me know as soon as you find out where mum is."

He watched the news on television for a little while, listening with some anxiety for the phone to ring. It was probably twenty minutes before it rang. He picked it up immediately.

"It's Graham, Sam. I'm at mum's. She's here. As I suspected she had the television on so high that she couldn't hear it ringing. I'll pass you over to her now."

"Hello Sam," his mother said. "Sorry you didn't manage to get through. I didn't hear the phone at all. Are you out of that hospital now? How do you feel?"

"Yes mum, I'm back home. I'm feeling a lot better; I'm still sore, but that should wear off in a while. They've given me some strong painkillers for the next few days. After that I should be ok."

"Well you should try to get some rest. Don't go into work for a few days."

"I'm already back, mum. I've been back in today."

"Oh, well that's up to you. But don't go rushing around. Take it easy for a while."

"I'll do what I can. We'll have to do something about that phone of yours."

"Graham said the same thing. He's talking about getting some kind of light that flashes when the phone rings. I usually hear it, but tonight there was a nature film and I couldn't tell what the man was saying, so I had to turn the volume up."

"Well, I'm glad you're ok, mum."

* * * * *

Cooper was in his kitchen making dinner later that evening; he was still emptying boxes after his move and couldn't find his favourite pan, so he felt a little annoyed, but after emptying several boxes he gave up and managed without it.

After eating he sat at the table with a notepad, writing down the various facts he had gathered in the past few days. Amongst the various notes he came across the scrap of paper on which was the Camden address Catherine Harper had mentioned earlier.

"Odd, she hasn't called me" he said to himself.

Out of curiosity he tapped the address into his laptop and a list of residents came up. It was obviously a building divided into several flats. She hadn't given him a flat number. He looked down the list, but none of the names meant anything. There was no James Clarke listed, but Catherine had said there was a new occupant.

He picked up the picture drawn by Angus; the newspaper cutting with the word 'Monica' written in the margin was still attached to it. He looked at it briefly and put it down, writing the word 'Renard' on his pad.

He suddenly put down his pen and went back to his computer screen, looking at the list of residents in the Camden apartment. He jumped up and walked to the corner of the room, picked up one of the boxes sitting there and tipped the contents onto the floor. The box had been full of books. Pushing through the heap he picked up an old, small blue book. It was his old French dictionary, from school. He flicked through the pages.

"Renard" he said aloud. "Renard is French for fox."

He looked back at the computer screen. The resident of flat one was Marcus Fox. He sat back, staring at the ceiling, the events of the past couple of weeks going through his mind. Then he started to write names on his pad, drawing connecting lines between them. Was he imagining things? Tina Marsh had an address in her book where someone called Marcus Fox lived; he drew a line connecting the two names. Her mother had been searching on Hampstead Heath for years, where Monique's body had been found. He wrote down 'Hampstead' and connected the name Monique and Hampstead. He then wrote down the names Angus Forsyth and Charles Edwards, drawing a connecting line between the two, and another one between Monique and Charles Edwards. Someone called Renard had been asking for pictures drawn by Angus Forsyth; he drew a connecting line between those two names. Renard was French for Fox, so he connected a line between Renard and Marcus Fox.

"So are Edwards and Renard connected, and did Angus Forsyth know Monique?" Cooper mused to himself.

After some more work he yawned; his painkillers were making him sleepy. He decided to have an early night.

He was in bed, half asleep when the telephone rang. He looked at the clock; it was almost eleven pm.

"Who the hell is this?" he muttered before picking up the phone.

"I'm sorry to bother you Inspector, this is Sergeant Jones here. We've had a call from a gentleman who was expecting to meet WPC Catherine Harper this evening, and he was worried that she hadn't turned up, nor had he been able to raise her on her telephone. He sounded very agitated, sir, so I tried to contact her myself but she isn't answering either her mobile phone or her home phone. She was on duty this afternoon, sir, but it seems now that she didn't call in at the end as expected. I've taken the

144

liberty of asking a car to call at her home to see if she is there, just in case she is ill or something, but the patrol has just reported to say no-one seems to be at home, although they could hear her little dog barking. I'm sorry to bother you with this, sir, but I am aware that she had been to speak to someone this afternoon at your request, and I wondered if you had spoken to her at all since then?"

"Who reported her missing?"

"His name is Andy Jones, sir. Do you know him?"

"I've met him. I have no idea where she might be. I asked her to call at an address in Camden today, and I had expected her to call but she hasn't. Get a car to go over there right away, and check if they did in fact see her."

Cooper gave the address to the duty sergeant, before ringing Mike Robinson.

"Hello Mike," he said as soon as it was answered, "sorry to bother you at this hour, but it seems that WPC Catherine Harper has gone missing, which seems uncharacteristic of her. It might be nothing of course, but she didn't turn up for a date with a boyfriend and her flat seems to be empty, except for the fact that her little dog is in there. I know she dotes on that dog, so it is unlikely she would go away and leave it alone. I've been asking her to help me to do some enquiries, to save me running around, and I wondered if you had spoken to her at all?"

"That's a bit unlikely guv; she disliked me a lot, so she's not likely to confide in me. What was she doing?"

"She picked up a story of another girl who disappeared from Hampstead about the same time as Monique. Catherine found an address in Camden where one of this girl's friends lived at the time and I asked her to call there today to speak to the current residents just to

145

see if they knew anything. It was unlikely but it was worth a shot."

"Is there a connection between these girls?"

"I don't know yet; I have a feeling there's something, but I'm not sure what as yet. What I can tell you is that one of the residents where she went is called Marcus Fox. The French for Fox is Renard."

"Renard? The French detective? That seems a strange co-incidence. So what do we do about Catherine?"

"I've asked Bill Jones to get a car down to Camden to see what they can find out."

"That's only round the corner from me. Shall I go down and take a look?"

"Why don't you do that? In the meantime I'll ring Catherine's boyfriend to see what he knows."

Cooper then hung up, and immediately called Andy Jones.

"Hello Mr Jones, DI Cooper here. I understand you've reported that Catherine seems to be missing."

"Hello inspector. Yes, I have. I hope it's just a false alarm, but I'm really worried about her. We spoke this morning and said we'd meet in a pub in Belsize Park, but she didn't show up. She knows where it is; we were there just the other evening. I waited for an hour in case she was held up, and I kept trying her mobile phone but it kept going straight to voicemail. I called the police station to see if she was out on an operation, but they told me she wasn't on duty. I then took a taxi to her apartment, but she wasn't there, although I could hear her dog barking. I'm mystified. If we'd had an argument or something I might understand she was avoiding me, but we hadn't. As of this morning she was looking forward to an evening out."

"You said you spoke to her this morning, did she say anything at all about what she was doing?"

"She just told me that she was going to go to Camden before heading off to Hampstead as usual, but she didn't say anything else."

"And you can't think of anywhere she might have gone?"

"Well she might have gone off to her mother's I suppose, but I'm not sure why she wouldn't call me first. I didn't want to ring her mother, who I've never met, and frighten her by asking questions about her daughter."

"Probably wise, but we might have to send a WPC there to check. Leave that with me. If you think of anything else, then please let me know immediately, whether any odd conversation or anything she mentioned at all."

"She didn't say anything to me about Camden, or what she was working on, if that's what you mean. Well, there was something we discussed a couple of days ago, but I don't think it's relevant."

"What's that?"

"You know that I asked Catherine about one of Angus's friends, a lady called Mrs Marsh?"

"Yes, I do."

"Well, it seems Angus had another friend that he kept secret. I mentioned this to Catherine and she seemed interested, but she hasn't mentioned it since. I only mention it in case it was something she was looking into."

"What was this friend's name?"

"Marcus. I'm afraid I don't have a surname, or know any more than that."

Cooper thanked him, put down the phone and looked at his pad. He wrote 'Marcus?' and connected a line to Angus Forsyth, and a dotted line to Marcus Fox.

Less than an hour after he had spoken to Robinson, he was on his way to the apartment in Camden. Robinson was waiting for him; Cooper had told him and the other officers not to approach the building until he arrived. He had spoken to the chief superintendent on the telephone and visited a nearby magistrate to obtain a search warrant for the ground floor flat. As a precaution he had requested an armed team, who were already waiting several hundred metres away from the property.

He met Robinson and the other officers, and briefed them on the operation. The door was to be broken down and two armed officers would enter first. Cooper and Robinson would follow them to make any arrests and to supervise the search. Two other officers would go to the rear of the building to ensure no-one left that way.

They then drove quietly to the end of the street, proceeding on foot for the last fifty metres to minimise noise. At a signal from Cooper, the door was broken in and the officers entered as arranged, with a loud shout to alert occupants that the police were entering the building. The property was in darkness but the lights worked and were switched on. The two armed officers entered the kitchen first, shouted that this room was clear, then entered the living room.

A shout from them alerted Cooper that they had found something and he ran in to see Catherine lying on the floor, her legs tied, her arms bound behind her, her mouth covered by some form of tape. She seemed to be bleeding from a head wound, and he shouted to Robinson to call an ambulance. The other officers in the meantime were carrying out a thorough search of the apartment, but there was no trace of anyone else.

Cooper gently pulled the tape from Catherine's mouth and she groaned. Robinson went into the kitchen and returned with a glass of water. Cooper held it to her lips and she took a small sip. He undid the tape from her arms and legs, laying her down in the recovery position to wait for the ambulance.

Within a few minutes the ambulance crew had arrived, and they began to check Catherine. She was drifting in and out of consciousness, but her breathing and heartbeat were regular. The ambulance crew then gently lifted her onto a stretcher, covered her with a blanket and carried her out to the waiting ambulance, after which the vehicle left, its siren piercing the still of the night.

As soon as the ambulance had gone Cooper telephoned the chief superintendent and then Andy Jones to let them know that Catherine had been found.

He then looked around the apartment. It had two bedrooms, old clothes scattered on the floor, boxes and bags of what appeared to be both rubbish and unopened items everywhere, on the floor, on every available surface, including the top of the bed.

"Where the hell did he sleep?" Robinson asked as they surveyed the scene.

The kitchen of the apartment was worse. The room was filthy as if it had not been cleaned for years, with dirty, greasy plates, bowls, cups, pots and pans in the sink, on the small table, on the floor. Cooper opened one of the drawers and noticed it contained an assortment of cutlery plus a large kitchen knife. He inspected the knife, noting it didn't match any of the others. He dropped it into a plastic bag for examination later. As he did so he remembered Andy Jones telling him that a knife had gone missing from the house in Hampstead. He made a mental note to check whether it was still missing. He looked in the other drawers and cupboards but it contained nothing of interest.

As he went back into the living room he took in a sight that could have been a jumble sale, with plastic rubbish bags full of assorted items, including clothes, soft toys, lamp shades, ornaments. Cooper noticed a door to an under stairs cupboard which he hadn't seen before, and he immediately pointed it out to two of the uniformed officers. The two of them approached it cautiously, pulling open the door and standing back, one shining a torch in at the same time. As no-one was hiding inside they took a step back, confirming to him that it was clear.

Robinson looked inside.

"This is interesting sir."

Cooper joined him. The shelves inside were full of cuttings from newspapers and assorted scraps of paper with drawings. He picked one of the drawings up. It looked exactly like one of the drawings from Angus. He handed it over to Robinson.

"This looks like Angus's work" Cooper said, "so it looks as if this is the same Marcus that Angus knew. I wonder if he is detective Renard as well. The question is; where is he now?"

Robinson looked through the pile, picking out a piece of paper with handwriting on it. He looked at it before handing it to Cooper.

"It's some kind of a poem."

Cooper glanced at it before putting it in his pocket to read later. He picked up some of the newspaper cuttings. They all appeared to be related to crimes, mainly but not only in the London area, and mostly of murders of young women, or of girls reported as missing.

As he was looking at them Robinson was looking at some old black and white photographs pinned to the inside of the door. He showed one to Cooper; it was a photograph of four young people standing in a group, talking. They seemed to be at a school or college.

"Isn't that Monique?" Cooper said.

Robinson looked at it closely.

"Yes I believe it is. And that could be a very young Charles Edwards with her. Who the other two are, I have no idea."

TEN

Cooper arrived at the hospital in the very early hours of the following morning; he hadn't yet been home, despite his plan for an early night. Before he went to see Catherine he found the doctor on duty and asked him how she was.

"I'm pleased to say that her skull isn't fractured, but she needed several stitches in what is still a nasty head wound. She's had quite a blow to the head, so we've given her something to keep her sedated, and we'll keep her that way for the next twenty four hours at least. Our biggest concern is that there might be some bleeding around the brain, so we are monitoring her carefully for that. She is certainly concussed, but hopefully she'll make a full recovery quickly. Right now she needs quiet, and rest."

For a while Cooper was standing quietly in the room where Catherine lay, near the door. He saw Catherine stir; Andy Jones, who was seated beside her, immediately sat up, a concerned look on his face. He had been holding her hand when Cooper arrived, and hadn't moved from her side for the last half hour. She looked pale and fragile; her head was heavily bandaged and she was wired to several monitors that made regular bleeping noises.

Catherine opened her eyes; it seemed to take a few seconds before she saw the two men close by.

"Hello beautiful."

"Hello Andy" she whispered. "My head feels very sore. Where am I?"

"You're in Hampstead Free Hospital, my love. DI Cooper here found you last night, thank God."

Cooper came over to the bed and smiled at her.

"Don't try and talk too much now Catherine. Get some rest and get yourself well. Then we can have a chat about what happened," he said in a very soft voice.

"Where did you find me, Sir?"

"In the apartment in Camden you went to visit. I know you spoke to the young couple upstairs; I suspect you then went to have a look at the ground floor apartment. But you can tell me what happened when you feel better."

"Yes. Yes I did go back. He hit me over the head with something, I'm not sure what, but it hurt."

"Well you have a concussion but no fracture. You'll be feeling better soon."

"Did you get him?"

"No. When we found you in his apartment you were alone. He had escaped. But we'll find him. Do you remember what he looks like?"

"Not really. He was tall and thin, I remember, but I didn't really see his face. Sorry."

"Don't be sorry. We'll get a description from the neighbours. He won't get far. You get some rest now."

It was almost midday by the time Cooper arrived at the police station. He asked Robinson to come to his office.

"Morning, sir. Did you manage to get any sleep last night?" Robinson remained standing.

"Not a great deal, no. I went straight to the hospital after I left you, and waited there with Andy Jones, who seems to be her boyfriend now, until she started to come round. I also spoke to the chief a couple of times while I was there to keep him up to speed with things, and I arranged for a forensics team to go to the apartment early this morning to search for any clues to the whereabouts and activities of Marcus Fox. After that I went to bed."

As he was speaking Robinson put a file with the newspaper clippings taken from Marcus Fox's apartment on his desk.

"Have you had a look through those?"

"I'm starting to catalogue them, sir. They are spread over twenty years, and are primarily in three categories. There are reports of murder, reports of girls gone missing, and reports of court cases that involve murder. They are spread over a good many years. There is a report about a search for Monique which is one of the earliest, if not the earliest. There are a few from the later nineteen seventies, a handful from the nineteen eighties, with just a couple from the nineties. I can see nothing after that."

"Any mention of either Tina Marsh or Paulette Dijon?"

"Yes. There's a report of Tina Marsh's disappearance here and, interestingly, there's a small article about Paulette Dijon, but it isn't about her going missing."

"What does it say?"

"It's an interview with her, saying how she loves being in Richmond. I presume it's from a local newspaper there."

"I wonder why he kept that."

"I don't know. Maybe he knew her?"

"Could be, I suppose. How many articles do we have in total?"

"Fifteen all told."

"We should check to see how many of the murders and missing girls are still unsolved."

"Are you thinking what I'm thinking, sir, that he could be involved in some of these disappearances? I've had a look through records, and there is no-one called Marcus Fox on the database that could be him. Assuming he always uses the same name of course. I've asked the passport office to see if they have a passport issued to that name at the Camden address, so we'll see what comes up. We're also making house to house enquiries this morning to get a description of Marcus Fox, so we'll see what that brings out."

"That's good, well done. Let's summarise what we know, shall we?"

As he said this Cooper pulled from his file the piece of paper on which he'd been connecting names the previous evening.

"Well, we start with our body on the heath, Monique Bertrand. She was in London because she had followed her boyfriend here; we don't have a full name from her brother but his first name was Charles, and we think he was Charles Edwards. Then we find several drawings by a man who committed suicide, who was related to Charles Edwards, and who we believe knew someone called Marcus. Then we have the disappearance of Tina Marsh a year later, the daughter of the elderly lady from Hampstead; her address book has an address in Camden listed, where one of the flats belongs to Marcus Fox. When WPC Harper visits this apartment, she gets a bang over the head for her trouble. We find a photograph of several people in the apartment; one of them seems to be Monique Bertrand, one of them may well be Charles Edwards, so it looks as if Fox may have known both of them. If it is Charles Edwards in the photograph, then that makes it certain he was Monique Bertrand's boyfriend, the one she came to see before she suddenly disappeared. Also in Fox's apartment we have a newspaper clipping referring to another girl who was later reported missing, in about nineteen eighty, Paulette Dijon. Finally we have a French so-called detective called Renard, which happens to be the French for fox, seemingly asking questions about the Monique case."

"We might of course be completely wrong about all three girls. It might be that Paulette Dijon came to his attention for some reason but he never met her, or he did know her but had nothing to do with her disappearance. With Tina Marsh, we have almost nothing to tell us what happened to her other than one of the names in her address book happened to be in the same building. Marcus Fox might never have met her either."

"It seems to me, sir, that we have two possible suspects, Charles Edwards and Marcus Fox, and three potential victims."

"I agree. It's time to talk to Charles Edwards; let's see what he knows about Monique, and about Marcus

156

Fox. It'll be interesting to hear what he thinks happened to Monique. She must have known Fox somehow as well, as her photograph is in his apartment, I'd like to know how. None of that however explains why Fox should attack WPC Harper unless he has something to hide. We need to find him. The fact that we've found drawings in his apartment, almost certainly by Angus Forsyth, gives me sufficient evidence to link the two of them, and if Mrs Marsh confirms any of them were the among the drawings she gave to Renard, then we have a link between Fox and Renard as well. I wonder what he wanted those drawings for?"

Robinson thought for a moment.

"Suppose he wanted to point us in the direction of Charles Edwards? Someone pushed a drawing through Diana Freedman's door. We've been assuming it was Angus Forsyth; suppose it was Fox? If he knew something about Monique's death, perhaps he was trying to give us a clue which would lead to Edwards."

"And why would he have tried to get the drawing back from Diana?"

"He wasn't. He just wanted to make sure we had it. If she'd given it to him, he would have found another way to get it to us."

"You're forgetting the drawings he took from Mrs Marsh. They may be among the ones we found there, as well as any Angus gave him directly."

"Again, he might have intended to let us have them in due course. I guess we'll just have to ask him."

"Edwards might have been involved somehow but Fox seems to be the common denominator here. I want to talk to him. We need to know what he's been up to, and more importantly where he is now. It'll be interesting to see what forensics find in his apartment."

"It could take them some time. It was virtually a rubbish tip" Robinson reminded him.

"Yes, he was quite a hoarder. I've asked them to look for fingerprints first, anyway, so we can see if he is on record anywhere, before they sift through the rubbish bags. Whilst I remember, will you do a search to see how long Fox has lived at that address, and where he was before he came to Camden."

Cooper picked up some of the newspaper clippings and leafed through them. As he did so the telephone rang. Robinson picked it up.

He listened to a voice at the other end, briefly answering "OK" before putting down the receiver.

"That was the duty desk" Robinson said. "They've found Catherine's bike."

"Where?" Cooper asked.

"Down an alley near Euston station."

"So Fox may have used it and then abandoned it there?"

"Sounds like it," Robinson answered. "They're bringing it in anyway, but where he went from there of course we don't know."

"He could have taken a train out of town, or the underground to anywhere in London. Get somebody to make some enquiries at the station, just to see if anyone saw anything."

"The duty desk have already organised that. They're dead keen to catch this guy; they all had a soft spot for Catherine."

"All except you, that is."

Robinson looked at him.

"I know I deserve that. I suppose you're right. I've always struggled with women as police officers."

He paused, looking up at Cooper, who was surprised to see that he looked quite emotional.

"I told you a while back that I was brought up by an aunt. The reality is that I was abandoned by my real mother when I was eight years old. Dad couldn't cope so I was brought up by his sister. For her I was a damn nuisance, and could never do anything right. She made my life hell, and I hated her for it. I've never found it easy to see good in any woman since then. I guess that's why I've never settled down and got married. Catherine is a good kid, I know that, and I'm glad she's ok."

Cooper let him recover his composure for a moment.

"Get the name Marcus Fox out into the press. I want him caught. And give Charles Edwards a call. Tell him we'll see him tomorrow, either at his office or at his home, his choice."

"I suspect he'll choose home" Robinson said.

"I imagine you're right. But we will speak to him tomorrow."

* * * * *

Diana was in the kitchen making a salad for her lunch and preparing some meat for Buster, when the telephone rang. Diana walked quickly to the hallway to answer it, wiping her hands on a towel as she did so; it was Amanda.

"Hello Amanda, how are you?"

"I'm fine mummy. I've just been talking to your cousin Marie."

"Have you? How is she?"

"She's fine; she's been really kind and helpful. We've been exchanging emails for the past few days, and she's suggesting I go over to Paris to see her so that we can look through some old family documents she has. She's promised to help me read them; apparently her sister-in-law works for the government as a historian, so she wants to introduce me to her as she knows a lot about the Paris uprising. I wondered if you wanted to come along too."

"I'd love to come darling, but I don't wish to leave Buster alone these days; he's getting on a bit you know, like me."

"You're not old, mummy. Can't you find someone to look after him for a few days? Marie would love to see you again, I'm sure."

"Why don't you invite Simon along? A spring break in Paris would be lovely for you."

"Are you sure you don't want to come? I'll ask Simon of course, but I'm sure Marie would rather you were there."

"No darling, you take Simon along, have a good look into our history, but also enjoy Paris with Simon."

"Well, I'll give him a call now and see. Marie will be disappointed though."

"She'll be happy to see you, so don't worry too much about that."

* * * * *

Cooper and Robinson arrived at the home of Charles and Isabelle Edwards at ten o'clock on the Friday morning. Cooper rang the bell at the gate and it swung open; as they approached the door Charles Edwards opened it.

To his surprise, Edwards greeted them with a smile and invited them in. He led him into his study, which had a couple of armchairs where he invited them to sit. Edwards took the seat at his desk, turning the chair to face Cooper. There was no sign of his wife.

"Tell me what you know about Monique Bertrand" Cooper said.

"I see you've worked it out. Yes she was a girlfriend of mine, a long time ago, before she disappeared. I thought she had gone back to France. It was a real shock when I read that her body had been found in Hampstead."

"Why don't you tell us how you came to know her in your own words, sir? The detective constable here will make notes."

"Of course. Well I first met Monique in nineteen sixty eight; I had just arrived in Nanterre. She was on my course and she was a good looking girl so difficult not to notice, but I had little to do with her at first. After a few weeks of the course I had made a few friends and went about with them. There was one girl I tended to sit with in the bars, but it was nothing serious. It was after a couple of months when Monique suddenly came up to me in a discotheque and asked me to dance with her. She was very direct. I was surprised, and flattered, although I soon found out that in fact she was trying to get rid of some geek who had been following her. A few weeks later the student demonstrations began in earnest. You may know there were serious riots on the streets of Paris that year, and a lot of universities were closed by the

161

authorities. Apparently it started with a demand that both sexes share the same accommodation; I thought it was unlikely, but a good idea if we got away with it, obviously. The situation became chaotic quite soon after that, and it escalated into a full scale riot including striking workers and the like. I wasn't sure what had caused it to get out of hand, nor frankly was I too interested in getting involved. I was only in Paris because I was on this course under pressure from my father; he wanted me to go into the family business, and he saw it as good training. I had no desire to be there, but couldn't get him to see that I had no interest in his damned business. I didn't want to be in Nanterre, so frankly if the course had been cancelled I wouldn't have worried too much. Anyway I digress. I met Monique again a little while after the dance. I can't remember how long, a couple of weeks, probably. As I said she had been trying to get rid of the geek. She was a good looking girl and seriously sexy and I was quite flattered that she took an interest in me, although frankly I had no plans to start a long term relationship at that point in my life. I was only there for a short while. After a few weeks we started sleeping together, which was fine by me of course, although I was even at that age a bit concerned that she seemed to be taking things so seriously. We were together for about three months; most of this time Paris was chaotic."

"You were involved in a car accident during this time?"

"Yes, you're well informed, inspector, we then had that bloody awful car accident, in which we were nearly all killed. It was a night of rioting in Paris. Would it help if I spoke about what was going on in Paris that evening?"

"Please do, sir."

"I started the evening alone in my apartment, watching the big football game, which was Manchester United versus Benfica in the European Cup Final. Monique wasn't particularly interested in watching it, and my French friends at university were too busy rioting on the streets just then to be interested in the game. When I say 'friends', they were just a bunch of boys I used to talk to at college, really. When things broke up we moved away and lost touch. I can't even remember most of their names now."

He looked at Cooper who returned his look without a smile, waiting for him to continue. Edwards was clearly trying to be amiable; he was determined neither to encourage nor discourage him.

"The match was incredibly exciting, and I must admit that I'm not sure how many beers I drank. There was an attempt on goal in the dying minutes which had seen a dramatic save from the Manchester goalkeeper, and the match went into extra time. Extra time played saw more goals from Manchester, and within half an hour they were European Champions for nineteen sixty eight. They were the first English club to win the trophy, you know. It was a big thing. I was ecstatic, and raced out to find my friends, who had told me they'd be joining the demonstrations on the streets yet again. Earlier that evening I'd seen the reports on television of the ultimatum by President de Gaulle; there had by this time been several weeks of strikes and riots by both students and workers. The president called it a civil war. The Latin Quarter, where my friends were, was effectively under siege, with the students behind barricades. As I headed down there I remember seeing a group of students from my university running towards me; I stopped one of them to ask what was going on. He told me they were sending in tanks; I thought he was making that up, but apparently it was true. Pompidou, the prime minister, has gone mad,

163

they said. I ran off in the direction of the action, determined to miss as little of the fun as possible."

Edwards paused for a moment, his eyes closed as if picturing the scene.

"I managed to get to the Latin Quarter, but I hadn't been there more than ten minutes when there was a police charge and a couple of gendarmes grabbed me and threw me in the back of a van. I tried to protest that I was English but they ignored me, and I soon found myself in a police cell somewhere. After another hour or so I was taken to an office and asked to show my papers. I had taken the precaution of carrying my passport with me, and not much later I was kicked out into the streets, almost literally. They were none too friendly. I eventually made my way to Jean Paul's house. When I arrived he rang Monique and somehow she managed to get there, although she said it took her an age because of police road blocks everywhere. We'd all been drinking, but Jean Paul said we needed more wine, so we ran to his car so that we could go and buy some. The two girls climbed into the back. We roared off down the street in his little old Citroen. The apartment was on the outskirts of Courbevoie, and we raced down towards the bridge over the river, turning down onto the road parallel to the Seine. We came to a narrow section where the road forked; we needed to go up to the bridge to cross the river but Jean Paul braked too late, completely misjudging the bend; the car hit the side of the wall, running alongside it briefly with a loud scraping sound before it tipped into its side violently, sliding along with a terrible squeal, followed by a bang when we hit something. I think I lost consciousness for maybe thirty seconds, I'm not sure. I managed to open my door, which was facing upwards, and climb out onto the road. There was glass everywhere, and people running around. I was dazed and confused, but then I saw a figure lying in the road. I thought we'd hit someone for a moment, but then I realised the car windscreen was completely shattered and it was Jean Paul in the road. No seatbelts in those days, of course. The two girls had been in the back of the car. Jean Paul's girlfriend had managed to climb out but Monique was still in there. I tried to help her but she was trapped in the wreckage. It took a while for the police and ambulance to get her out. I went to the hospital with her; the police told me that Jean Paul was dead. They had to operate on Monique; they told me afterwards they had amputated a couple of fingers on her left hand."

Again he paused. Cooper said nothing.

"She got awfully shitty with me after that, and we fought a lot. Shortly after the accident the university closed down the course, so my parents came over to take me home on the boat train. I'd been home for several weeks when the phone rang and it was Monique. She was in tears, telling me how she loved me and wanted me back, but I said it was over, she should find someone else. I wanted to move on; as I said, for me it wasn't a lifelong love story, even if I was very fond of her and missed her more than I expected. A couple of weeks after that she rang again, saying the geek who'd been following her had contacted her and wanted to see her. He really gave her the creeps, I knew that. She said a friend was taking an English course in London, and could she come over and spend some time here to get away from him. By then I was going out with Isabelle, and the family were already talking about wedding plans, so I told her that if she came I would see her, but in secret. I was in a trap really; I didn't love Isabelle either but it was made plain to me that a wedding was what the family expected, and large sums of money were being promised if I did what I was told. It sounds bizarre I know, but I had no source of income and I knew that if I was thrown out then I should end up with nothing. Isabelle wasn't so bad, so I went along with it, even though I knew Monique was in love with me, and I still missed her. Things came to a head several weeks later. I'd told Monique I was marrying Isabelle out of convenience and for money, but not love. Monique was always headstrong and fiery, and she took it into her head to come to where Isabelle was living to confront her. When I opened the door she went berserk, threatening to kill Isabelle. The threat wasn't real, it was rage, I knew. The next thing was that Isabelle arrived from the kitchen with a knife in her hands. She waved it at Monique, and Monique jumped back out of the way. Monique then ran off. I never saw her again after that. She made no attempt to contact me. It was a relief, because I was for weeks afraid she would come back again, but she never did. I didn't see her again."

"What did you think when you found out she was dead, sir?"

Edwards looked at them, tears forming in his eyes.

"I'm sorry" he said, "it's a long time ago but it's still painful. Perhaps I did love her."

"But you didn't try to contact anyone, not even her family, who had no idea what had happened to her for all these years?"

"I didn't know she was missing, inspector. I never met her family; Monique didn't want to introduce me to them. She said they were very poor. I think she was a little ashamed, I don't know why. I guess she saw me as very rich. Isabelle thinks I was just a meal ticket, but I think it was a lot more than that."

"When the car accident happened in Paris, who was driving the car?"

"My friend, Jean Paul."

166

Cooper pulled out from his folder the photograph found in Marcus Fox's apartment, and handed it to him.

Edwards put on his reading glasses. As he looked at it closely, his eyes opened wide.

"I haven't seen this before. Where on earth did you get it from?"

"Who is in the photograph, Sir?"

"This is me with Monique, Jean Paul and his girlfriend. It must have been taken at the university, and was probably not long before the accident. Where did you get it from?"

"What was the name of Jean Paul's girlfriend?"

"Good question. Sophie something or other. Can't remember the rest I'm afraid. It's a long time ago."

"Was she hurt in the accident?"

"I think she escaped scot free. She didn't even attend the hospital as I recall, she just went home to clean herself up."

"Jean Paul was killed?"

"Yes, he was. Poor sod. He was very drunk."

Robinson spoke up.

"You stated that Monique was being followed by someone you described as a geek. Why a geek?"

"I didn't know him, I just saw him a few times. He was tall and lanky, usually had his head in a book, or at least pretending he did. In reality he seemed to be sneaking a look at the girls, although he wouldn't have stood a chance."

"Why was that?"

"He was dirty. He never washed. You could smell him coming before seeing him."

"Did you ever speak to him?"

"Only once when I saw him peering at Monique. I told him to beggar off."

"How did he react?"

"He just told me to mind my own business before walking away pompously. He thought he was really smart. He was well connected I was told, but I never knew how."

"He told you in French I presume?" Robinson asked.

"No, no. He was English. There were a few English guys there at that point."

Robinson looked at Cooper.

"Do you remember his name by any chance?"

Edwards paused.

"I'm not sure I do. Monique did mention it, but I can't remember."

"It wasn't Marcus, by any chance?" Cooper asked, more out of hope than of conviction that he was going to be their man.

Edwards' eyes opened in astonishment.

"Yes. Marcus, it was Marcus. Marcus Clarke was his name. Did he give you the photograph? Now I come to think of it, he often walked around with a camera."

"Marcus Clarke?" Robinson asked. "Are you sure it was Clarke?"

"Yes, quite sure. Monique had a letter from him, and I told her to hand it to the police, although I don't think she ever did."

"Do you believe the story, sir?" Robinson asked as they were driving away.

"We know Monique was injured in a car accident, so that stacks up, as does the bit about her following him back to London. I want to speak to this Marcus. He's our only other lead right now."

"What about Edwards' wife?"

"He was certainly keen to pin some blame on her, with mention of a knife. But I don't want to talk to her just yet. Let them sweat for a little while."

ELEVEN

It was late on the Friday afternoon; Cooper was at his desk in the police station when Robinson knocked on his door.

"Got a minute, Inspector?"

He nodded and Robinson went to sit but then seemed to change his mind, standing instead.

"I've had a dig into the background of Marcus Clarke, and it's quite interesting. We have him on file. I've also got a photograph of Marcus Fox from the passport office. Marcus Clarke was born in nineteen forty seven, on the third of July, which matches the date of birth shown in Marcus Fox's passport, so my belief is it's the same person."

"Let me see."

Robinson handed Cooper a copy of Fox's passport photograph which was of a man who looked older than sixty three, with untidy hair and a heavily lined, slightly gaunt face.

"What do we know about him?"

"The report to the court says that Fox's parents were the Honourable Henry Clarke and Felicity, maiden name Romney. His father is the third son of a Marquis, apparently. Fox was confined in a mental hospital when he was aged eight, in September nineteen fifty five. As Marcus Clarke he was convicted by the court of the manslaughter of his sister. It was quite a thing in the press at the time."

Cooper looked at him as he spoke, his mouth slightly open in astonishment.

"What happened?"

"He was convicted of drowning his sister in the bath. She was only four at the time. His mother came to the bathroom to find him holding her under the water. It seems he wanted to see what happened when someone drowned. Because of his age and the fact that he was deemed not to have realised how serious it was, he was charged with manslaughter, not murder, and put into psychiatric care."

"When was he released?"

"He was released from the hospital into the hands of a psychiatrist after five years, in March nineteen sixty, aged twelve. Just six months later, when he turned thirteen, he went to Harrow. He really does have friends in high places."

"Harrow? Didn't Charles Edwards go there as well?"

"Yes, he did. I wondered if they knew each other."

"He said he knew his name, but he didn't say he knew him. We'll have to bear that in mind. What then?"

"At the end of his time there he won a place at Cambridge, so he's obviously not stupid. He only did a year at Cambridge however before leaving, and that seems to have coincided with a relapse of his mental illness. He was convicted for possession of the drug LSD during his brief stay at Cambridge, in March nineteen sixty six, and given a twelve month suspended sentence.

Whether he was an addict or not I don't know, but straight after that he spent a year in a private clinic somewhere in Europe. I don't have an address but Switzerland is mentioned in the notes at one point, so it may have been there; the notes also mention the same psychiatrist he was in the care of as a child. He didn't go back to Cambridge that I can see. He then spent about a year in Paris between nineteen sixty seven and eight, which fits with the story told to us by Charles Edwards and I assume is when he met Monique. The doctor he had been seeing all along was a psychiatrist based in Harley Street, a doctor Jeremy Portman."

"And what became of him after that, and when did he change his name to Fox?"

"I can't see any mention of a Marcus Clarke after that, and as Marcus Fox he seems to have kept a low profile except he was once mentioned in a report into animal rights activists."

"Doing what?"

"He's mentioned in a report from an undercover officer into an animal rights organisation. The report says Fox loved animals and hated the people that harmed them with an intensity that had alienated him from many other supporters of the group. He had reportedly argued that as humans were destroying the planet for all animals, people were therefore dispensable. He had been a leading protestor in the movement but after that statement they had classed him as too extreme and he left. There's no report after that. I suspect he changed his name to lessen the risk of his past coming out. I have a search under way to find out when he changed his name, but it must have been after he went to Paris, given Charles Edwards knew him as Clarke, not Fox."

"When WPC Harper looked at Tina Marsh's address book, there was mention of a man called James

Clarke. She was trying to trace him when she came across Marcus Fox. I wonder if there is a connection, or whether it's just a coincidence?"

"There've been more coincidences than usual on this case."

"It seems so. Could you check to see if Marcus Clarke had a brother, or perhaps a cousin with the name James Clarke? I'd also like to talk to that psychiatrist; maybe he was a young man then, or perhaps someone else took over the care of Marcus Clarke after him. It's over fifty years ago so he may not still be alive, but check it out just in case."

"Also I've heard from the police in Richmond, about Paulette Dijon and Terence Brown, sir."

"Have you? What did they have to say?"

"The constable I spoke to said they seemed genuine enough. He's an elderly gentleman, living in a nice house in a respectable area; apparently his wife is confined to a wheelchair. He said when he asked if the name Paulette Dijon meant anything to them the wife looked startled, and asked him what happened to her. It seems Paulette came to stay with them for a few months. She was with them from just after New Year in nineteen eighty. They had been advertising a room to let and the school rang them to say that they had this girl, Paulette, who was urgently in need of a room. She came and they agreed to rent her a room for three months but just before the three months were up she disappeared completely. They had a note from her to say she had found a boyfriend and had decided to move in with him, and would call to collect her things after a few days. They never saw anything of her again after that. They told the constable they kept her things for a while, but she never came to collect anything. There wasn't much left, just a couple of jumpers, some underwear, and a couple of books. And some shoes. They kept them for a few years in a box in the attic, just in case she returned for them, but she never did, so in the end they gave the stuff away to a charity shop. They said they weren't sure what happened to the note she left for them."

"Did they report her missing?"

"No, they didn't report her missing, they said, because they knew she had moved to be with her boyfriend. She didn't owe them any money, she had paid for the accommodation in advance, so they didn't think too much of it. The constable asked them if they had a name for the boyfriend but they couldn't remember. He also asked if there'd been an address on the note, but they said there wasn't one, or they would have sent the stuff on to her. They also said she didn't talk about boys much, and they were a bit surprised when she went off like that. She was a sweet young girl."

"Marcus Fox had a newspaper clipping about her, so he certainly knew something about her."

"Looks that way."

"We need to find him."

* * * * *

It had been a long week and Cooper was looking forward to his weekend and seeing Melanie again, even if he wouldn't see her until Saturday evening, but on his way home he called at the hospital to see how Catherine Harper was. She had been moved since his last visit, so a nurse took him down to her bed on a female ward, which had the curtain pulled around it. When he walked in she looked to be asleep, but he sat down quietly at the bedside; the nurse left him, pulling the curtain closed behind her. Catherine was sitting, propped on a number of pillows. He noticed the wires monitoring her had been removed. She certainly had a little more colour in her cheeks. Catherine stirred and opened her eyes. She saw him and smiled.

"How are you feeling, Catherine?"

"I seem to keep dozing off, sir. My head still aches, and I'm feeling sore all over. The last time I woke up it took me a while to remember where I was, and why I was here. I have no idea of the time, whether it's daytime or in the middle of the night, as I can't see a window from here with the curtain closed. What time is it now?"

"It's seven in the evening on Friday."

She lifted her head from the pillows momentarily, but it seemed a great effort because she immediately lay back on the pillows again. Her eyes closed; for a moment Cooper thought she had gone back to sleep but then she opened her eyes again and smiled at him.

"I know I've been very lucky; I could have been badly injured or killed. Some small details have started to come back to me. I'm trying to remember the sequence of events. I remember that after I spoke to Mrs Marsh I looked through Tina's address book, and found the name James Clarke in Camden. There was nothing on him in the police computer, and you asked me to visit the address to see if the current owners knew him or anything about him. The apartment was on the top floor, a lot of narrow stairs. There was a young Polish woman in the apartment. She didn't know anything, but she told me the name of the letting agent. When I left I went to see the agent to ask if they knew anything about James Clarke. They didn't know the name, but they gave me the name of the current owner. I don't remember the name,

175

although I must have made a note of it. It wasn't Clarke. I'm very thirsty."

Cooper poured a glass of water for her and put it into her hands; they looked very small.

"There is something I should remember, something important, but I can't remember what" she said. "I asked the agency who the current owner had bought the apartment from; they had sold it to him but the lady didn't know; she said the name would be in their archives, and it would take her a couple of days to get the file sent to her. I remember coming out of the agency and getting on my bicycle. I had intended to return to Hampstead, but something stopped me. When I'd been with the Polish lady I had looked out of the window down onto the garden and asked if she ever used it. She said it belonged to the man on the ground floor; the woman said she didn't like him. She said he was English and thought he had been living in the ground floor apartment for a long time. It occurred to me it was possible he might know James Clarke, so I decided to go back and ask. I don't remember anything after that. There is something else I should remember."

Catherine closed her eyes. Cooper waited for a few minutes but she was asleep. He left the bedside and closed the curtain behind him.

* * * * *

The police patrol car was parked in a small side street of Portsmouth as the pubs started to empty and the clubs were beginning to open. The night air was mild but humid, with a fine rain blowing in the air making all surfaces glisten under the streetlights. The two officers inside the car had to use the wipers occasionally so they could keep an eye on the major road in front of them for pub goers who had had a drink or two but who had decided to drive the car home anyway. It had been a quiet evening, but it was early yet. It was about this time that things usually started to get busier; so far they had stopped two drivers who they had suspected might have had a drink. One of them had been driving a scruffy car with one of the side lights not working. They had stopped him, but he proved negative from the breathalyser. He had been quiet, polite and helpful, and had told them he owned a boat in the area which he was on his way to. They had let him go with a caution, and the officer noted the name of Marcus Fox in his notebook.

After this they had settled down to watch the increasing number of cars in the area once more until the end of their shift came and they headed back to the station. The officers checked in with the sergeant and finished writing up their reports before heading home. The sergeant looked at the reports briefly, putting them into a folder whilst greeting some police officers arriving for the early shift. He then left for home himself.

As he drove home he listened to the local radio, with a news bulletin coming on the half hour which included an item on the attack on Catherine. He wasn't listening too closely, but then he heard the name the police were seeking. He pulled his car into a side street, turned the vehicle around, and headed back to the police station. He walked back in and picked up the folder of reports, still on the table where he had left it. He looked through, and found the one he had remembered seeing earlier. He took it to the duty sergeant.

"You'd better have a look at this."

* * * * *

As the Friday evening Eurostar train drew near to the centre of Paris, people started to stand, getting bags and coats down from the racks, readying themselves to leave the train. Simon stood up and did the same, passing a small overnight bag down to Amanda. A short while later they emerged from the station looking for a taxi. Amanda gave the address of her Aunt where they would be staying for the weekend as they climbed in.

The evening was much milder than it had been in London; the tourists were wearing a variety of clothing from heavy winter coats to light waterproof jackets. It was that time of year when no-one seemed quite sure what to wear. The locals, always obvious owing to their more elegant attire, were lightly dressed, the ladies in long overcoats with shawls over their shoulders, the men generally wearing jackets with a scarf but without overcoats. They passed endless street-side cafes and small restaurants, full of people eating indoors as it was still too cool to eat out, before they drove into a quieter, more residential area, stopping shortly afterwards outside an elegant early twentieth century apartment building.

They walked up the steps to be met by a porter, who telephoned the apartment of Amanda's Aunt and, when satisfied, called the lift for them. He slid back the outer cage door of the lift and they stepped inside, the lift then juddering before beginning its ascent, causing Amanda to hold Simon's arm in alarm. He smiled at her and after a few moments he slid open the cage door and they stepped onto an elegant, belle époque hallway lit by a wonderful chandelier, the floor covered in swirling marble. Amanda rang the bell outside the door into her Aunt's apartment.

The door opened almost immediately and Amanda's Aunt Marie greeted them both with a kiss and a hug. "Come in, come in" she said and they stepped into an elegantly furnished apartment, immediately struck by the view over the roofs of Paris to the Eiffel Tower.

"It's a wonderful sight" she smiled at them, "the view was what made me determined to own this apartment in the nineteen fifties. It was not so fashionable then. I couldn't afford to buy it now. But I do love it here. It is a quiet area and yet central to everything. The neighbours are charming too, and I have many friends in this area. For me, it is ideal."

She then took them through a small corridor to where one of the guest bedrooms was. This room was almost as large as Amanda's entire apartment.

"This is lovely" Amanda told her Aunt.

Marie left them and they unpacked their clothes, before joining Marie in the drawing room.

"I have arranged a little supper for us here" Marie told them, "as I didn't want to book a restaurant for you in case you were delayed, or too tired to go out. I thought you might want to take a walk out alone together to enjoy the Paris evening, so I suggest that I'll leave you alone to do that after supper if you wish. Tomorrow morning we'll have a look through some of our family papers. I hope it won't be too boring for you Simon. Will you want to stay with us?"

"Yes, I'm happy to do that. I can always take a little walk or read if it gets too much."

"Splendid. Now I also promised I would introduce you to my sister-in-law Beatrice. She works for the French government, advising on historical preservation of buildings. She is something of an expert on the history of Paris, so it may be interesting to chat to her about what life was like in those times. If it is all right with you I have invited her to lunch here with us tomorrow afternoon."

Amanda smiled to indicate her agreement and Marie then led them into the dining room, with three places laid with a selection of meats and cheeses with salad and fresh bread; two bottles of wine were open on the table, one red and one white.

"Welcome to Paris" Simon whispered to Amanda.

* * * * *

As the ferry slipped its moorings exactly on time at eleven pm on the Friday evening and made its way out of Portsmouth harbour into the Channel, most of the passengers were inside the various lounges and bars, preparing for the overnight sail to Le Havre. A few young couples were enjoying being huddled together against the cold night air, although one older man, tall and thin, who appeared to be alone, was at the stern of the ferry, looking at the lights of Portsmouth receding into the distance. Only when the last of the lights disappeared into the darkness of the night did he move and descend the stairwell into one of the noisier bars, where music was playing loudly and there were several groups of young people, including a group of young women who appeared to be on a 'hen' party as they were all dressed identically. All were drinking heavily and enjoying themselves; all were oblivious to the man who slipped quietly into a corner seat, taking only a soft drink. After a few minutes he turned his chair slightly sideways to one group of girls and pretended to look at a newspaper so he could watch them without being too obvious; this was a manoeuvre he had perfected over many years. As the bar gradually quietened down and people either fell asleep or went to other parts of the ship, the man remained in the same position, although he now put down the newspaper and half closed his eyes to feign sleep.

The tannoy system of the ferry the next morning announced their pending arrival in Le Havre; the group of girls he had been watching gradually made their way to the bathrooms and then descended the steps to the disembarkation area, oblivious to the man who had joined the crowd of people standing close by them; he was however close enough to hear their conversation and learnt that they were to get the bus into town. He and the other foot passengers made their way down the ramp and followed the signs for the bus; he made sure he was as close to the group of girls as he could. As they boarded he pushed his way in amongst them and sat himself in the seat next to one of them.

* * * * *

That evening Cooper went to eat a pizza alone at a restaurant near his flat as he didn't feel like cooking; he rang Melanie from his mobile phone but it went straight to her voicemail so he just left a brief message saying he was looking forward to the weekend.

He was asleep when his mobile phone rang. He looked at the clock as he reached for the phone; it was two in the morning.

"Sorry to bother you, inspector, it's Sergeant Jones here. We've just had a call from Portsmouth police. One of their cars stopped a man for driving with one light not working just before midnight. They breathalysed him but he was in the clear, so they gave him a verbal warning and let him go. His name was Marcus Fox, and his driving licence showed an address in Camden, the same address where WPC Harper was attacked the other evening. The duty sergeant there is apologetic but the report wasn't filed until just now, and the name wasn't picked up."

"Did they ask him anything? Did he say where he was going?"

"He told them he owned a boat in the area, and he was on his way there."

"Get back onto them. Tell them I'll be driving down first thing tomorrow morning, and I'll need some help from their CID to track him down, so get someone to meet me there tomorrow. DC Robinson will be with me, so tell them we need two clean hotel rooms for tomorrow night. Can you also ask them to get onto the local marinas to see if any of them have a boat registered in any of these names: Marcus Fox or Marcus Clarke? If they get anything, call me straight back, whatever time it is."

"Will do, sir. Is there anything else I can be doing to help?"

"Not that I can think of for now."

"OK sir. Goodnight. Good luck for tomorrow."

TWELVE

Cooper's plan for the Saturday had been to go to the hairdresser to get his hair cut which was long overdue, and to buy a book for his history course from his usual bookshop, after which he was going to have a quiet afternoon before going out for the evening with Melanie. Instead of this, by seven that morning he was sitting in Mike Robinson's car; they were heading down to Portsmouth to co-ordinate the search for Marcus Fox. As Robinson drove down the motorway, Cooper received a call from the detective in Portsmouth assigned to work with him.

"We're pleased to work with you, sir. We're starting to contact the local marinas looking for any boat registered to the names you gave us. Most of the ones we've spoken to so far have someone on duty to keep watch but the office isn't open yet, so that might take a while I'm afraid. I also have a group of constables calling the local hotels and guest houses to check the guest names, however there are literally hundreds of those and that could take more than the weekend."

"OK, keep me informed. Has someone sent you his photograph?"

"Yes, sir, we have that. It's been given out to all our patrols going out this morning; they're out looking to find his car as well. If he's still near here, we should find him."

"Let me know as soon as you hear anything."

A while later Cooper's phone rang again.

"Hello inspector, it's Catherine."

"Catherine! How are you? Shouldn't you be in bed?"

"I'm feeling a little bit better, although I'm sure I should still be in bed. The nurse isn't very happy with me. I needed to call you, sir, as I remembered when I woke up this morning that my assailant told me he was heading back to avenge his first love. I don't know what he meant by that, but he said his first love, and he definitely used the word avenge. He then said he thought Paris was much nicer than London. I'm convinced that the two are connected, and that he's making his way to Paris."

"Catherine, you're a star. Now go back to bed."

"Thank you sir. I will."

Cooper called the detective in Portsmouth once more.

"Will you get your people to focus on the hotels closest to the ferry terminals first? I have had a tip off that he might be heading to France. Could you also get on to the ferries to provide passenger lists as soon as possible? Lastly will you check that a search for the car that your men stopped the previous evening has been organised, and again concentrate on the area around the ferry terminals."

"No problem sir, we'll get onto it."

An hour later they were driving into the outskirts of Portsmouth when Cooper's phone rang. It was the local detective; they had now received the passenger lists of all the ferries that had left since the previous evening. Neither Marcus Fox nor Marcus Clarke was amongst the passengers.

"Could you have a look if you have any other Fox, and could you try Renard as well?"

The detective confirmed the spelling, promising to call back as soon as they had looked again.

Within ten minutes the local detective called him back. They hadn't found a passenger called Fox, but there was one called Renard, Pierre Renard.

"Where was this Pierre Renard travelling to?"

"He took the eleven pm ferry to Le Havre last night."

"When does it get to Le Havre?"

"It arrived at eight this morning, local time, so seven am here."

Cooper looked at his watch. It was almost nine am.

"Did it arrive on time?"

"I don't know. We'll have to check."

"Please do that. Could you also get onto the French police to look for his car?"

"If this is the man we're looking for, he hasn't taken his car, sir, because Pierre Renard was just a foot passenger."

"In that case can you find out if there are trains directly to Paris from Le Havre and if so ask the French if they can have someone ready to meet the next train in Paris? I'm sure they can find an excuse to check the passengers as they leave. Could you also send over the photograph of him that we have, and ask them to check if they can find a photograph of the passport of Pierre Renard, if one exists?"

Cooper looked at Robinson after he ended the call. "I think he may be travelling as Pierre Renard; if I'm right then he's in France, on foot. I assume then from what Catherine told me he's heading for Paris. What I'd like to know is why Paris?"

"Do you want them to stop searching for him here?" Robinson asked.

"Absolutely not. Not until we're sure it's him." He paused. "Let's go and get some breakfast" he said. "I don't think well on an empty stomach."

* * * * *

Amanda sat up in bed and looked at the time; nine thirty in Paris. Simon was already out of bed and in the bathroom. She stepped out of bed and padded across the room to the window, which she opened wide to let some fresh air into the room. The cool air was filled with the scents and sounds of Paris, and she was reminded of a weekend she had taken here with her parents as a small girl. She wondered why she had not met Marie at the time, but perhaps she had been away.

She looked around the room they had been given. The house in Hampstead was large, but this room, as all the rooms in the apartment, was of grand proportions and high ceilings, features that she loved. The furniture was antique and very French.

Simon appeared from the bathroom in a dressing gown, his hair still wet from the shower.

"Why don't you go for a walk this morning darling?" she said. "I don't think you'll be terribly interested in our family history, and I suspect we'll be talking a lot about ancient, long dead relatives. You may as well take some fresh air or see one of the museums."

"If you're sure you don't mind, I may do just that."

They took breakfast in the kitchen where the housekeeper had laid out some fresh bread, with various meats and preserves.

After breakfast Simon went out to take a walk around some of the weekend flea markets to see what he could find to add to his collection of books, whilst Marie and Amanda sat together going through a lot of family papers, which Amanda found fascinating. There were documents of christenings, weddings and funerals of the family going back into the mid eighteenth century, and Amanda made lots of notes, and promised Marie that she would enlarge the family tree and send it over to her when completed.

Simon returned just after midday and at a few minutes after one o'clock Beatrice, Marie's sister-in-law, arrived for lunch. After the introductions they went along to the dining room and sat down. Amanda wondered, half aloud, why the French could make a simple lunch with just a few ingredients so tasty and appetising; a feat that was near impossible in England. The two French ladies merely smiled.

Both during and after lunch Beatrice spent some time explaining the history of the French revolution and the subsequent upheavals. Amanda asked lots of questions and found Beatrice fascinating. After some time they began to talk about London and she asked Amanda where she lived.

"Well I have a small apartment in St John's Wood at the moment, but I spent most of my life in Hampstead where my mother still lives."

"Ah, yes I know Hampstead. I believe it was in the news recently as well, with the discovery of the poor French girl who was murdered on the heath."

Amanda wasn't sure what to say, but Marie answered anyway.

"Diana was the poor lady who discovered the body. It was an awful shock for her."

Beatrice looked at Amanda in surprise.

"Oh, your poor mother. What must she have felt? It's quite a coincidence really, because only the other day I was talking to a good friend of mine called Florence; we were discussing the news and it seems Florence has a cousin that used to know the murdered girl."

Amanda thought she would rather not know too much about the victim, but Simon was more curious. "Did she really?" he asked. "How did she know her?"

"Well it was before you were born, but Florence's cousin, Sophie, and Monique, the murdered girl, were both at university in Paris in nineteen sixty eight. Florence told me that Sophie and Monique had got to know each other quite well."

"Did she say why Monique was in London?" Simon asked.

"That year was very difficult in Paris because of the riots at the time; then the university closed down. Monique went to London to study, but also to follow her boyfriend."

"Did Sophie go over to London as well?"

"It seems not, because Sophie and Monique had fallen out. You see they had both been involved in a car accident in which Sophie's boyfriend had been killed. It seems that Monique's boyfriend had been driving the car, but Monique had lied to the police by telling them that it was Sophie's boyfriend who had been driving. As he was dead, he couldn't say anything, of course."

"Why did she do that?"

"Sophie said Monique did this in order to keep her boyfriend out of prison; they had all had too much to drink to be driving. Sophie had been furious with Monique; Florence told me she didn't speak to her or see her at all after the university closed and they all moved away."

"Didn't Sophie tell the police?" Amanda asked.

"I think she only found out about the lie some weeks later, and anyway she wouldn't have gone to the police. Those times were very difficult, you see, and relations between young people and the police were very poor. It is not easy to explain now, but those times were very dangerous."

"So no-one knows what happened to Monique after she went to England?" Simon asked.

"No; Florence said it was years later when another friend mentioned to Sophie that Monique had never returned from the UK; apparently no-one knew what had happened to her."

"How odd. I wonder what did happen to her."

"Would you care to meet Sophie? She's a very nice lady; I have met her several times in these years. I would have to ask Florence as well, of course, but she might be happy to meet you to talk about those times a little more, if you are interested."

"I'm not sure" Amanda replied. "What do you think, Simon?"

"I think you may regret it if you don't meet her whilst you have the chance."

"Well perhaps you're right. Yes, I should like to meet her. Thank you."

She said it out of curiosity, although something inside her told her that she might regret it.

* * * * *

During the first part of Saturday morning Cooper and Robinson sat in an office assigned to them in the main police station in Portsmouth, talking to the local detectives who had been drafted in to assist on the case; Cooper had made various telephone calls including two back to the chief in London. After some delay he had been given permission to travel to France if events demanded it. He had then spoken to a contact in Paris who had agreed to act as the main liaison, if only because he spoke perfect English and so would be extremely helpful in any event; Cooper's French was rusty, to say the least.

It was mid morning when one of the detectives came into the office.

"We've found a boat registered to a Marcus Fox who lives in London. We've a car waiting for us downstairs."

"Right, let's go."

They hurried down to meet the other waiting officers, getting into two marked police cars. Soon they were being whisked through the streets of Portsmouth towards one of the marinas, the police drivers driving at maximum speed, sirens blaring to warn other road users of their approach.

Cooper asked them to silence the sirens as they approached, and they drove quietly into the far side of the marina. They were greeted by the manager of the yard who had been asked to keep a distance from the boat but to keep a discreet watch if at all possible.

"No-one has entered or left the boat since I called" the manager told Cooper after he was introduced.

"Can you point out exactly which boat it is?"

"Yes. If you look at the second pontoon on the far side, you'll see a white hulled sailing yacht; it's the one with the grey inflatable dinghy upside down on the cabin roof."

"Yes, I see it. Do you know who owns the boats on either side, and are they likely to be on board?"

"Yes, I do. I don't believe anyone's on those boats right now; the owners live in town, both of them, but I haven't seen them this weekend."

"How well do you know Mr Fox?"

"I know him reasonably well. He isn't a frequent sailor now. There was a time when he was here every weekend a few years ago, but he sails a lot less now."

"Could you describe him?"

"He's about sixty, I'd say, quite tall, very thin grey hair, and quite slender."

Cooper and Robinson exchanged glances at the description. Cooper then showed him the photograph.

"Yes, that's definitely him" the manager confirmed.

"Have you seen him at all in the past few days?"

"No, I haven't seen him here in quite a few weeks."

"Do you have a small boat that some of the officers could use to approach the yacht from the water?"

"I have a dinghy they could use but, as the yachts are moored stern to, your officers would have to get onto it by the bow which wouldn't be easy. They'll need to use a rope, I would suggest."

"I think you're right, it would take time and be too noisy to clamber up the front of the boat from a dinghy. Well let's have two men in a dinghy approach the yacht from the water, and be on standby. When they are in position, two men will board each yacht adjacent to Mr Fox's yacht to act as back up, three men will board Mr Fox's yacht directly from the pontoon."

Within five minutes all were in position, including two officers paddling a dinghy, and Cooper gave the signal to proceed. Two armed officers boarded each yacht positioned either side of Fox's yacht as silently as possible. At the signal three armed officers jumped onto Fox's yacht, shouting that they were police officers, and banged on the hatch entrance into the cabin of the yacht. They broke open the hatch and went down, guns at the ready.

After a moment they re-appeared. All was quiet on board, with no signs of life at all.

Cooper and Robinson ran over as soon as the armed officers came out, and they boarded the vessel. The interior of the yacht was certainly tidier than the house in Camden. They began a search of the yacht, both interior and exterior; one of the constables gave a shout and Cooper went to see what had been found. One of the exterior lockers contained a plastic case, which he opened. Inside was a large kitchen knife, plus a small hacksaw. Cooper put the case to one side and looked inside the locker. It contained a number of rolls of new plastic bags, the type used for waste bins.

He turned to one of the local detectives.

"Can you get forensics down here please to go over this boat carefully?"

As he spoke, Robinson shouted.

"Blood stains here, sir."

Cooper went back inside the cabin. Under the small table in the middle of the cabin Robinson had lifted a small carpet; there were dried blood stains on the floorboards underneath.

"All right everyone; let's get off the yacht now. Organise a guard over this yacht please, until forensics have been over it."

As they left the marina in one of the cars, Cooper rang London to update the chief on progress. As he finished the call his mobile phone bleeped to tell him that he had a message.

"Delacroix, my contact in Paris, must have called whilst I was talking to London. He needs to talk to me urgently" he told Robinson.

He then listened to the message.

"The French police say a young girl has gone missing in Le Havre" he told Robinson. "They are conducting a search now. I'm going to go over there."

"Do you want to scale down the search for him here?"

"No, because we can't be certain that this incident in France has anything to do with him, and even if it has, he may then double back and return here. If he has left his car here, as seems likely, then I want to find it. If this is a wild goose chase I'm going on, at least we'll be looking here as well. Let's keep looking."

* * * * *

Cooper arrived in Le Havre by the fast ferry at six thirty in the afternoon, local time. The local police met him and took him straight to the police headquarters. He entered the grand building just off the main square and was shown into a waiting room, where he sat waiting for someone to speak to him for almost an hour. He understood he was not in charge of this particular operation, and was here strictly as an observer and as a liaison with the police in the UK, however he wanted to know what was happening and was feeling frustrated. Marcus Fox, or Pierre Renard as he now seemed to be calling himself, could be on his way to Paris by now. It was very likely he would be on the move already.

Just then the door opened and a severe looking old woman came in. She was small, overweight, dressed in black and looked old enough to be his mother. She spoke in excellent English but with a strong accent.

"The inspector can see you now."

He followed her as she made her way with surprising agility up a broad flight of stone steps that followed a sweeping curve up to the next floor, then entered a large office in need of redecoration, with an impressive but slightly battered oak desk on a dark tiled floor, behind which sat a slightly overweight man with thinning grey hair swept back from his forehead. Cooper guessed he was in his late fifties. As he entered the man stood up, smiled and extended his hand.

"Good evening Inspector Cooper. I am Inspector Mercier."

They shook hands.

"Please call me Sam."

"Certainly. Please call me Bernard."

Mercier indicated to one of the chairs by his desk, and he sat down. Mercier sat in the chair behind his desk, an old leather chair that had seen better days.

"I am pleased that you are here" he began, "but right now there's not a great deal to tell you. The girl that has been reported as missing is called Bernadette Guillaume. She travelled to Le Havre on the ferry from the UK overnight with a group of girlfriends who had been to London for the weekend. Bernadette and the group had travelled by the ferry from here to Portsmouth and from there by train to London. They returned the same way. When they arrived back in Le Havre yesterday the group of girls took the bus from the ferry into the town centre here, after which they went their separate ways, mainly to their homes. We are told that Bernadette had said to a friend that she needed to do something before going home, but what that something was we do not know. She was reported missing by her mother when she did not get home after several hours and could not be reached on her mobile telephone. None of her friends have seen her since they left the bus. We have now contacted them all and had statements from them all. We now have another small group of young people that were also on the same ferry and have come in because they think they might have seen something. I am about to go down to speak to them, if you would like to accompany me?"

"Yes, please, I should be interested in that."

"Very good. Follow me please."

They went down a flight of steps and along corridors, their footsteps echoing, to a large interview room. Several people were in there, including four teenage girls, two boys, and a couple of adults who were introduced as parents.

The inspector began by asking them who they were, and what they had seen. He then asked them if they would explain a little of their story in English. Cooper would have preferred to see them individually, but said nothing. They looked at each other, then one spoke up who seemed to be the main spokesperson for the group; he was one of the boys, who looked slightly older than the others.

"The ferry left England at eleven pm on Friday evening. It made its way out of the harbour and out to sea. Most of the passengers were inside, in the bars, but a few people were enjoying being huddled together against the cold night air."

"You stayed out on deck?" the inspector asked.

"Yes, I did."

"Who was with you?"

The boy hesitated, looking at the group. "Alice" he said, at which the face of one of the girls turned a pinkish red. The others smiled but said nothing, glancing at each other.

"I see, please continue" the inspector said.

"As we left the harbour in England I noticed an old man, quite tall and very thin, who appeared to be alone, at the back of the ferry. He was standing still, just looking at the lights as they became smaller. He stood still for a long time, just looking. It soon got cold and I, I mean we, went down to join the others in the bar. By that time most of the other passengers were down; the old man was virtually the only person still outside. Inside the music was playing loudly, it was difficult to talk and there were several groups of people, including a group of girls. It was only quite a while later that I noticed the same man, who was sitting alone in a corner seat. He was drinking what looked like just a coke, so he was not getting drunk like everyone else. I am pretty sure it was the same man that I had seen outside because he was very thin, but I didn't take so much notice. It was a long time later that I noticed him again; he was looking at a newspaper and I wondered how he could read with all the noise. Something about him made me watch him and I realised he was not reading at all, he was watching the group of girls."

"How long did he stay like that?" the inspector asked him.

"I don't know, maybe a couple of hours. People were gradually going to sleep in the chairs, although I couldn't sleep. Again I noticed the man remained in the same place, although he had now put down the newspaper and closed his eyes. I got the impression that his eyes were not really closed, as once as I was looking in his direction he opened them to look around quickly before closing them again."

"Did he stay in the chair all night?"

"I didn't see him move. I couldn't sleep. I never sleep well sitting in a chair. I wasn't looking so carefully though, so he might have taken a walk at some point. Certainly by the time the ferry arrived he was still in the same chair."

"What happened next?"

"The ferry arrived at Le Havre. The group of girls he had been watching went down to the disembarkation area in front of us, and again I saw the thin man immediately behind them, not too far in front of us. When the ferry stopped we went down past passport control, and went out to get the bus into town. As we went on board the bus I saw him push his way in amongst the girls and he sat in the seat next to one of them."

"Did he speak to her at all?"

"No. He ignored her until the bus was almost in Le Havre. I saw that he took a look at her as she spoke to one of the other girls in the group. She was possibly the youngest in the group; she only looked a similar age to us, about sixteen or seventeen, but the other girls looked older, in their twenties perhaps."

"What did she look like, what was she wearing, the girl he sat next to?"

"She had long blonde hair and was wearing a yellow top and blue jeans."

"And the man, how would you describe him?"

"As I said, he was quite old, probably old enough to be a grandfather. He was tall, and very thin. He had hair that needed a cut. He had a dark coloured raincoat on when he left the ferry; it was dark grey I think."

The inspector looked at Cooper.

"Is there anything you would like to ask them, inspector?"

Cooper looked at the youth.

"You say this man was tall and thin. Can you tell me how tall?"

"He was taller than me; I would guess he was a little less than two metres."

The inspector thanked them for coming in, and he and Cooper returned to his office.

"We are searching the local river, the harbour and the woods, but so far we have found nothing. Ordinarily we would have waited a little longer as girls have a habit of visiting boys but not telling their mothers, however in the light of your information about a possible murderer being on the same ferry then we are taking no chances."

"And can you tell me what is being done to find Marcus Fox, or Pierre Renard as he is also known?"

"My focus, as you will understand, is on finding the missing girl. The photograph you supplied has been circulated amongst all my officers with the instruction that they are to alert me personally if he is seen and to follow him but not apprehend him. In addition we are reviewing the hotel registers to see if we can find a Monsieur Renard staying anywhere here."

"Is anyone watching the train stations, or contacting the local car hire companies?"

"Right now, no. My manpower resources are stretched already, and as I have said my first priority is to find the missing girl, I hope alive. When we have done that then more resources can be allocated to the search for this man."

"What about bringing in resources from elsewhere? Are there no local towns that can spare some resource to assist?"

"I have asked the question already, but there was a large football match taking place today, so the town is full of people who may make trouble, as you will understand. Other resources I might ordinarily use are already fully stretched. I am sorry, Monsieur Cooper, I understand your frustration in not being able to bring more focus on catching your suspect, but we are doing all that we can right now. I would like to help more, but right now I cannot. Now if you will excuse me I am due to go to a briefing with my commissioner and I shall need to leave shortly."

Cooper was escorted back down the stairs to a waiting police car, which took him to his hotel. By this time it was almost midnight, and he collapsed gratefully into the bed, falling asleep within moments.

THIRTEEN

Cooper woke early on the Sunday morning, the sun shining through the window of his hotel room. He had arrived too tired to take much notice last night, but now he sat up and looked around. The pale green painted room was large but sparsely furnished; the metal framed bed, a single cupboard at the side on which he had dropped his watch and loose change last night, and an old fashioned stand-alone wardrobe in the corner were all it contained. The floor was tiled; he remembered it feeling cold on his bare feet as he undressed. A door in the corner led into a bathroom with a large bath with a shower above it. He picked up his watch; it was seven thirty French time, which meant that it was six thirty in the UK. He remembered that breakfast was served from seven thirty, so he got out of bed, putting his bare feet into his shoes to avoid the cold floor.

Once showered and dressed, he went down to the dining room, where several elderly couples were already eating. He ordered a cafe au lait and took a croissant. Waiting for his coffee he checked his phone for messages and emails. He started when he saw a missed call and a message from Melanie. The message had arrived the previous evening; he had put his phone on silent when he had arrived at the French police station, and had then forgotten about it.

"It is almost nine o'clock and I have decided I have waited far too long already. You have obviously forgotten me, as you have not had the courtesy to call, or return my call. I have been feeling like a prostitute, sitting in a bar alone, dressed to kill, pretending to be waiting for someone. Thank you for that."

He slapped his hand on his forehead.

"Oh no. Damn me. I'd completely forgotten to call her to let her know where I was. Oh God, what do I do now?" he muttered to himself.

He looked at his watch. It was eight fifteen in the morning, which meant it was seven fifteen in the morning in the UK; it wouldn't do his case any good by calling her so early on a Sunday morning. He decided there was little he could do at this hour, so he finished his coffee and went back to his room to review his notes and wait for the local police to collect him once more, all the while wondering what he could do to make up to her.

"Fine way to treat your guardian angel, you dimwit" he said to himself as he worked, cursing himself.

He tried Melanie's mobile phone after another hour and left a message, but the phone seemed to be switched off. She didn't call him back.

* * * * *

Beatrice's acquaintance, Sophie, lived in a small but elegant apartment in the Neuilly district of Paris. As she walked out early on that sunny Sunday morning and down onto the street she might have been aware of a man standing across the road who seemed to be waiting for someone, but if so she took little notice, and certainly didn't look in his direction.

Marcus Fox saw her clearly enough. He thought her as beautiful as ever. His mind went back to when he had first seen her; it had been the first day of university and she had been looking lost. His French had been good enough then to ask her if she needed help; she had smiled at him and thanked him. After that she had often smiled at him when they passed each other, which he had made sure was most days. After a while he had taken enough courage to go into a bar where he knew she was with some friends; she had allowed him to buy a drink, and they began to talk. It had only been for a few minutes, perhaps half an hour, but it had been heaven for Marcus. He understood that Sophie had become wary of him during that conversation, as most people did, but she had seemed friendly enough. After a few weeks however she began to be less pleased by his attention and had started to avoid him. One time he had found the courage to ask why.

"It's mainly your views about other people, Marcus. You can't hate people the way you do. It isn't right. It's best if we don't meet again" she had said.

Marcus watched her walk down the street, and then he started to follow her at a discreet distance.

* * * * *

Amanda and Simon were also awake relatively early on the Sunday morning. They had arranged to meet Beatrice and Sophie for a late breakfast at a Parisian cafe later that morning, so they had to pack before taking the train back to London in the late afternoon. Marie wasn't able to join them so they strolled alone through the streets of Paris to the Le Marais area and, after a little while, found the cafe they were to meet in. There was no sign of Beatrice as they were a few minutes early, but they took a table for four people anyway and started to look at the brunch menu.

Five minutes or so later Beatrice entered with Sophie. Amanda thought she looked to be in her fifties although she knew she must have been over sixty. She was elegantly dressed and spoke to them in perfect English. She gave Amanda a warm smile, and gave Simon a polite kiss which he obviously enjoyed. She had been, and still was, a good looking woman. Beatrice had commented that Sophie had never married; Amanda wondered why.

They ordered some breakfast, Simon ordering a good deal more than the others as it was well past his normal breakfast time and he suspected he might not get too much lunch.

"So Amanda, this is Sophie, my good friend's cousin, as I explained to you the other day" Beatrice began after they had ordered. "She used to be a friend of Monique Bertrand, although they didn't see each other after university. I think she was very curious when Florence told her that I was with the daughter of the lady who had discovered Monique's body in London."

"Yes, I was very curious to know how your mother came to find Monique," Sophie assented, "and I thought perhaps I could tell you a little about her as well, as I am sure you are curious about her."

"I guess we are" Amanda began. "I can tell you what I know. My mother lives in Hampstead and has done so since before I was born; she has a little dog that she takes for a walk on Hampstead Heath every day. On that particular day in January it had been raining all day, and the weather for the previous few days had been very wet, but nonetheless my mother went out for her walk with the dog as usual in the afternoon. Because it was raining so heavily she decided to take a shorter walk, so went on a different part of the heath than usual. It was while they were taking this route that the little dog ran off and started to dig at the ground. When he wouldn't come away and was barking incessantly, my mother went to him and saw a few bones protruding from the ground. Some soil had been washed away by the rain and then partly dug away by the dog, exposing the bones, which turned out to be a hand, it seems. She found it very shocking, I know. My mother then called the police, of course."

"It must have been very frightening for her" Beatrice said.

"It was. The police came to interview her, of course, but she couldn't tell them anything except that which I've just told you. It was only weeks later that we found out through the news, along with everyone else, that it was the body of a girl and that she was from France, but apart from that we know very little. My mother has spoken to the police three or four times since the discovery of the body, but as yet we haven't heard that they know who killed her."

"That I can tell you."

Sophie spoke with a passion that took both Amanda and Simon by surprise.

"I know exactly who was responsible for her murder, and why."

After a couple of hours listening to Sophie's story Amanda and Simon walked out of the cafe and into a taxi which took them to the Gare du Nord to catch the train to London. As they climbed into the taxi Simon noticed the slightly scruffy, tall and thin man standing looking in the shop window across the street, but then forgot about it as the taxi pulled away.

* * * * *

As Amanda and Simon were having breakfast with Sophie, Cooper was back in the waiting area of the police station in the centre of Le Havre, which he was coming to know and detest. He passed the time watching people come and go; you saw all life go through a police station, he decided after an hour had passed. He sat quietly, as he knew the local police had their orders and he was not going to be able to influence that, no matter how much he would like to.

He made one call to the chief, who was sympathetic and said he understood his frustration, but Cooper knew the chief was not going to make too much of a fuss at a higher level in France. The chief's view was that they had a fugitive that might have committed one crime as a child, but against whom they did not have any evidence as yet; certainly not enough to ask the local police to ease off their search for a missing girl and to concentrate on looking for Marcus Fox.

Cooper waited.

It was late morning when Mike Robinson called him; he was relieved to have someone to speak to.

"Hello sir, how are things there?"

"Quiet. What about there?"

"Not quiet. I've just got back from the Camden apartment where WPC Harper was attacked by Marcus

Fox. Fred from pathology was waiting for me. He told me it has been a bit of a challenge, to say the least. The place is a hoarder's paradise. He mustn't have thrown anything away for years, nor made any attempt to clean up in that time either. Fred told me he has a theory why he may have wanted to do that, though."

"Oh, what's that?"

"He was trying to discourage visitors, or at least make sure that the smell of the place overpowered any other smell that may have been present."

"I'm not sure I follow you."

"Well, if you had, for example, something hidden that could have caused a smell after a while, and if someone wanted to visit you, say a social worker or some official for example, then if the apartment itself was fairly smelly then it would have disguised the smell he didn't want others to detect."

"And what smell did he not want others to detect?"

"He has been disposing of body parts down the drain. When forensics lifted the covers of the drains and took some samples they found traces of human remains in them."

Cooper whistled.

"No wonder he reacted when WPC Harper arrived at his apartment. Could they tell you anything about what they've found? Any clues as to sex, age and how long he or she's been dead?"

"They know they are human remains, but beyond that they know very little as yet, although they say they'll know more during the next week. It may be that young WPC Harper was lucky that Fox decided to run away when he did."

"Where else have they looked? What about the garden?"

"Well the recommendation is that they continue to sift through the contents of the apartment, to dig up the garden to see if there are further human remains, and I also suggest we may need to take a look under the concrete floor of the extension that seems to have been added in recent years, if we think it was built whilst Marcus Fox lived here. What do you think, sir?"

"Tell them to do whatever is necessary. I'll clear it with the chief."

* * * * *

Sophie had had her mind on other things that beautiful morning as she took the metro from Neuilly to Le Marais, then walked the short distance to the cafe where she had been invited to meet Beatrice and the daughter of the lady who had discovered Monique's body. She went with a mixture of curiosity and sadness; she was sad because the conversation with Beatrice had brought back all sorts of memories of those days in Paris and the car accident. She had been deeply in love; she had seen Jean Paul killed, and had suffered bad dreams about it for years afterwards. She had met other men of course, but somehow she had never fallen in love in quite the same way again.

She knew who had killed her greatest love, and she had never forgiven him.

After the breakfast, and after Amanda and Simon had gone off in their taxi, Beatrice and Sophie had stayed for a while chatting, before taking a walk through Le

Marais down to Place de Vosges, admiring the shops along the way. Beatrice then took a taxi home, leaving Sophie to walk some more.

After another half an hour Sophie arrived back at her apartment. As she opened the door she noticed something odd; the door to her bedroom was closed. It was normally held open by a small paperweight, because she disliked being closed in during the night. She walked over to the bedroom door, pushing it open once more and looking behind the door for the small weight. As she did so a hand was placed over her mouth and she felt something sharp against her throat.

"Hello Sophie. It's been a long time" Marcus said.

* * * * *

Cooper was still in the waiting room of the police station. He decided to call Melanie once more and was just taking his phone out of his pocket when Inspector Mercier came down the stairs and gestured to him. Cooper walked over. The inspector leaned towards him, speaking in a low voice so as not to be overheard by the members of the public assembled in the waiting room.

"Someone has found a body" he said, "and we are just going down there now. If you wish to come along as an observer you are welcome."

Cooper followed the inspector outside. As he climbed into the back of the police car his mobile phone rang; he looked at the screen. It was Melanie calling. He reluctantly pushed the red button to decline the call and put his phone onto silent, as the French police car swept through the local roads and out into the countryside towards where the body lay, the late spring sun glinting on the fields. He had the feeling it was going to be a while before he could call Melanie once more, if she ever accepted his call again.

The girl's body had been found by a man walking his dog. She was hidden among some bushes alongside a small country lane a mile or so outside of the town. As they looked at the scene Cooper became conscious of the scent of the nearby bushes, the branches moving gently in the breeze. There was silence for a short while as everyone took in the scene, respecting the body lying prostrate in front of them.

Inspector Mercier told him that this was an area popular with young lovers, often parking their cars in the area at night.

"I wonder how he knew about it?"

"I don't know. Perhaps whoever did this has been here before, or perhaps he followed her here."

She was lying face down. Cooper approached and crouched over the body looking at her carefully; Inspector Mercier was at his side. The body had multiple wounds, certainly with a knife.

"Does this look like the work of your suspect?"

"It's too early for me to tell, yet. We have connected him to the disappearance of at least two girls, possibly more. A search of his house has found traces of body parts; forensics are still working on an identity. I think he is a dangerous man. Whether he is connected to this case, I can't be sure, but I think he may be. I feel it in my bones."

* * * * *

Sophie sat staring at Marcus, wondering what he was doing here, why he had broken into her flat, what he wanted with her, trying to recall events from over forty years earlier. At first she hadn't recognised him, but when he spoke he knew her name, then she remembered. It gave her a chill down her spine when she recognised him; he wasn't easy to forget, although she had given him little thought since those days.

She had been sitting in a dining room chair for the entire night, her hands bound tightly behind her back with some form of tape that Marcus had taken from his pocket, her ankles bound tightly to the chair with the same. He had offered to leave her mouth uncovered if she promised to be quiet; if she broke that promise he had told her, in a quiet voice that had made her chill to the spine, he would cut her throat and sever her breathing tube, although in an odd kind of way he had been quite gentle with her, taking care she felt no pain as he bound her, as if he were doing this reluctantly, as if compelled by some higher authority to act against his will. When he spoke however there was a real menace in his voice, even if he spoke very calmly and quietly.

For most of the night he had been sitting quite still in a chair, staring into space as if she were not there, so that at one point she thought he had fallen asleep, but for the past hour he had been pacing up and down the room, talking to himself, ignoring her. If there had been anyone else present, Sophie would have said they were having a heated argument.

"What do you think he wants?" she heard him say. "He's been free for all these years, what's the point in changing that now?" Then a pause, as if he were listening to something. "Yes, but that was a long time ago. Anyway, she had nothing to do with it. We should just ask her and then act."

During the silence that followed, Sophie watched Marcus as he stared out through the window down onto the square below. The early morning light was casting a golden sheen across the leaves. Sophie longed to see it; the early hours were her favourite time of day, when the air was still and cold. She wondered if she would ever see it again. He suddenly turned from the window and walked to her, sitting down in a chair he had placed facing her almost an hour earlier, but until now had left empty.

Marcus leant towards her, looking at her intently.

"What happened on that night?" he suddenly asked.

Sophie looked at him, confused as to what he was talking about.

"Which night?"

"The night of the accident. What happened, really?"

Sophie realised that he was referring to the car accident. She wasn't aware that Marcus knew about it at all, and even more puzzled as to why he wanted to know about it after all this time.

"What do you want to know?" she asked him, "and why do you want to know? It was all a very long time ago. I have almost forgotten about it myself."

"I want to know exactly what happened, and who did what."

Marcus did not address the question as to why; Sophie decided she had little choice so she began to tell the story.

"I was with my boyfriend at the time, Jean Paul" Sophie began.

"Yes, I know all about him" Marcus interrupted.

"Well, I was with him on that evening. You know that there were a lot of crowds in Paris that night, a lot of police, and a lot of trouble. I tried to persuade Jean Paul to stay away but he wanted to see what was happening. We managed to get quite close but then one Gendarme saw us and began to run towards us, shouting for us to stop. We ran away as fast as we could, down some small alleyways and hid in a doorway. After a while we had seen nothing so we crept out; the Gendarme had gone away so we ran back towards his apartment as fast as we could, laughing all the way. When we arrived we began to drink heavily, and we were quite drunk when the doorbell rang; when we opened the door Jean Paul's friend, Charles Edwards, stood there. He had been arrested but then released, probably because he was English, and he had been unable to get home so he came to stay with us. He and Jean Paul carried on drinking; I decided they were being stupid so I went to the bathroom to have a bath; when I came out they were still drinking champagne but by then I had had enough. I rang Charles girlfriend, Monique, and told her Charles was with us. She said she would come over. I was hoping that she would be able to calm Charles down."

Sophie noticed that, as soon as she mentioned the name of Monique, Marcus sat bolt upright, his hands covering and uncovering his eyes as if he had some image in his mind that he didn't want to see.

"After Monique arrived" she continued, "Charles was shouting that we needed to buy some more drink, and he and Jean Paul went down to the car. Monique and I ran after them, trying to stop them as we said they were too drunk to drive. Charles insisted, saying that he would drive, so eventually we all climbed in. I was terrified, although Monique seemed terribly calm. As we drove along I knew we were going too fast and I shouted for

Charles to slow down, but it was too late. The car hit something and then tipped over. It slid on one side. None of us was wearing a seat belt of course, they didn't exist in those days. I ended on top of Monique, who had her hand caught underneath the car as it slid along. She was screaming; I think she had her arm out of the window just before we crashed. I remember a terrible bang as the car hit something and stopped very suddenly; I discovered later that it was the bridge we hit. I was thrown against the back of the front seat which saved me from being injured. I remember terrible screams and a crashing of glass which must have been poor Jean Paul as he was thrown through the windscreen. He was killed instantly, I was told. I managed to climb out through the door; I wasn't hurt, and I wanted to get to Jean Paul. I rushed over but he was dead; his head was turned at a peculiar angle, and I knew his neck had been broken. It was a horrible sight. I was too shocked to do anything; I just sat on the pavement and cried. An ambulance arrived very quickly, and the three of them were taken to hospital. I was just dazed and a bit scratched, so I said I didn't want to go in the ambulance. After the ambulance left, I sat by the road, not knowing what to do. I presume I was in shock. I must then have made my way back to the apartment because I woke up there with a terrible headache the next day. I don't remember how I got home; I assume I walked."

"What happened after that?"

"I knew that Jean Paul had been killed, and I really didn't know what to do. I decided just to go home to my parents, so I rang my mother later that day, and they drove all the way to Paris that evening and took me home. It was a couple of weeks later when I felt well enough to go back to Paris. I went to see Monique to see how she was. We had an argument, and I went straight back home to my parents. I never saw her again after that. I knew that Jean Paul was dead of course, but I didn't know his family, so I didn't want to try to see them, and I didn't attend his funeral. I hadn't wanted to see Charles because I blamed him for the accident; I think he went back to England shortly after that."

"The funeral was private. Only family."

"Was it? I suppose I wouldn't have been welcome at the funeral even if I had wanted to go."

"Probably not."

Sophie looked at him. "How did you know it was private?"

"I watched from a distance. Only family. The newspaper report said that Jean Paul was driving. Why did they say that?"

Sophie hesitated, not sure what to say.

"I said I want to know everything," Marcus said to her. "I know you did nothing wrong. Please tell me the truth. I need to know so that we can decide what to do."

Sophie wondered who 'we' were. "I fell out with Monique" she continued, reluctantly, "because she had told the police that Jean Paul was driving the car, and had caused the accident. She wanted to keep Charles out of prison."

Marcus looked at her with a strange look in his eyes. "Why did she lie about him? Did Charles ask her to lie?"

Sophie looked down at the floor, reluctant to answer. She wasn't sure what this was leading to. Marcus suddenly leaned forward, pulling her hair with his left hand, making her head jerk back, and holding his knife to her throat with his right hand.

"Why did she lie?" he repeated, speaking in a soft voice that sent shivers down her spine.

"She told me that he asked her to lie for him. He knew that he would have been arrested if the police thought he had been drunk and driving, so he persuaded her to lie for him."

"Then why did he kill her? Had she been threatening to tell the truth?"

Sophie looked at him, wide eyed.

"I don't know what they said to each other. I don't know what happened to her. I don't know if he had anything to do with it. I didn't see her or speak to her after we had the argument. It was a long time later when I heard she had disappeared."

Marcus let go of her hair, and put his knife back into his pocket. Once more he went to the window, looking down at the square outside. He stood, looking down at the square outside, saying nothing. Finally he turned to her.

"You were kind to me once, so I am being kind to you now. You have been helpful today, and I now need to do some things. I am going to leave. But I shall wait outside your door for a while. Maybe a minute, maybe an hour. You will sit here quietly; if you don't and I hear you shout then I shall come back in through the door and I shall kill you. So sit quietly and you will not be harmed. After a while I shall call the porter downstairs and ask him to come and untie you. Until then, do what I say. Goodbye Sophie."

With that he went out and closed the door.

FOURTEEN

It was Monday morning and Diana Freedman was in her kitchen emptying the dishwasher, a job she detested even if it was preferable to washing the dishes by hand, when the telephone rang. It was Amanda.

"Hello darling, are you back home? How was Paris?"

"Paris is always marvellous mummy, especially in spring. The weather is wonderful there, and it's so nice walking around in the evening, even if the air goes cool quite quickly at this time of year."

"And how was Marie? Have you made much progress with the family tree and our mysterious ancestor?"

"Marie is lovely, and she made us feel very welcome. I think poor Simon was a little bored with my obsession with ancient history, so he went out walking whilst I was going through dusty old papers, but I found some interesting facts as well, so I think it was a successful weekend. I've got a lot more of the tree complete. I'll bring it over this evening and you can take a look. Marie was also kind enough to invite her sister-in-law Beatrice over for lunch on Sunday; she has a huge knowledge of the French Revolution and the period around then. She also has a lot of books on the subject and she let me have a few, although some of them are difficult French – I'll need a good dictionary."

"Well I'm pleased that it's been worthwhile for you. I'm looking forward to hearing all about it when you come over, and you can show me what you've found."

"I'm not sure if you want to know this mummy, but during lunch Beatrice asked where we lived, and when I mentioned Hampstead she asked about the body of the girl on the Heath. I wasn't really going to say anything but then Marie mentioned during the conversation that you were unfortunate enough to have discovered the body."

"Marie was never very subtle, I'm afraid."

"Did you two not get on?"

"It's a long story dear. When we were much younger we fell out over a few things. Well mainly about one boy. I'm afraid I never really got on with Marie after that."

"So that's why you didn't want to go to Paris?"

"I thought you'd get on better without me being there. I also meant what I said when I thought it was a nice opportunity for you and Simon to spend some time together, even if he did decide to leave you to it for a while. Anyway, do go on with your story, dear."

"Beatrice then told us that, incredibly, she had a friend whose cousin had known the poor girl who was murdered. They were together at university apparently. She then asked if we would like to meet this cousin, and I agreed, although I was a little reluctant, so yesterday we had breakfast together. She had a story to tell about that girl Monique, and even more importantly has a theory as to why she was killed."

Diana listened to Amanda, making notes on a pad as she did so. After she had finished the call she took a walk around the garden, Buster trotting beside her as she went; she was deep in thought.

* * * * *

After seeing the girl's body in Le Havre, Cooper had called the chief to report on what he had seen. He had sought and, after some debate, received permission to go to Paris. He was convinced that Marcus Fox had gone there.

He had spent the Sunday night in the hotel in Le Havre and was now standing on a cold station platform waiting for the train to Paris. He had already spoken to a detective based there, Maurice Delacroix, who he once met on a training course; they had got on well, and last year when Delacroix and his wife had spent a weekend in London, he and Carol had spent a day with them. Cooper had already exchanged emails with him several times in the past few days to keep him informed.

"Hello Maurice, it's Sam."

"Hi Sam. Are you still in Le Havre?"

"I'm about to leave; I'm catching the train to Paris, because I'm convinced my man is now there."

"We've issued his photo to all the force here, Sam, so if he is here in Paris we'll find him. We've checked all the hotels; no-one called Fox or Renard has signed any register as yet, but we'll keep an eye on that as well. If you let me know what time your train arrives then I'll have someone meet you and bring you here."

Cooper gave him the details. Shortly afterwards his train pulled into the station. He boarded and settled down for the journey. He wanted to clear his head, to think what else he could do to apprehend Fox, but all the while he was wondering what he could say to Melanie. When his phone rang he answered it immediately without checking the caller's number, half hoping it might be her.

"Hello Inspector, I hope you don't mind me calling you on your mobile. It's Diana Freedman here."

For a moment he couldn't place the name; the lady in Hampstead. His mind was elsewhere.

"No problem at all, Mrs. Freedman. What can I do for you?"

"If you remember our conversation when you were last here, my daughter Amanda has been to Paris to visit my cousin, to research our family history. Whilst there she met some people, one of whom told her something I thought you ought to know."

Cooper hoped it wasn't going to be a long call. He had left more messages for Melanie that morning; he dreaded to think she was trying to call him just then.

"In Paris?"

"Yes, that's right. Whilst she was there with my cousin she encountered a lady who, when she discovered she came from Hampstead, asked her about the discovery of the body on the heath; it was I know well publicised in France, especially after it was known that the girl was from Paris. The dead girl was called Monique, I seem to remember. To cut a long story short, it seems this lady knew Monique from her university days and, more importantly, she told my daughter that she knows who the killer is."

Cooper suddenly paid more attention.

"She knows the killer? Who does she say it is?"

"She claims it was Monique's boyfriend. She and Monique were at university together in nineteen sixty eight. It seems that she and Monique were out together one evening, with their respective boyfriends. Whilst they were out there was a car accident, as a result of which this lady's boyfriend was killed outright. Monique was injured and needed hospital treatment, but this lady and Monique's boyfriend walked away with a few scratches. Monique's boyfriend had been driving the car and, according to the lady, he caused the accident by being drunk at the time. Apparently after the accident Monique's boyfriend was frightened of going to prison, so he lied to the police, telling them the other boy had been driving. He persuaded Monique to lie as well, to back him up. As the other boy had been killed he was a convenient scapegoat, of course. Apparently the lady telling this story to Amanda only discovered later what had been said to the police, so it seems he got away with it."

"Do you have the name of this boyfriend?"

"Yes, she did name him. She said he is called Charles Edwards. She also said he used to be a junior minister in the British Government. I think I met him at a dinner party once, but that must be twenty years ago."

"So what happened after the accident?"

"Shortly after that Charles returned to England and soon left her for another girl. Monique then followed him over here. Whilst here she wrote a letter to this lady, telling her she had confronted him and threatened to go to the police. The lady heard nothing more from her; she discovered some years after that she was missing."

"So the assumption is that she was killed to prevent her telling the truth."

221

"So this lady says. I must admit I thought it a bit far-fetched, but this lady was adamant. She says she knows he killed her. He had been violent before, apparently, and he was desperate not to lose a significant inheritance from his family. Quite how she knows that I'm not sure, but that is her story."

"Do you know this lady's name?"

"She is called Sophie Renard."

Cooper paused. "Did you say Renard?"

"Yes. It's odd isn't it; the man who called a while ago pretending to be a French policeman said his name was Renard. Quite a coincidence."

He wasn't sure it was such a coincidence.

"I'd like to talk to her, if possible, Mrs Freedman. Do you have a telephone number for her?"

"I don't have a number for Sophie Renard, I'm afraid, but I can give you my cousin Marie's number. She can find it for you."

"Thank you for letting me know, Mrs Freedman. This is very interesting."

* * * * *

Cooper rang Delacroix.

"Hi Maurice, Sam again. Do you remember the case of the car accident in Paris that Mike Robinson was chasing you about? If you remember, your file had three names in it, although you believed there was a fourth person, a girl, that had not been seen by the police at the time. Well, I think I have her name, which is Sophie Renard."

"Renard? That is the name Fox is using?"

"Yes, exactly. This Sophie Renard has told someone that she believes she knows who killed Monique Bertrand. She says it wasn't our Mr Fox, but one of the other passengers in the car, Charles Edwards. I think we should speak to this Sophie Renard as soon as I get to Paris. The second reason for the call is that I think it possible that Fox has gone there to see her. He's mixed up in all this somehow, I can't figure out how yet, but he is linked to this. If he is trying to see Sophie, then she may be in danger. Can you get someone to her as soon as possible, to make sure she is safe?"

"You think all of this was triggered by the discovery of Monique's body?"

"Yes, I do. If Fox was in love with Monique, and it seems she was very attractive, then it may be that the realisation she is dead has triggered this reaction. You have to remember that he told my constable he wanted to avenge his first love."

"I'll contact this Sophie Renard now. Do you have an address?"

"I don't, but I can give you the name and telephone number of someone who can give it to you."

* * * * *

Cooper then rang Robinson.

"We have a theory about who killed Monique and why, or so Mrs Freedman tells me."

"Mrs Freedman? The woman who found the body on the Heath?"

"Yes, it's a long story, but Mrs Freedman has some family in Paris, and apparently one of them has a friend who turns out to be the fourth passenger in the car that crashed, injuring Monique. Her name is Sophie Renard."

"Sophie Renard? Was that her name? The same surname as Marcus Fox has been using?"

"Exactly. She told Mrs Freedman's daughter that Charles Edwards killed Monique."

"Edwards killed her? Not Fox?"

"So she says. She claims that Edwards caused this car accident by driving whilst drunk and Monique lied to the French police to protect him. Afterwards, when he tried to leave her, she threatened to go to the police."

"Can we talk to her? She might be able to tell us a lot more than we already know." Robinson said.

"Yes, I know. I've asked the Paris police to talk to her. I'm on my way to Paris now. I'm worried there's a link between Sophie Renard and Fox; they both knew Monique at about the same time, and I don't think Fox's use of the name Renard is just a coincidence."

"Do you think she is the girl in the photo that we found in Fox's house? If you remember it was of Charles Edwards with Monique and another couple. If they were close friends as Mrs Freedman suggests, then it might well be the four that were in the car."

"Yes you may well be right, I hadn't thought of that." Cooper paused. "If so then Fox definitely knew her as well."

"Could it possibly be that Fox took the photograph not because of Monique but because of the other girl, and that other girl was Sophie Renard?"

"That's another possibility. We need to catch this guy. I've asked Paris to keep a watch on her apartment."

"So you're heading for Paris now?"

"Yes, nearly there. Are the UK border agency on the lookout for Fox, just in case he heads back to the UK?"

"Yes, sir. All airports and ports are looking out for him. I'm heading off out shortly. I want to follow up on the visit WPC Harper made, to track down this James Clarke. He may be able to shed some light on Fox, if we can track him down."

"Fine, keep me informed. I'll let you know what happens here."

＊ ＊ ＊ ＊ ＊

His train arrived in Paris; it was almost five on the Monday evening. It was going dark and it had been raining. Cooper was met by a uniformed officer and was driven to the police station; they drove in silence, as his very rusty French seemed incomprehensible to the officer, and his driver either could not or would not speak English, so he gave up and sat in silence as they whisked through the crowded Parisian streets. He sat looking in wonder at the brightly coloured lights of the various shops and restaurants reflecting on the street as they drove along at breakneck speed. His thoughts turned to Melanie; he wondered what she was doing right then.

When they pulled up outside the police station Cooper entered the building and was shown straight to Delacroix's office, where he shook his hand and was invited to sit.

"Did you manage to track down Sophie Renard?"

"Two officers have called at the apartment but it was in darkness. There was no answer when they rang the bell. They didn't attempt to enter by force as they had no warrant, nor any reason to suspect anything other than the lady was out. We'll keep an eye on the flat, but at this point there is little we can do except to continue the search for Fox."

"Have you circulated his photograph outside Paris, just in case he heads elsewhere?"

"Yes, it has been circulated all over France now."

Cooper pondered his next move. It occurred to him that Sophie's friend might know where she was. He decided to ring Mrs Freedman to get her number.

"Hello Mrs Freedman. We have been trying to contact the lady that your daughter spoke to in Paris, Sophie Renard. She appears to be away and doesn't answer her door. Do you happen to know if she was going away somewhere?"

"I don't know I'm afraid, but my daughter Amanda might do. She is here with me at the moment, telling me what she discovered about our family over there. Wait a moment and I'll pass you over to her."

Cooper waited.

"Hello Inspector, it's Amanda. I'm afraid I don't know about Sophie's plans, but when we left she was still with Beatrice. It might be that she has some idea."

"Would you be able to give me a telephone number for Beatrice?"

"Give me a moment. She gave me her card, and it's in my bag."

He could hear a scrabbling sound as she emptied the contents of her bag onto a table.

"Here it is, at the bottom of the bag, of course."

Cooper thanked her for the number, and rang off. He passed the number to Delacroix who was sitting opposite him.

Delacroix dialled the number and spoke to the lady; Cooper's French wasn't good enough to follow what was being said, so he waited patiently for him to finish. Delacroix finished the call and held up his hand to Cooper as he dialled another number; he spoke for a few minutes more before putting down the phone.

"I spoke to Beatrice" Delacroix said, "and she tells me that she too has been trying to contact Sophie Renard. She says that Sophie did not mention any plans to go away and she too is anxious as to her whereabouts. I have just spoken to my senior officer and we now have been given permission to enter Sophie Renard's apartment by force if necessary. Let's go there now and see what we find."

Much to his frustration Cooper was asked to wait on the ground floor of the apartment building where Sophie Renard lived whilst six French officers, who were of course armed as they always were, went up the stairs to the front door of Sophie's apartment with Delacroix.

Inspector Delacroix had tried the telephone number of Sophie once again before they had arrived, but there had been no reply. The French gendarmes did not wait to knock at the door, they simply aimed a stout block at the lock and broke the door open before running in, guns at the ready.

At a signal from Delacroix he ran up the stairs and entered the apartment. A woman was sitting in a chair, with her hands tied behind her back. One of the gendarmes was removing a tape from her mouth as he entered, Delacroix was untying her arms and ankles. As the inspector spoke gently to her, Cooper went to get a glass of water from her kitchen. She confirmed that she was Sophie Renard. She could only stand with assistance but she seemed remarkably well given her ordeal, and managed to thank Delacroix for arriving when he did; Delacroix translated for him as they spoke. After a few sips of water she recovered some strength. She insisted on speaking further to Delacroix and Cooper before going down with the ambulance staff who had arrived minutes after being called.

"His name is Marcus Clarke" she said, in perfect English. "I think he is very dangerous. I knew him when we were at university together, and he tried to get me to date him at the beginning of our time there. We spoke a few times but I didn't like him and didn't get to know him so well. I haven't seen him since then, but then yesterday I arrived home and he had somehow managed to get in here. He was waiting for me when I walked in."

"Did he say what he wanted, madam?" Delacroix asked.

"He talked a lot before asking me questions about the death of a girl who had been at university with us, Monique Bertrand. That seemed to be all he wanted, to know more about her. She was of course the girl that the British police found buried in Hampstead all these years after she disappeared. He kept asking me what happened in a car accident we were involved in; that was back in

228

nineteen sixty eight. Monique and I were both in the car with our boyfriends, Jean Paul and Charles. In the accident Jean Paul was killed, Monique was injured but Charles and I were not. Charles was driving but he blamed Jean Paul for the accident, saying that he had been the driver, which wasn't true. It seems all this took place at the hospital. Because I wasn't injured I didn't go to hospital; I just wanted to go home to my family, which is what I did. It was only a while later that I discovered what Charles had said to the police; I was very angry with him and with Monique. I thought of telling the truth to the police but by then he had already returned to the UK."

"What is Charles' last name?" Delacroix asked her.

"Edwards. His name is Charles Edwards. Marcus was very interested in all of this because I think he was in love with Monique and has wanted to know the truth about her death all these years. I suppose the fact that she was killed and left in such a pitiful way triggered these questions for him. He is very strange, inspector, and I think very dangerous. I think he could have killed me very easily if he had wanted to. He told me that himself, and he had a knife, but he also said he spared me because I was kind to him when we were at college together."

"Did he say what he intended to do next? Did he say he was going back to England?" Delacroix asked her.

"No, he didn't say what he was going to do exactly, he just said he needed to make some decisions. Actually, that isn't true; he said that we need to make some decisions."

"We?"

"That's what he said. I don't know who else he was referring to, but I think he talks to himself a lot. There is something else you need to know" Sophie added. "I did not tell this to Marcus, but just before she disappeared I received a letter from Monique. She had gone to London to follow Charles; she was obsessed by him. She told me in the letter that she was going to threaten Charles that she would tell the authorities if he didn't take her back, because he had dropped her for someone else. I wrote back to her to tell her that she was mad to do that, but I never had a reply."

"Do you still have the letter?" asked Delacroix.

She walked over to a desk and took an envelope from her drawer. She handed it to Delacroix who took out the letter and read it.

"It is not very long," he said, translating from French, "but she says that she is in England and hopes to see you soon and we can be friends again. She says she has tried to see Charles but he has found someone else, and she is desperate. She says she is going to confront him and try to persuade him, but if that doesn't work then she might return to Paris."

He looked at the date.

"It wasn't long after this that she disappeared. Did you tell anyone about the letter at the time?"

"No, I'm afraid I did not. I was angry with her and I almost threw the letter away. I'm not sure why I did not. I spent some time away from Paris; in fact it was years later when I saw another friend from those days who told me that Monique had never returned from England."

"You told the young couple from England that Charles killed her. What makes you say that?" asked Delacroix.

Sophie looked surprised for a moment and looked at Cooper before continuing.

"Monique told me one evening that Charles hoped to inherit a lot of money from his family, but he had to behave himself and join the family business to inherit. It was a condition of his grandfather's will that if any of the grandchildren had disgraced themselves or tarnished the family name, then they would be, how do you say, disinherited. I also know Charles and Monique had terrible fights. They were both very hot headed you see; he had a terrible temper. I remember being with them on one occasion when he threatened to push her off a bridge into the river. He was in a rage at the time, and I knew he was not joking, but Monique just continued to tease him and argue. I think she was lucky that he chose to walk away that night, but I did wonder if she had provoked him one time too many when she was in England. I believe that when she threatened to expose him for lying to the police he was afraid of losing his inheritance and he killed her. Perhaps we'll never know the truth."

Cooper spoke up. "May I ask you a question, madam?"

"Certainly," she replied.

"You said that Marcus was in love with Monique, but some years ago he changed his name to Fox, so we know him as Marcus Fox. Fox, as you will know, is the English for Renard. He has also been using the name Renard at times. For example we believe he impersonated a police detective at one point using that name, and he certainly used that name when he booked himself on a ferry from England to France. Do you think he might have been in love with you and not Monique?"

Sophie looked thoughtful and didn't answer for a moment.

"I don't think he was in love with me" she eventually replied. "He said that I treated him kindly, so he would be kind to me. If he had been in love, surely he would have said that instead?"

"So you think he was in love with Monique. Then why use your name?"

"I don't really know, inspector. I assumed he was in love with Monique because all the boys were fascinated by her. She was very beautiful and very sexy. I wonder.."

She hesitated.

"What do you wonder, madam?"

"He mentioned Jean Paul's funeral. It seems he went along to see. He told me it was a private family affair but he had seen it from a distance. I wonder why he did that?"

* * * * *

Isabelle Edwards awoke with a start, her body damp with perspiration, her nightdress wrapped tightly around her, pinning her arms down uncomfortably by her side. For a moment she struggled to move, but then managing to free one arm she threw the bedclothes aside so that she could sit up and pull her nightdress straight. She slid out of bed and felt her way to the bathroom without switching on the light so as to avoid waking Charles, there washing her face in cool water, the sensation pleasant on her skin.

She had been having the dream again; it was always the same dream.

Her dream was she supposed what others would call a nightmare, but she knew what it meant and she knew why she dreamt about it. There had been different versions of the dream; sometimes she had been swimming against a strong tide, shouting for help but no-one could hear her shout. Another time she would be running through an empty building, being chased by something she could hear but could not see. Each version of the dream however would have the same scene; she always saw a ghostly figure at some point. The ghost did not speak, but looked at her and slowly raised an arm, pointing a finger. The figure was vague and she never saw a face as the head and body was cover with a white cloth, wrapping around her - for Isabelle was certain it was a woman - and billowing around, moved by a breeze that was only present where the ghost was.

Isabelle sat on the edge of the bath, patting a towel against her face, gently drying her skin. She had first had the dream a few weeks after that terrible evening many years ago. For the first year she had seen her ghost almost every evening, but then the dream had become less frequent, although sometimes the dream had been more vivid than ever. Over the past few years the dream had become much rarer; she couldn't actually remember the last time she had it, but she was sure it was more than a year ago. She also knew why the dream had come back to her.

It had been the visit from the police.

She couldn't carry on like this.

The sound of Charles coughing brought Isabelle back to the present; she washed her hands, dried them with the towel and went back to bed.

FIFTEEN

It was the following morning and Cooper was back in Delacroix's office when his phone rang once again; this time it was the chief.

"I need to talk to you about that damned idiot, DC Mike Robinson. I've just about had enough of him. He really doesn't know how to behave. I don't think he'd know a good policeman if he fell over one."

He was taken aback; this tirade was obviously going to lead to some allegation about Robinson, he couldn't think what.

"What's he been up to, sir?"

"As he passed the front desk on his way out of the building yesterday afternoon, it's been reported to me that he said to the duty sergeant "I'm off to Camden to follow up on something that WPC Harper was asking about before she got bumped on the head. If anyone wants me you know where I am." The duty sergeant replied "Mind you don't get bumped on the head as well then." To which Robinson said "I don't have the boobs for that." Now, as you know, he has a reputation for making sexually offensive remarks to or about women, and the sergeant found this remark especially offensive towards an injured officer, and frankly so do I. He has already been dealt with under the complaints procedure;

as a result he is already on a written warning. This really isn't good enough, Sam. I'm calling to tell you that my intention is to speak to him shortly to give him a final warning, with the clear message that if he so much as breathes out of place then he'll be out on his ear. I've driven up to Camden this morning and put myself in your office. I'm just waiting for another senior officer to be available and I'll call him up."

"Would you call me back as soon as you've spoken to him, sir, to let me know how it went?"

"Yes of course."

Cooper put down the phone and looked at Delacroix.

He repeated what he had been told.

"It sounds as if Robinson has blown it, this time. He probably won't survive. I'm sorry, in a way. I think Robinson is competent; we don't have much in common, but that isn't the end of the world. Perhaps Robinson would be better off outside the force after all."

He began to think who might replace him if he did leave.

About thirty minutes later the chief rang back.

"I've just spoken to DC Robinson. I told him that over these past months I've received a number of comments about his attitude and behaviour towards female colleagues that I find unacceptable. I said it seems that he is incapable of talking to, or about, a female member of the force without making some form of derogatory comment, some of which are described as mean, some as offensive. I told him I am well aware that he has faced disciplinary action before, due to an allegation of improper behaviour to a female colleague that he did not deny. Because of that I would have expected him to behave with extreme care towards female officers, but it seems he can't. I said he must be aware that the police force is determined to stamp out prejudice of all kinds from the force, whether against colour, race, religion or sex. I then told him that the reason I'd asked him to see me was that he is alleged to have made a remark yesterday about an injured woman police officer, and that this remark had been witnessed by several officers. The remark would have been considered careless and unkind by any right thinking person, but coming from him was found by several of them to be especially offensive, knowing his attitude to women officers in general. To his credit he didn't deny making the comment, and said that he knew the remark I was referring to. He said he deeply regretted it as soon as he said it but he felt it was too late to say anything to retract the comment. He said that in hindsight he should have apologised immediately, but did not. He then apologised to me and said he is prepared to apologise to WPC Harper once she returns. I told him he is a valued member of this force but we cannot tolerate this kind of behaviour. I then told him he had a choice, Sam; either we suspend him from duty immediately pending a formal investigation, or he agrees to attend an anger management course, to see if it helps to control his behaviour. I told him that if he agreed to attend the course then we would put this conversation on record, and give him a final written warning about his behaviour. He said he would like to try the course, and I told him that he had one last chance. Between you and me, Sam, I think it's a waste of bloody time, and that he's got to go, but I have to follow procedure. You never know, he might surprise us, although I doubt it."

"He's basically a good police officer, sir; I think he has considerable intelligence and works hard, but he has without doubt this aspect of his personality that makes him difficult to like and, more importantly, work with. If colleagues won't work with him and don't trust or respect him then that puts him in a very difficult position."

"Well he has been warned once before and now he's on his final warning. We'll have to make a decision before very long as to whether he leaves the force altogether or is put back onto uniform duties."

"I'm not sure that putting him back in uniform will work, sir. If he has a problem with how he perceives, and is perceived by, his fellow officers, especially the female officers, then in my view he either works this through, or he leaves."

"Well that decision needs to be made in the next few days, certainly within the next two weeks. To keep DC Robinson waiting for a decision from us, if we have in reality decided to remove him from the force, is not fair on him nor on the rest of his colleagues. I've sent him home for now."

* * * * *

Cooper took some time to consider what he should say to Robinson before he called him.

"Hello Mike, I understand you've had a conversation with the Chief."

"Hello sir, yes I have. I suppose you know what happened. It was my own stupid fault. I opened my big mouth yet again; I knew as soon as I spoke that I'd end up in trouble, so I wasn't surprised really."

"This is very serious now, Mike, you do appreciate that?"

"Yes sir, I'm well aware of that. I did agree to go on this course to try to help myself."

"And do you think it will help?"

There was a pause as Robinson thought about the question.

"I'm not sure, sir. I would like to think so, and I realise the consequences if it doesn't help. I want to give it a go."

"I think you need to think about it, because it might be easier for everyone, especially you, if you decide before you go on this course whether you can change or not."

"Do I still have your support, sir?"

"I said to the chief this morning Mike that I think you are a good, intelligent and hard working officer. The fact is however that if your behaviour doesn't change then I can't support you any longer. We've had a conversation once before about all this, and I told you then that your attitude towards female officers was unacceptable. My belief is that you cannot stay in the force with things as they are, however good you are as a detective. I want you to think carefully about this over the next forty eight hours. You then need to tell me if you think you'll be able to change. If you will, then you'll have my full support as long as you do change. If you decide you can't change, then we need to discuss you leaving the force."

"I understand, sir."

"Good. Now in the meantime, let's talk about this case. What progress?"

"I've been digging into Marcus Fox's background. He has an elder brother, a Richard Clarke who lives in

Lancashire. It seems that it's some kind of huge manor house."

"Didn't Charles Edwards mention the fact that Fox seemed to be well connected?"

"Yes, he did."

"Let's see what we can find out on Richard Clarke, then. Let's see what we're dealing with here."

"Yes, sir. When I went out yesterday afternoon, and got myself into trouble as I did so, I was going to follow up on the enquiry that Catherine Harper had been making when she came across Marcus Fox. You'll remember she'd been to that address in Tina Marsh's address book looking for a certain James Clarke. I briefly spoke to Catherine yesterday. When she went there she spoke to a young Polish lady who now lives at the address. She didn't know James Clarke but had suggested Catherine talk to the letting agent. Catherine told me she had been there, and asked them for the name of the owner, who isn't James Clarke. They confirmed they'd sold the property to the current owner, who bought it as a rental investment some years ago. Catherine had asked them to dig out the vendor's name from their archives, so yesterday I went to talk to the agent. They had found the name and confirmed to me that a James Clarke had sold the apartment to the current owner. They've given me the address they had in the archive. It was sold in May nineteen seventy, which was a month or so before Tina Marsh disappeared. The address given for correspondence was the same address of Richard Clarke, Marcus Fox's brother, so it's clearly the same family. However I don't think it'll help us at all. I've just discovered that James Clarke died in nineteen seventy four. The death certificate states that he died of pneumonia; he was also convicted a couple of years earlier of possessing heroin, so my guess is that he was a

239

drug addict; he was only thirty one when he died. I also did a search of the land registry. It seems that the Clarke family owned all the apartments in that building in Camden at one time; the land registry shows that James Clarke and Marcus Fox's grandfather bought the building in nineteen thirty two. When he died, half went to Clarke's father, and half to Fox's father. When Clarke's father died in the late nineteen sixties he inherited it. Fox inherited his apartment a few years after that."

"Catherine was looking into Tina's disappearance," Cooper said, "because Tina had the name of James Clarke in her diary. Maybe they were friends, or perhaps he was selling her drugs. So we have another possible connection between Tina Marsh and Marcus Fox. I suppose it's possible she went there to see Clarke from time to time and met Fox sometime while she was there."

"If she did, then it might be her remains that Fred has found in the apartment."

"Then we should do a DNA test to see if we can establish a link."

"I'll get onto that" Robinson said. "My next item is the psychiatrist who was looking after Fox at one point, Dr Jeremy Portman. I have managed to track him down. He has long since retired, in fact I believe he's about eighty, but he still has a small number of clients that he looks after, and maintains rooms in Harley Street where he meets them. I have spoken to his secretary this morning, and she called me a short while ago to say that I have an appointment to go see him tomorrow morning. Interestingly, I could have sworn I heard a sharp intake of breath from his secretary when I mentioned Fox's name."

"Did you? Well that's interesting. Maybe they have some idea of what Fox is up to right now. Well done, that's good progress. It'll be interesting to see what he knows, or at least what he will tell us."

"Another development sir. That blood sample from Fox's boat. We've found a match."

"Have you? Whose blood was it?"

"A girl named Monica Gascoigne. She was reported missing from Portsmouth eighteen months ago."

"Monica? Bloody hell, the name on the paper?"

"Yes, sir, my thought exactly."

"And from Portsmouth, where Fox kept his boat?"

"Yes, sir."

"So, we have another potential victim of Fox. If he killed her on his boat, of course, her body could be anywhere, including in the English Channel."

"It looks that way, sir. There's been one other development," Robinson said.

"What's that?"

"Well, the name Marcus Fox has been on the radio and TV news, and suddenly we've been contacted by a solicitor representing Isabelle Edwards. She wants to make a statement to us."

"Charles Edwards' wife?"

"Yes, that's the one."

"What did you tell him?"

"I just said that I would need to speak to you and I'd get back to him."

"Well, I'm definitely going to be in the station the day after tomorrow, so give him a call and get her in as soon as possible then. I can't wait to hear what she has to say. I wonder if her husband knows about this."

"No idea, sir."

"Anything else?"

"No, sir, that's all for the moment."

"I'll probably be leaving France soon. I think Fox will have left Paris now, and may well be on his way back to the UK. As a precaution, will you speak to the chief about arranging a watch outside Edwards' house please?"

"I'm not sure the chief will be happy to hear my voice, sir, but I'll call him now."

"Let me know if you have any problems. I don't think you will."

"Will do, sir."

* * * * *

Cooper decided he would return to the UK in the morning as the Eurostar train was fully booked. Delacroix offered to buy him dinner at a small restaurant which was close by his hotel for the night. He accepted gratefully. When they arrived Delacroix was greeted by the proprietor as an old friend, with an embrace and kisses on both cheeks; the proprietor was a little more formal with Cooper, who was pleased to avoid the kisses. They sat at a small table in one corner close to the window. The restaurant was clearly popular with locals, as the proprietor seemed to know everyone who came in, and greeted them all as long lost friends. As far as Cooper could tell it was full of locals; he seemed to be the only foreigner in the place. He thought that was a good sign;

he was right; the food was excellent, and the wine Delacroix ordered was particularly fine if more oaked than Cooper was used to.

"What will you do next, Sam?" Delacroix asked him, as they sipped coffee.

"Well, try to make it up to my new girlfriend to start. I was meant to see her on Saturday evening, and I forgot to let her know that I'd gone down to the south coast to find this character, and I then jumped on a ferry to follow him over to Le Havre. As always, I got so wrapped up in the investigation that the rest of the world didn't exist, for a while. That's how life is for me."

"Are you serious about each other?"

"I'm not sure yet, but I guess it might have become serious. Whether it will now is anyone's guess. I take her seriously, that's for sure."

As Cooper climbed into bed it was almost midnight; he was exhausted but when he heard a beep from his phone he climbed out of bed to check it. There was a short message from Melanie.

"Thanks for the flowers."

He typed "Sorry my love, I ought to have sent flowers, but I didn't. I'm caught up in an enquiry, in France as I said in my message. Very intense here, but home tomorrow. Speak soon I hope."

As soon as he pressed send he lay down and was asleep within seconds.

Early the next morning Cooper headed for the train. As he sat on board waiting for the train to leave

Paris he sent a message to Melanie to confirm he was on his way back to the UK.

"I'll call tomorrow when I can. Life full of surprises at the moment, so I won't promise anything this time, but I'll do my best. PS did you find out who sent those flowers?"

Within a minute a reply came.

"No idea who sent flowers. I thought you had, but if not then I really don't know."

* * * * *

At ten o'clock in the morning precisely, Robinson walked up to the Harley Street surgery of Doctor Jeremy Portman. To one side of the black wooden door was a steel panel with a number of buttons; Robinson inspected the names against each button and pressed the relevant one. After he said his name a buzzer sounded and he pushed the door to go in.

The door led into a large square entrance hall, carpeted in pale green and with wooden panelling on the walls. Robinson felt as if he had entered some kind of stately home. He took the staircase and walked up one flight of stairs, where there was a door off to the right with the doctor's name above it. Through the door he entered a short corridor, at the end of which were a couple of easy chairs, a coffee table and two doors, one of which was open; he could hear the sounds of someone making photocopies as he approached the open door and looked in.

The room was much smaller than the grand entrance hall, containing a small desk and a number of filing cabinets, as well as the photocopier. A late middle aged woman was standing by it as he entered; she looked at him and asked him to take a seat outside and wait.

"I'm DC Robinson" Robinson began.

"Yes, I know" she said, somewhat abruptly but giving no hint of approval or disapproval. "Please take a seat in the waiting room."

Robinson retreated to the corridor which served as a waiting room and sat in one of the easy chairs. After a few minutes the second door opened, and a well dressed, elderly but elegant man walked out. He spoke briefly to his secretary before he greeted Robinson with a pleasant smile, shaking his hand and waving him into his consulting room.

This was a much more comfortable room, with a large walnut desk and a number of paintings of an antique appearance on the wall. Whether the paintings were valuable originals or modern copies Robinson had no idea. As a matter of courtesy Robinson showed his ID card to the doctor to confirm his identity.

"Thank you. Please sit down. I understand from my secretary that you wish to speak to me about one of my patients, Marcus Fox?"

"Yes that's right."

"May I ask what this enquiry is about before I answer your questions?"

"We have two issues that we are making enquiries about. One is an assault on a female police officer, where we believe that Marcus Fox, or Marcus Clarke as he used to call himself, can help us with our enquiries. The second issue concerns an enquiry into the disappearance of a number of women over a number of years. Again we would like to question him on those matters, as we believe he can help us with our enquiries there."

"So you do not at this moment know where he is?"

"He is not in custody. We have some idea as to his whereabouts, but as yet we have not been able to speak to him."

"And how can I help, exactly?"

"According to our records Marcus Fox was a patient of yours. We are of course well aware of his conviction as a child. We are trying to understand what his state of health was like then, how he is now, and whether he has expressed any tendency towards violence at all since his conviction. In short, doctor, we are trying to piece together a picture of this man, and anything you may be able to tell us about him."

"I trust that his name hasn't come to your attention due to his history as a child? That was a long time ago and is hardly relevant today."

"I can assure you, doctor, his name came to our attention as Marcus Fox. It was only after making quite a lot of enquiries that we discovered that he used to be called Clarke, and after that we found his court record. Our intention is to seek to know him better, so we can understand what might be motivating him."

"I see."

Whilst Robinson had been speaking the doctor had pulled a small folder from his desk and was looking through it.

"I see" he said again, seeming almost absent minded. Robinson waited for him to gather his thoughts.

"He was, and still is, a patient of mine" the doctor continued. "I must tell you now that I have spoken to his elder brother, who has charge of his affairs by a court order, as Marcus has not been considered fit to manage his own affairs since childhood. His elder brother has given me express permission to be open with you and to co-operate in any way that I may. Marcus has been causing concern to his brother and to me for some time now. He has a diminished mental capability, with psychopathic tendencies, in that he hears voices and sometimes acts as if someone is instructing him. Neither his brother nor I have seen Marcus for almost a year; he has ignored all attempts at contact, so we are concerned to hear that he is subject to your enquiries and want to help in any way possible. Whilst Marcus has a limited mental capacity, by which I mean he has very little empathy with, and understanding of, other human beings, he is nonetheless capable of being extremely calculating."

"Has he shown violence to any person, especially to any female?"

"Not since his conviction that I am aware of. At one time I believe he was a member of an animal rights group so he has been against violence, at least to animals. A number of years ago he did tell me of some fantasies of violence against women he had, but he was a young teenager then, no more than thirteen or fourteen, and he told me at the time he didn't actually carry out any of these fantasies. He hasn't mentioned them since. He seemed to be more stable in his later teens, but then he had a relapse of hearing voices. That was about the time he was convicted in court, and he was using drugs. I believed that the drugs were causing some kind of hallucinations in him, which caused him to fantasise and his psychosis deteriorated. He was in and out of clinics during a period of about twenty years, but that was to treat him for his schizophrenia. In the past few years since then he has seemed stable; he is certainly eccentric in his ways, but he is on regular medication which helps him enormously. Whether he is still taking the drugs I'm afraid I don't know; as I said I haven't seen him for about a year."

"Is there anything else about his condition we should be aware of?"

"Nothing that I think will be relevant."

"And you have no idea of his whereabouts right now?"

"I have no idea. I was hoping that his brother would have heard from him, but as I said he has seen and heard nothing for over a year."

"Can you tell me please what dates he was in a clinic?"

The doctor consulted his records.

"He went into his first clinic in March nineteen sixty six, after his conviction for drug use. He was there for almost exactly a year. After that he was re-admitted in July nineteen seventy, at his own request. Again he was in the same clinic for about a year. He was also in the clinic from September nineteen seventy seven, for twelve months until September seventy eight, and finally from May nineteen eighty to December of that year."

Robinson thanked the doctor and left. He consulted his notebook as he sat on the underground train back to Camden. Tina Marsh had disappeared in June nineteen seventy, a month before Fox was admitted to the clinic. Paulette Dijon disappeared in March or April of nineteen eighty, a month or so before his final stay. What had triggered the need to go to a clinic? Was he seeking help after committing murder? If so, what had triggered the stay in the clinic in March nineteen seventy seven? Was there another body somewhere?

* * * * *

Cooper arrived home in the late afternoon. He decided against going to the station; he needed a shower, to buy some food for himself and to unpack his bag. He called Melanie but she was reluctant to talk to him.

"I need a few days to think, Sam" she said. Give me a call later in the week."

"I know I upset you, and I'm sorry. I'd really like to see you soon."

"I need a few days. Call me in a few days."

She hung up.

Cooper put down the phone and looked out of the window. He knew he had ruined his chances of a relationship with her. He sighed and sat for a while, his head in his hands. It was best to leave her be for a while; his instinct was to rush over to see her, but that might be the last straw.

"Be patient, Sam, be patient" he said to himself.

He needed to think about something else. He called Mike Robinson to get an update on his visit to see Fox's doctor.

"So you think something triggered each visit to a clinic, and that something could have been a murder?"

"I don't know, but it seems a strong set of co-incidences."

"Why don't you check any girls who went missing in nineteen seventy seven, to see what turns up?"

"I will do, but before I do there is one other thing, sir. I've been thinking about my conversation with the chief, and what you said to me the other day about reforming my character. The thing is that I'm proud to be a police officer, and I enjoy my job, but I'm not sure I will ever be politically correct enough for the force. I know I give some of the women a hard time and they don't always deserve it, but sometimes I like to be the joker and I don't think the force can cope with that. I guess what I'm trying to tell you, sir, is that I don't think I'll survive much longer in the force whether I do this course or not, so I may as well quit whilst I can leave with dignity, rather than be slung out at some point in the future."

"You're sure about this? It's a big decision, Mike."

"Yes, sir, I know. I've given it a lot of thought, but I've made my mind up. I need to leave."

"I see. I'm sorry it's come to this, Mike. I hope you're making the right decision; I understand what you're saying and I won't try to change your mind. I'll give the chief a call and let him know what you're planning. Do you have any idea what you'll do afterwards?"

"I've had a chat with a few friends, and one of them got me an interview yesterday with a guy who runs a private security firm. He rang me this morning offering me a job running one of his operations, and I've accepted."

SIXTEEN

At the agreed time the next morning Cooper and Robinson walked down to the interview room, where Isabelle Edwards was waiting with her solicitor. They took a seat on the opposite side of the small table.

"I am Nicholas Saunders" the solicitor began, "and I believe you are aware that my client has come here voluntarily as she wishes to make a statement."

He reached into a battered brown leather briefcase at the side of his chair, and pulled out a file with a piece of paper clipped into it.

"She has made this written statement which I suggest you read, after which Mrs Edwards has agreed to answer any questions you may have."

Cooper took the paper and read through the statement carefully before handing it to Robinson.

"Before we start to go through this statement, is there anything else which you wish to add that you think we should know?"

Isabelle looked nervously at her solicitor, but he just smiled in encouragement.

"Not at this time, no I haven't anything to add. I think everything is in there."

"Would you like to tell me in your own words what happened?"

"Yes, I want to explain everything about that evening. It has been on my mind for 40 years, inspector. You have to remember that it was an accident. We behaved very foolishly, probably we were a little drunk, and we were young and naive. Charles had been cooking bacon, because he always liked to eat something after an evening drinking in the pub with his friends; I hadn't gone with him that evening because my cousin's small son had been staying with us. You know his name, inspector. It was Angus Forsyth."

"Ah, the artist."

Isabelle looked at him blankly.

"He was an artist?"

Cooper turned to Robinson.

"Do we have an example of his art?"

Robinson opened a folder and took out the drawing that had been sent to Diana Freedman, handing it to him; he looked at it briefly before showing it to Isabelle.

"I'm not sure it's a good likeness of your husband. I assume it is him holding the spade? By the way, did Angus know Monique? What did he call her? Monica?"

Isabelle started. Tears formed in Isabelle's eyes, her cheeks and neck turned pink and her hands shook visibly.

"He must have seen something, or heard something that night. I thought he was asleep."

"This was pushed through the door of the lady unfortunate enough to have found Monique's body. She was fairly shocked too. We think Angus drew this shortly before he hung himself."

The solicitor intervened.

"Was there a suicide note, inspector?"

"No, there was not."

"Then you cannot possibly know what motivated a disabled young man to take his own life. Nor do you know when this drawing was made, so do not try to associate his death with an incident that occurred 40 years ago, and which my client has come here to explain to you of her own volition."

"Why don't you continue, Mrs Edwards?" Cooper suggested.

"We had been standing in the kitchen to the little flat we then lived in; I had been cutting some bread for Charles when the doorbell rang. Before Charles could get to the door the bell rang again. Someone was clearly impatient or angry; somehow I knew it was Monique. I then heard her voice. Monique started shouting loudly, so I ran from the kitchen to be with Charles. I had met Monique only once before, which was before Charles and I had started to be serious about one another, when he and Monique had still been lovers. Charles had never been serious about Monique, but Monique had been desperately in love with him; I had always known that Monique would not go away quietly, whatever Charles had said at the time. As I arrived in the hallway, I saw that Charles had hold of Monique's arm and was trying to push her back out of the door. I was oblivious to the fact that I was still holding the knife I had been using to cut the bread. Before I knew what was happening Monique had taken my hand and was trying to pull the knife from me. Charles grabbed her arm, then we both pushed at Monique."

Isabelle stopped speaking, her eyes closed, tears running down her cheeks.

"So what happened then, Mrs Edwards?"

Isabelle opened her eyes and looked straight at Cooper. If she was looking for pity, she found none. She cast her eyes down to the floor.

"Monique screamed out as she fell backwards, tumbling down the stairs that led up to our front door. Her head hit several of the stairs. Her body rolled down and down. When it stopped her legs were at an odd angle. Suddenly everything went very still and quiet. I couldn't move. It was horrible, looking at Monique lying there, completely still."

"Was the knife still in her?"

Isabelle paused.

"No. No, Charles was holding it. He was dumbstruck with horror. He had just been trying to get it off her, and in the struggle he had stabbed her. At first I didn't understand what was going on, but then I looked at the blade. It was covered in blood."

"What happened then?"

"Charles ran down the steps. He turned to me and said he thought she was dead. I recovered my senses and ran down to see. Charles had started to lift her and rolled her onto her back. Monique's eyes were open, her tongue out of her mouth as if she had been trying to lick her lips. I couldn't take my eyes off her face."

As she said this she closed her eyes as if not wanting to see her face even now.

"I asked Charles what we should do, whether we should call the police. He said absolutely not. How would we explain this? Did I think they would believe that she was trying to grab the knife? How do we tell them she was stabbed? He asked me to go and get a blanket, quickly. I wasn't sure even then what he planned.

254

Somewhere in my mind I thought he wanted to keep her warm, as if she was still alive. But I went for the blanket. Charles then used it to wrap around the body. He then said we were to put her in the car. I obeyed, I was too distraught to argue with him, too numb to be able to think what else we could do. I just wanted the problem to go away. Charles ran out and I waited for what seemed an age before I heard the car engine. He had then run back to the door. He told me to help him to carry her. The body seemed incredibly heavy. Charles had left the back door of the car open, and we somehow managed to lay the body across the back seat. He ran back into the flat, telling me to wait in the car. I was terrified, still half expecting Monique to sit up and start shouting again. Charles ran back and opened the boot, putting something in, then closed it and jumped into the driving seat. I asked him where we were going to take her. He said up to the heath. I thought then that Charles was just going to leave her on there, as if she had been robbed or something. He parked the car in a remote spot near the heath. By now it was well past midnight and, apart from the occasional car driving past, the area was deserted. As quickly as we could, we opened the rear door to the car and pulled the body out. I slipped as I tried to help and the body fell to the floor with a thud. Charles picked it up and carried it alone into the bushes beyond the edge of the road. He shouted to me to bring the shovel. I didn't understand for a moment, then realised that he had brought the shovel in order to bury her. That was what he had put into the boot. I asked him why we couldn't just leave her there, but he said she might have told someone she was going to see us. We couldn't take the risk. We were in too deep now to turn back, and Charles was in a rage; he wasn't going to listen to reason. He said it would be far better if she simply disappeared. If we did this right then she would never be found."

She became silent.

"So you buried her on the heath, and hoped she would never be found again," Cooper said, little sympathy in his voice.

Isabelle nodded.

"But you came out of the kitchen with the knife. Isn't the truth that you wanted her dead, wanted her out of the way?"

His voice was raised; he looked directly into Isabelle's eyes.

"No," she replied.

She remained calm, but he noticed she averted her eyes; she wouldn't look at him.

"No, that isn't true" she continued. "I just ran to make sure Charles wasn't going to.."

Her voice trailed away.

"He wasn't going to do what? Wasn't going to kill her?"

"No, that he wasn't going to get hurt. She was a wicked girl, inspector."

"But your husband told us that you had appeared with a knife, and she had run away, frightened of you."

"She didn't run away. That isn't true. I wish it were."

Isabelle sat with her head bowed. Robinson offered her a glass of water. She accepted it gratefully.

"When did your husband first meet Monique Bertrand?" Cooper asked her, after she had taken a drink and looked slightly more composed.

"He met her while they were both at university in Nanterre in Paris. My husband had gone there to improve his French as much as anything; he was sent by his father to do a course on business. It was during the time of the Paris riots, in the late nineteen sixties. He had another girlfriend at first, but then Monique wanted him. What she wanted, she usually got, particularly with men. She was very..."

Isabelle's voice faltered and she took another sip of water.

"Please take your time" Robinson told her, in a gentle voice.

She looked at him.

"Thank you. She was very beautiful. I think every boy in the university was chasing her. But for whatever reason she chose Charles. She was very possessive though."

"In what way?" Cooper demanded.

"She would hardly let him out of her sight. She insisted they do everything together, and after a while Charles became tired of her. He tried to break with her, but she became hysterical and threatened to kill herself. I think Charles was quite afraid of her."

"How did the car accident happen, Mrs Edwards?"

"I'm not sure I can add anything you don't already know."

"Nonetheless, I'm interested to hear what you were told."

"Very well. From what I know, Charles was a passenger in a friend's car. He made an error on a bend in the road, resulting in the accident. The friend driving was killed, and Monique was badly hurt. She lost two fingers on her hand."

She paused.

"Was Charles injured at all?"

"Not badly, no. He had cuts and bruises, that's all. He left the university after that, and came back to the UK, which is when I met him."

"You were living in the UK?"

"No, I am a second cousin to him; I came over to do a course in English and I stayed with his parents for a little while, which is when we met. Things just developed from there really."

"And did you know Monique at this time?"

"Not when I arrived. I had been here for about a month when she arrived. She joined my course. I had no idea who she was until Charles saw her, and told me everything that had happened. She had come onto the course to follow him across to England. She was determined to get him back again. At that point she started to threaten to tell the police about him."

"Tell what to the police?"

Isabelle paused once again to take a sip of water. "Charles' friend was driving at the time of the accident. Monique, because of her jealousy and out of spite, was threatening to tell the police that Charles had been driving. Charles was afraid of being held by the police if they thought he had been driving the car. Monique knew that of course, and kept threatening to tell them he was driving whilst drunk and had caused the accident. Charles told me Monique was drunk and she would have had no idea who was driving."

"So what did Charles do?"

"He tried to reason with her, but she was not a person to be reasoned with. She became very threatening, and I was very scared. Charles was desperate that his family didn't find out; his mother had been distraught enough without all that. And then she appeared at our flat door. The events after that are as I have written down."

"So the fact that Monique was stabbed, and died, was very convenient for your husband. It solved his problem of the story coming out. It might interest you to know, Mrs Edwards, that I have a witness who says that your husband was indeed driving that night. So in fact Monique was telling the truth. He lied to the police."

Isabelle stared at him; she seemed bewildered. Her solicitor put a hand on her arm.

"My client was not there that evening, inspector. There is little to be gained by trying to continue a conversation about who may or may not be telling the truth of an event forty years ago."

"So you say your husband killed Monique, by accident. But isn't the truth that he killed her because she threatened to tell the truth about the accident in France, when he killed someone but claimed the dead boy was driving? Isn't the truth that he killed her because he stood to lose his inheritance if he brought disgrace to the family name under the terms of his grandfather's will?"

She gasped.

"No, no that isn't true. It was an accident."

She sobbed continuously, her head bowed again, her strained breathing filling the room.

Cooper picked up the statement once more.

"This is your statement, Mrs Edwards. Does your husband know that you are here?"

"Yes, he knows."

"But he chose not to come with you. Why not?"

"Because he didn't think it was necessary."

"Not necessary to tell the truth?"

At this point the solicitor put a hand onto Isabelle's arm once again.

"My client has made a full statement, inspector, and answered your questions as best as she can. Any questions as to the thoughts and motives of her husband should be addressed to him, not to her."

"Very well," Cooper said, "then we will put those questions to Mr Edwards. We will wish to see him as soon as possible."

"I shall contact him and let you know."

Cooper then turned to Mrs. Edwards.

"Thank you for your co-operation, Mrs Edwards. If we have further questions..."

"Please address those to me, inspector. I wish to accompany my client if you have further questions for her."

"Then we'll be in touch."

* * * * *

Cooper made himself a light meal that evening; he was pleased to be home and to be able to relax after travelling around for the past week. He put on some Mozart and read for a while until his mobile phone rang. It was an unknown number.

"Is that Sam?" asked an unfamiliar female voice.

He had no idea who it was.

"Yes, this is Sam Cooper. Can I help you?"

"This is Margaret Brooks here, Melanie's mother."

"Hello Mrs Brooks. What can I do for you?"

"I was wondering if Melanie was there with you."

"No, I haven't seen her at all today, or for a few days in fact. Why do you ask?"

"Well I have her little girl here, and she was supposed to come and collect her after her shift finished at seven, but she hasn't appeared. It's very unlike her; she wouldn't leave her little girl here without making sure I had everything for her. I'm not sure where she can have got to. I've called her mobile and she doesn't answer, and the hospital says she left on time. I'm really worried about her."

"Where are you, Mrs. Brooks?"

She gave him her address.

"Look I'll see what I can do to find her. Can I call you back on this number?"

"Yes, please do."

"And if you see Melanie or hear from her, please let me know right away."

Cooper first rang the police station, asking them to check with local hospitals if anyone of Melanie's description had been taken in after an accident. He then rang the Great Ormond Street hospital to speak to staff to see if she was still on her shift. After a few minutes he managed to speak to a senior nurse who confirmed that Catherine had left the hospital at seven.

He looked at the clock. It was ten o'clock. He picked up his coat and car keys, and went out to drive to Melanie's apartment. He had been out for five minutes when his mobile phone rang again.

"You can call off the cavalry."

261

It was Melanie.

"Oh, it's you. Thank goodness, you had me worried for a while."

"Yes, I'm really sorry. I tried to call Mum to tell her I'd been invited out and would be late, but she was on the phone. In fact I must have tried three times in half an hour but she was constantly on the phone; it seems she was chatting to her sister. In the end I sent her a text message because the battery on my phone was finished, but Mum kept calling me from her home phone and didn't think to check her mobile phone, so she never saw the message. I'm sorry she panicked and called you. I'd forgotten I'd given her your number once."

"Well, at least you're safe. That's all that matters."

"Sam I owe you an explanation. I need to tell you where I was. I was having dinner with my ex boyfriend. He called me a couple of days ago to ask if I would see him again, and I agreed. To cut a long story short he told me he wants to get back together with me again. We've discussed our relationship a lot over the past couple of days, and I want to tell you that I've agreed to go back to him."

She hesitated.

"In fact he has asked me to marry him and I have accepted."

Cooper was stunned into silence for a moment. There wasn't much to say; he hadn't treated her well and he knew when he was beaten. He felt as if he had let himself down, too. Not for the first time.

"So I guess he sent the flowers?"

"Yes, it was. He didn't attach a card, so I thought they were from you. I'm sorry for that."

"No need to apologise. I should have sent some, after what I did to you. Well Melanie, thanks for being honest with me. You're a lovely girl, and he's a very lucky guy. I'm very envious. If you change your mind then you know where I am, but if not then good luck to you."

"Thank you Sam. I hope you get what you want out of life, I really do. I'm sorry it ended so quickly, but I wanted to tell you straight away and not make a fool out of you. You don't deserve that. I ought to go now. Good bye Sam."

With that, Melanie rang off. He turned the car around with a heavy heart and headed back home.

SEVENTEEN

As soon as Cooper walked in to the police station the duty sergeant spoke to him.

"There's someone here you'll be pleased to see, sir" he said.

He looked through the glass partition at the desks beyond him; WPC Catherine Harper was sitting in a chair, looking at him with a smile on her face. He walked through into the office.

"Good to see you back" he said to her.

"Thank you, sir. I'm doing some work for the sergeant here before going down to the records office to help with the day's queries and filing needs. It isn't a job I relish doing to be honest, but I know I won't be allowed back out on duty until I'm completely fit."

"How are you feeling?" he asked.

"I'm feeling a lot better. I'd rather be here than stuck at home."

"We'll look after her sir, don't worry" the sergeant said to him.

He smiled; he believed that he would.

He had not been at his desk long when an officer put his head around the door and told him that the chief was in the building. After two minutes there was a brief knock at his door and the door opened. The chief walked in and sat in his visitor chair. He sat back and then leant forward quickly.

"Damn me, Sam. This chair's not very bloody comfortable. Why don't you get a new one?"

Cooper murmured a response; he didn't want to admit that it was part of his image he enjoyed. Perhaps he really would have to replace it soon.

"We need to talk to Catherine Harper and Robinson," the chief told him.

He called the front desk. After a couple of minutes, during which time he briefed the chief on the case, Robinson appeared in the doorway and Cooper waved him to enter. He saw Catherine Harper standing behind him and told her to come in as well. They both stood, Catherine smiling but Robinson saying nothing, looking at the wall.

"Welcome back Catherine" the chief said. "It's nice to see you back. I need to inform you that Mike Robinson has told us he's decided to resign from the force with immediate effect, for personal reasons that I can't go into. Because of that, and because we've been impressed with the way you've handled yourself recently, we want to offer you the opportunity to move into the plain clothes branch as a detective constable. You've expressed an interest in that during your past reviews, I know. If you accept this role, as I hope you will, then we have asked DC Robinson to hand over his papers and update you on the current investigation this morning, which he has agreed to do. Just to be absolutely clear, DC Robinson has not been asked to leave, and he leaves the force with honour and with our best wishes for the future. I need to know if you're prepared to accept this role."

Catherine looked stunned, her cheeks flushing, glancing at Robinson and then at Cooper, who nodded at her in encouragement.

"I am very pleased and honoured to accept this opportunity, sir. Thank you for your faith in me."

"That's excellent. You will of course get a formal letter and all that as soon as possible, and I shall be putting out a note to inform the officers here today, but you are as of now acting DC Harper. Congratulations. I'll leave you all now as I have another bloody budget meeting to go to. Good luck."

He shook hands with each one of them and went out.

"Well done Catherine. Now let's get straight down to business" Cooper began, as soon as the chief had gone. "I know that the two of you have not always seen eye to eye, but we have just a few hours to be briefed on the current state of this investigation. Mike needs to brief me as well, so he might as well brief us together. Mike, you will then be free to clear your desk and go as Catherine and I will then need to put our heads together to determine the next move, so you don't need to stay after the briefing."

"That's fine by me, sir. For the record, I have nothing against WPC, sorry, DC Harper, and I wish her the best in her new role. Obviously I am sorry to go, but I think it's for the best in the end."

"Thanks" Catherine responded.

By midday Robinson and Cooper left his office and went to Robinson's desk. No-one took any particular notice as he put a few effects into his battered sports bag as they stood talking

"I'm sorry it turned out like this, Mike," he said, "but perhaps it will be the best for you. I wish you all the best, and if you want a personal reference from me then do let me know. Keep in touch."

They shook hands, and Robinson walked out of the building, a couple of officers looking on, wondering what was happening.

* * * * *

"Hello mum, how are you?"

"Hello Sam, I'm feeling better today. I haven't heard from you for a while."

"I had to go to France at short notice, so I've been away for the last few days."

"France? What were you doing in France?"

"It was connected to this case I'm working on. One of the suspects went across to Le Havre and so I went over to help the French police. He then went to Paris so I ended up there."

"Well, at least Paris must be nice. Did you get chance to see much?"

"I didn't get much time for sightseeing, mum. I did manage to have a very nice meal in a restaurant on my last evening there."

"That's nice. And how is your new girlfriend?"

"I'm afraid she isn't my girlfriend any more. Her ex partner asked her to go back with him, and she decided she would. In fact they are going to get married."

"I'm sorry to hear that Sam, she sounded a nice girl. I was looking forward to meeting her. Never mind, there are plenty more fish in the sea."

"Yes, I know that mum. I'm sorry too. I liked her a lot. How is Graham?"

"Your brother is fine; he carries on as ever, nothing seems to change for him. Chalk and cheese you two, you always were. Still, I wouldn't have you any other way."

Cooper smiled. Was that a compliment?

"You'd still like to marry me off, though."

"Only if you're happy, Sam. You'll get another girl soon, don't worry."

"I'm sure I will, mum. And I'm not worried, so you don't worry either."

* * * * *

It was a cold, crisp evening as a tall, thin man walked through the Bassin Napoleon port area of Boulogne on the north French coast. Anyone watching might think he seemed to be acting in a strange manner, as if he were either drunk or deliberately trying not to be seen; he was walking a circuitous route through the shadows, where the light from the lamps atop the tall poles above the port did not fully penetrate the dark.

The man finally crossed to the car park and down a ramp to the marina area, where a number of yachts were moored. He walked swiftly to where the smaller sailing boats were gently bobbing on the water, pausing to survey an older, less well maintained wooden-hulled vessel that, judging by the white deposits left by seagulls across the roof of the cabin, seemed to have been moored for a while. He stepped on board; taking a knife from his pocket and with very little noise or effort he forced open the hatchway down into the main saloon. He paused to listen for a moment before going down the steps, knife in hand, going quickly through to the small cabin at the bow to ensure no-one was asleep on board. All was quiet. The boat had clearly not been used for a while.

Marcus Fox sat at a small chart table and opened the drawers; he soon found what he was looking for, a spare key to the engine. Returning on deck, looking carefully to see if anyone was in sight, he inserted the key to start the diesel engine which throbbed and spluttered a little before settling down. He moved swiftly forwards and aft, letting go the mooring lines, and slowly eased the little boat away from its mooring, through the marina and out towards the gap in the harbour wall. He had not put on any lights at this point, using the moonlight to see his way between the other silently moored boats. Nothing was stirring; only as he reached the outer wall did he switch on the navigation lights. Then the small yacht was clear of the harbour and heading out to the English Channel.

Fox did not stop the engine and raise a sail until he was well out into the Channel as the wind was very light; he also wanted to reduce the radar signature. He knew however that in one of the busiest shipping lanes in the world he would have to stay alert all night if he wasn't to finish his voyage in the wreckage of a small boat hit by a passing supertanker.

He had spent many years sailing the coast of the south of England, and he knew it well. He set his course and sat back, tiller in hand, to make his way back to England with only an occasional glance back to the fading lights of France to ensure nothing was following him. With a favourable wind he expected to reach his destination before dawn.

The crossing was uneventful; he had used the engine at one point as he passed between two large container ships, but there had been no other excitement. The wind began to freshen during the night, but it was from the South West which helped speed his journey.

He recognised the lights of Hastings in the small hours of the morning, and headed for the shore to the east of the town where he knew there was an uninhabited, wooded beach area. As he reached the middle of the bay the wind started to swirl around in a confused way; the wind was against the ebbing tide so the waves were quite choppy.

As he approached the shore it became distinctly uncomfortable; in the moonlight he could just make out the white foam as large rollers hit the beaches and rocks. He had no choice but to try to land on the beach as he did not want the boat to be seen in any marina; he had to assume that an alarm would have been raised by now about the missing boat. He put on a life jacket as he was pretty sure he would have to swim at some point.

He steered the little craft towards the shore, the engine revving as the propeller came out of the water each time the yacht reached the crest of a wave. As he reached within twenty metres of the beach he heard the boat's keel start to drag on the sea bed; within seconds the boat was listing to one side. He quickly moved the tiller over so the boat was swinging back out to sea and put the engine on full power, before jumping over the side into neck high water, the waves going over his head as he half swam, half waded towards the shore. The waves helped him towards the rocky beach until he was in shallower water, the lifejacket lifting him back to the surface each time he was submerged in icy cold water. After a few minutes he was able to clamber on to the shingle and crawl up the gradual slope out of reach of the breakers.

He lay still until he managed to get his strength back, exhausted, cold and drenched, but then forced himself to get up and walk into the trees and out of sight. As he did so he looked out to sea; he could make out the little yacht which was now listing at a severe angle and partially submerged, the keel well fast in the sand offshore, the boat unable to move despite the engine still turning the propeller, the ebb and flow of the waves spinning the craft left and right with each successive movement. It clearly would not be long before the boat broke up.

Fox turned and walked into the trees, determined to put as much distance as possible between him and the boat before daylight.

* * * * *

The early morning orange ball of a sun was still low in the sky, made dim by a thin grey mist, as a man walked with his dog through the wooded area down to the beach. He pulled his scarf tighter around his neck to keep out the damp air as he watched the black labrador scamper off across the sand, barking excitedly at seagulls who screamed in protest as it hurtled towards them, forcing them into the air. The dog's barks were lost as waves rolling onto the beach and the wind in his ears drowned the sound out completely.

As the man stood to wait for the dog, his feet sinking slightly into the soft sand, he took a pair of binoculars from a bag slung over his shoulder and started to watch some of the birds bobbing about on the water, scanning the shore to see if there was anything of interest. As he looked farther out he noticed something white a hundred metres or so offshore. Focussing his binoculars on the spot, he realised it looked like part of a boat. He looked closely and he could see more pieces on the water, and then he saw the remains of a hull wedged onto nearby rocks, disappearing under the water and then surfacing momentarily with the ebb and flow of the waves.

He walked closer to the water's edge and scanned the water with his binoculars once again, seeing after a moment another large piece that could well have been from the same boat. Unsure what to do, he decided to call a friend who had, until he retired, worked for the coastguard.

The former coastguard decided to play safe and alerted the authorities that wreckage had been seen, after which a fast inshore lifeboat was quickly dispatched to the scene to investigate. They found quite a few pieces of wreckage and soon a search of the coastline was underway which continued for several hours until it was called off, no sign of any bodies having been found.

* * * * *

It was late afternoon by the time Cooper was alerted to the finding of wreckage.

"Where was it found exactly?" he asked, reaching for a road atlas at the same time. "Hastings Country

Park? I assume that's not far from Hastings? Ah yes, here it is" he said as Catherine found it and pointed it out to him.

"Could you find out which station in London the train from Hastings arrives at?" he said to Catherine as he listened to the information from the other end. "No body and no signs of life?" he spoke into the telephone to the coastguard. "Is there any way of getting the name of the boat? We have it; well then, what is it? Then it's a boat from France? Do we know where in France it was kept? Boulogne? And it was stolen? That's very helpful. I'll talk to the French police. Thank you for your help."

"Trains from Hastings go to London Bridge and on to Waterloo, sir" Catherine informed him.

"Get onto British Transport police and get them to keep an eye out for Marcus Fox please. I'm going to find him, this time"

* * * * *

Twenty four hours later Catherine was at her desk when the duty sergeant called over to her.

"Someone looking for DC Robinson. Do you want to take the call?"

"Yes please."

She waited for the click as the call came through.

"I'm afraid that DC Robinson is on leave" she said. "Can I help? I am DC Harper."

"Yes, I hope so. My name is Richard Clarke. I know from my good friend Dr Portman that DC

Robinson was keen to find the whereabouts of my brother, Marcus Fox as he now calls himself, as part of an investigation. I wanted to let him know that Marcus called me this morning."

"He did? Thank you for letting us know, sir. Do you know where he is, and can you tell me what he said?"

"He didn't tell me where he was calling from, but he did say he'd recently arrived back in the UK from Paris where he had seen an old friend, and that he wanted to renew an old acquaintance here in the UK. I didn't fully understand what he was trying to tell me but he sounded both confused and quite angry."

"You don't know what he might have meant by that, or who this acquaintance might be?"

"I'm afraid not."

"Did he say anything else, sir?"

"No, that was about it. I called his doctor this morning, who has been looking after him for many years, and he suggested I call DC Robinson."

"I see. There is nothing more you can add that might help us to find him? We are very concerned about him, you must know that."

There was a moment of hesitation.

"Yes, I do understand. Marcus can be very strange, I know, and his doctor and I have been particularly worried about him over this past year. If I think of anything then I shall of course let you know."

"Please do, let me know of anything at all that might help us to find him. Is there anywhere he could conceivably be headed for?"

Again there was a pause.

"Not really; I assume you're keeping an eye on his apartment. I have only one other thought, although I suspect it unlikely. We have an elderly aunt, who lives in Knightsbridge in London, close by Harrods. It's possible I suppose he might head there if he has it in mind to get back to London. I can't think of anywhere else he might go, other than here in the north, and he never liked it here. He always preferred London."

"Thank you for sharing that, sir. Could you give me the name and address of this aunt, please?"

After the call she headed up the stairs to talk to Cooper. She passed the sergeant on the way, who gave her the thumbs up sign. Puzzled, she stopped to ask what he meant.

"He's finally replaced that chair. We all reckon it's because you're with him now, and he can't for shame have you stand all the time. So well done, the bugger's finally got a new one. We've burnt the old one anyway, just in case he changes his mind."

Catherine laughed and carried on up the stairs. She wasn't convinced it was anything to do with her, but she wouldn't argue.

Cooper was speaking on the phone but waved to her to come in. They were right; a new visitor chair had appeared in his office. She smiled as she sat in it, wondering what had really triggered the purchase, but decided against making a comment.

"How are you feeling?" he asked when he had finished the call.

"Not too bad, sir."

Catherine then briefed him on the call she had received from Richard Clarke.

"Will you arrange for someone to keep an eye on that aunt's house, just in case Fox heads there? Will you also check that we have someone at the Edwards' home at all times now?"

"Yes sir. Do you want me to head over to Cadogan Place now to see if this aunt has heard from him?"

"No, it's time you went home; I don't want you working too late just yet. Send a car round to check if she is there. If there are no signs of life then you can go over there tomorrow morning. Something else has just cropped up; do you feel up to a ride to Hampstead? They've found a body floating in the pond on the heath. We'll leave in half an hour to take a look and then I'll drop you home."

They parked in a side street close by a narrow alleyway that led directly onto the Heath, not far from Hampstead Pond, and walked through. The body had been found by a swimmer; it was in some reeds at the far end of the pond, away from the busiest areas.

The area around the pond had been cordoned off by a line of blue police tape; a constable standing guard lifted the tape to allow Cooper and Catherine to walk through. As they walked to the edge of the pond he could see Fred, the pathologist, standing behind a mobile screen, speaking to another constable, a body covered in a white sheet lying on the ground beside them. He shook hands with Fred and introduced him to Catherine.

"She's my new assistant" he said.

The pathologist glanced at her briefly.

"What do you have for us?" Cooper continued.

"It's the body of a middle aged woman. She's been in here for just a few hours I should say. Fewer than twenty four hours, certainly."

"What time was she found?"

The constable answered.

"We took a call saying a body had been found at three seventeen this afternoon, sir."

"Do we have an identity, constable?" Cooper asked him.

"Yes sir." The constable pulled out his notebook. "We found a handbag near the shore, and it contained a driving licence with a photograph, so I believe it belonged to the deceased lady. Her name is Isabelle Edwards."

Cooper looked at Catherine, then at the pathologist.

"We'd better see the body, Fred."

The pathologist bent forward and pulled back the sheet to enable them to see what lay underneath.

Cooper looked down on the pale face, barely recognisable as the woman he had spoken to only a week before.

"Any signs she died of anything other than drowning?"

"No obvious signs, so I'll reserve judgement until we can have a look."

"And you think she's been in the water for several hours?"

"First view is for several hours, perhaps as many as twenty four, but no more than that."

Cooper walked away and the pathologist replaced the sheet over the body; Catherine followed behind, stopping only to take the handbag from the constable who was clearly happy not to have to hold it, and checking with him to be sure he had made a note of the contents. Cooper was deep in thought.

* * * * *

The formalities of the identification of his wife's body completed, Charles Edwards was driven home by the police. When Cooper arrived at the Kensington house it was late evening; a marked police patrol car was parked on the road outside the house, Edwards' large BMW was parked on the driveway.

He walked up to the front gate and pressed the buzzer. A woman police constable appeared out of the door of the house and came down the steps to open the gate for him. Cooper walked up and into the house, followed by the constable. He stepped into the large hallway and the constable then led him past the staircase leading up to the first floor, towards the main living room where Charles Edwards was sitting. As he walked past the stairs he stopped. He bent down to examine the first step. The floor of the hallway was in wood, but the stairs had a pale grey carpet fitted. The constable realised he had stopped and returned to him to see what he was looking at.

"Have either of you been up stairs at all?"

"No sir, we've been in the living room, keeping Mister Edwards company. He is in quite a state."

"There's part of a footprint on the stair; looks like someone came in with muddy shoes."

"Well it wasn't made by either of us, sir. We've only just come on duty."

Cooper straightened up and gestured for the constable to take him to see Charles Edwards.

"Good afternoon, Mister Edwards. I'm very sorry about your wife's death. Is there anything we can do at all?"

"No, not right now. I need time to think, that's all. Difficult to take in all this, you know."

"I'm sure. I shall need to ask you a few questions to try to establish what happened before too long. Do you feel up to that?"

Charles looked at him, his eyes red. "Yes, inspector. I'll be fine."

"When did you last see your wife?"

"She was here this morning at breakfast. Then she went out. I haven't seen her after that, not until..." Edwards voice trailed away.

"Do you want to take me through what you both did this morning?"

"Of course. We woke up at about seven, as normal. I looked out of the window and your patrol car was already outside. We got up and got dressed. Isabelle went into the kitchen and started to make breakfast. She suggested I should ask your officers if they wanted anything, as they were probably cold, so I went out to them. They accepted a cup of tea, so I suggested they come inside, which they did. They came into the kitchen and we were chatting whilst they drank their tea. They were two nice young men. They said they would be leaving shortly afterwards as their shift was ending, and another car would be coming shortly. After they went back outside Isabelle went upstairs and came back down dressed to go out. She hadn't mentioned anything so I was surprised, but she said she needed some air and wanted to think a bit, so I didn't protest. She had been very tense of late, as you can imagine, so I hoped a little quiet time alone would do her good. She then went out. After that I sat and did some work, and then a little reading. I thought Isabelle would be back after an hour or perhaps two. When by lunch time she hadn't returned I called her mobile phone several times but it went straight to her voice mail; it was switched off I suppose."

"She had given no indication where she was going?"

"None at all. I assumed into town to walk around the shops. She often does."

"Did you leave a message on her voicemail at all?"

"No, I did not. I was thinking that she had switched it off because she didn't want to be disturbed. Obviously that wasn't true."

Cooper noticed that through all of this speech Charles Edwards had not seemed emotional at all, until the very last few words where he bent forward, tears in his eyes. He had the distinct impression that Edwards had decided he needed to look more sorrowful.

"I understand that you didn't report her missing at all?"

"No. I was surprised she hadn't thought to call but I thought she had perhaps decided to take lunch with someone. However it was a little after six this evening when the constables who by then were sitting outside came in and explained what had happened."

Cooper decided to leave him for the moment. He would need to see the result of the post-mortem before deciding what to do next.

As he went to leave, Cooper said "You have a very nice garden, sir. Do you look after it yourself?"

"No, I don't have the time or the talent. We have a gardener who comes here three mornings a week. Isabelle takes...used to take care of it."

This time he looked genuinely distressed. Cooper walked back through the hallway, stopping to take another look at the footprint, before returning to the living room.

"I'm sorry, Mister Edwards, but can I ask you when you last went upstairs?"

Edwards looked at him curiously.

"Upstairs? Well, Isabelle went up there obviously before she left, but I don't remember having been up there since breakfast. Why?"

"Do you mind if my constables take a look around up there, sir?"

"What are they looking for?"

"I just want to be sure there isn't anyone else in the house, sir."

The constables looked at each other and went out to go upstairs.

"What makes you think that, inspector?" Edwards asked him in a hushed voice.

Cooper said nothing, waiting for the constables to return. After a few minutes waiting, they came back down.

"All clear upstairs sir. No signs of anyone, or of any entry at all" the WPC assured him.

"Fine. I'm sorry about that, Mister Edwards, but I noticed a muddy footprint on the first stair and I wanted to make sure it wasn't someone who had entered while you were working. The print seems too large for a ladies' shoe. Can you explain how it got there?"

"I have no idea. Perhaps it may have been when I came in yesterday evening."

"Had you been somewhere that was muddy, sir?"

"Not that I recall, but it must have been me I suppose."

"I see, sir. Well, I'll leave you now. Good evening."

* * * * *

After the visit to the pond, Cooper had dropped Catherine home. She kept Isabelle Edwards' handbag with her.

After she had eaten she emptied the contents of the bag onto her table; the only thing of any interest was an address book. As she leafed through it she noticed one name had been blacked out with a felt tipped pen. She held the page up to the light; the name and phone number weren't visible at all.

She put the contents apart from the address book back into the bag. She thought for a while, then she decided she would drop it off with the laboratory in the morning; perhaps they would be able to tell her the name that had been blacked out.

EIGHTEEN

The sky was full of heavy grey clouds, threatening rain, and a strong wind was blowing as Catherine Harper drove to the apartment of Marcus Fox's elderly aunt in central London the next morning, arriving in the garden square of large, red brick villas to meet a marked police car with two armed officers inside. She spoke to them briefly, insisting that she should go to the door, with them on standby in the street.

"We are dealing with an elderly lady here. I don't want to frighten her to death."

Catherine went up the steps to the front door and rang the buzzer to the apartment, but there was no answer. She knocked on the door at which an elderly man opened it, who introduced himself as the caretaker for the building. After showing him her identity card he allowed her and the other officers into a large hallway with a marble floor, a glass chandelier hanging from a thick chain. Catherine told the caretaker to remain on the ground floor while with the constables she ascended a broad sweeping staircase to the third floor; she identified the correct apartment and knocked on the door. There was no answer. It seemed that the old lady wasn't there.

Catherine sent one of the constables down to ask the caretaker for a key, but he returned to say that he didn't have one; the management company didn't allow him to keep them.

Catherine pondered her next move. She had no authority to force an entry, but she needed to be sure the old lady was indeed away and that Fox wasn't hiding inside. She called Richard Clarke, explaining where she was.

"Your aunt doesn't appear to be here sir, and we don't believe she was here yesterday evening. Do you know if she is likely to have gone away?"

"I'm not sure. My cousin, her son, lives down in Hampshire. Perhaps she's staying with him. Would you like me to call him now, to see if she is there, or if he knows where she might be?"

"If you could give me the number then I will do that."

Clarke gave her the number, which Catherine called immediately.

"Good morning, sir, I'm sorry to disturb you. This is Detective Constable Catherine Harper from the Metropolitan Police. I have just been speaking to your cousin, Richard Clarke. For reasons I can't go into right now, we are interested in speaking to Marcus Fox, who is a cousin of yours I understand. Mr Clarke suggested he might be visiting your mother; I am outside of her property in Cadogan Place right now, but there appears to be no-one at home. Do you know where your mother is at the moment?"

"My mother's here, spending a few days with us. Do you need to speak to her?"

"Not necessarily, sir, if you can confirm she is with you. We would however like to have a look inside your mother's apartment to check it, but the caretaker here

284

tells us he doesn't have a key at all. Is there anyone else from whom we could get a key?"

"She has a housekeeper who goes along every day to do some cooking and cleaning for her; she goes every day whether she is there or not. I believe she should be along very soon."

"What is her name, sir?"

"Her name is Wilkins, Ruth Wilkins. I need to also tell you, detective, that my cousin Marcus was here staying with us two nights ago."

Catherine was stunned into silence for a moment.

"He stayed with you?"

"Yes, he stayed with us the night before last. He turned up looking quite ill. He looked as if he'd been sleeping in the same clothes for days, and his clothes were quite damp. He said he'd had an accident and fallen, but we weren't sure we believed him. My aunt said she wanted to call a doctor as Marcus looked quite ill, but Marcus became quite agitated so we agreed we would not. He had a hot bath, a good meal and some clean clothes. He slept here that night, but the following morning he didn't come down to breakfast. We left him to sleep for a while, thinking he must be exhausted, but when I eventually checked his room to make sure he was ok, he had gone. We assume he must have gone out in the early hours, although we heard nothing."

"Do you have any idea what time he might have left?"

"Not really, no. We left him sleeping, so we thought, until after ten o'clock in the morning. He could have left at any time during the night."

"I shall need to know what clothes he was wearing when he left. Do you know?"

Catherine was given a description of a pair of corduroy trousers and a heavy wool jumper in dark blue. He had also taken a black overcoat.

"What did he say to you when he arrived, sir?"

"Frankly he said very little. As I said, he seemed exhausted so we fed him and put him to bed, expecting to learn more the next morning, but he had gone."

"You said he was wet when he arrived?"

"Yes, I was surprised at that as it hadn't been raining at all."

"I see. If we see the housekeeper, sir, I would like to look around the apartment to make sure your cousin is not hiding in there. Could I have your permission to do that, please?"

"Yes, of course. I will speak to my mother and explain what is going on, but yes you have my permission to have a look inside. I assume you won't have to break in, of course."

"That won't be necessary, sir, don't worry. If you should hear anything further from Mr. Fox, then please let me know straight away."

Catherine gave him her number to call. She then called Cooper.

"I'm at the apartment of Marcus Fox's aunt in Knightsbridge, sir, but there are no signs of life. I've just spoken to Richard Clarke and then to his cousin, the lady's son. The lady is staying with him at the moment, so the house should be empty. However we've been given permission to get the key from a housekeeper who comes every day to check the apartment, so I propose to wait here until she arrives, which should be shortly. We will then go in to make sure the apartment is clear and our friend Marcus Fox isn't hiding inside. One other piece of information sir, is that Fox was staying with his cousin the night before last."

"Staying with his cousin? Where?"

"At their home, in Hampshire."

"And he stayed with this cousin for just the one night?"

"Yes sir, that's what the cousin said."

"What did he tell you?"

"When Fox arrived at his cousin's his clothes were damp, and he looked as if he had slept in them for days, which he probably had. They gave him a hot bath and a change of clothes and he went to bed. They left him sleeping until late, or so they thought, but when he didn't come down the cousin checked the bedroom and he had vanished. They have no idea what time Fox left."

"We're one step behind him all the time" Cooper mused. "He's a smart character, I'll give him that. Where will he go next, I wonder?"

"I don't know, sir. He may come here of course, but he may just lie low for a little while, or he may try to strike quickly."

"Strike at Charles Edwards, you mean?"

"Yes sir. I presume that is his target."

"I'm assuming so too. My next question is: who killed Isabelle Edwards?"

Catherine started. "Are you saying her death wasn't suicide, sir?"

"The autopsy has shown there was no water in her lungs. She was dead before she went in the water. She had been suffocated. Not sure how as there were no bruises. She'd been dead for several hours before she went into the pond."

"Oh no! Poor woman! Will you talk to Charles Edwards again?"

"I wanted to see how you got on before I went over there. Even if he killed his wife, he isn't likely to murder anyone else, so he can wait for an hour or two. One other thing, to bring you up to date; I've just spoken to Fred about the search of Fox's property in Camden. He has had the results from the tests on the traces of remains found in the drains there. He is certain there are definitely the remains of one person there; he also says it is a man."

Catherine was silent for a second as the news sank in.

"It's a man? So that means it can't be either of the missing girls, Tina and Paulette? We're no further forward with finding what happened to them?"

"No, it seems not. We still need to find Fox, though."

It was almost ten o'clock in the morning when Catherine saw a middle aged woman, carrying a couple of shopping bags, approaching the apartment in Knightsbridge. Catherine was sitting in the front of the police car with the two constables, parked across the street from the apartment. As Catherine watched, the woman went to the front door of the apartment building and put down the shopping bags as she began to look through her handbag; Catherine assumed she was looking for a key.

Catherine jumped out of the car and walked quickly over to the woman.

"Are you Mrs. Wilkins?"

The woman turned to face Catherine, then saw the constables getting out of the car behind her. She looked very alarmed.

Catherine repeated the question, and the woman nodded confirmation.

"I'm sorry to startle you. I'm a police officer. I'm DC Catherine Harper. We have been speaking to Mrs. Clarke, the owner of the apartment here, number seven, and we should like to take a look inside, if you wouldn't mind giving me the key please."

"I'd rather let you in when I go in."

"No, I'm sorry; you're not to go inside until we've taken a look."

The woman looked very confused, but handed Catherine the key.

"Well, I suppose you can, if Mrs Clarke says it's ok."

"Thank you."

Catherine signalled to the constables and they walked quickly over to join her. Asking the woman to wait, she opened the door to the communal hallway, and they took the stairs to the third floor. At the doorway to the apartment, Catherine opened the door with the key, but then stood back as the armed officers entered with their weapons in their hands. She stood outside of the doorway while they quickly checked the rooms. After a few moments they declared the apartment safe and Catherine walked in, donning gloves. An inspection of the apartment showed no signs of anyone having been there, or forced an entry. Catherine sent one of the constables down to tell the woman that she could now come up; she walked over to the window to look down onto the street. As she did so she noticed a letter on the desk in the sitting room.

It was addressed to DI Cooper.

* * * * *

After speaking to Catherine, Cooper drove out to Kensington to see Charles Edwards. He found him in his study; on his way through the hall he had noted that the stair had been cleaned.

"Could I ask you to go over with me again your wife's movements yesterday?"

"Yes, of course. We woke up at about seven; I always have the alarm set for the same time. When we went downstairs Isabelle went into the kitchen and started to make breakfast and I collected the post. Your officers then came into the kitchen and we were chatting whilst they drank their tea. They then left shortly after that. Isabelle went upstairs and a while later came back down dressed to go out. She seemed fine at that point; she didn't seem upset or anything. After that I sat and did some work, and a little reading. I thought Isabelle would be back after an hour or perhaps two. I rang her towards lunchtime to see if she was planning to be home for lunch but didn't get through. Her phone seemed to be switched off. When she hadn't returned by mid afternoon I began to be a bit worried. I rang her mobile after that several times but still didn't get a response."

"You didn't think to talk to the police outside at that point?"

"Yes, I thought about it. But I kept putting it off as I thought she had probably just decided to have a day in town and I didn't want to bother them over nothing. She enjoyed walking around the shops; I detest it myself. I then thought she might perhaps have arranged to meet with a friend. I'd called her another few times but then the officers outside knocked on the door to tell me she's been found."

"Did you speak to anyone else, or see anyone else, yesterday, sir?"

"No, I was at home the entire day."

"I'm afraid I must tell you, sir, that I have spoken to the doctor who has carried out a post-mortem on your wife. Your wife did not drown. She was suffocated in some way before she went into the water."

Charles Edwards gasped and sat back in his chair. He closed his eyes and covered his face with his hands. Cooper waited, letting the news sink in, watching his reaction carefully. He gave nothing away, sitting with his eyes closed, breathing heavily as though recovering from a shock.

"Is there anything else that you want to tell me, sir?"

Charles opened his eyes and looked at him.

"No, I've told you everything I know. Who could have done that to her?"

At that moment Cooper's mobile phone rang. He looked at the number; it was Catherine.

"Excuse me sir, I need to take this call."

He walked into the hallway, leaving Edwards to his thoughts in his study.

"Yes, Catherine" he said.

"Sorry to disturb you, sir. I've now gained entry into the old lady's apartment here. There is no-one here, as we suspected. But I think Fox has been inside. He may have stayed here overnight, although if he did he hasn't left much evidence."

"What makes you think he's been there?"

"I've discovered a letter here, addressed to you. I can only imagine that Fox would write it. No-one else knows you."

"What does it say?"

"I haven't opened it. Do you want me to do that?"

"Yes, open it now."

Cooper waited; he could hear the letter being opened.

"Yes, it is from Fox. Let me read it to you. 'Dear Inspector. I assume by now you have discovered the remains of a former friend of mine in Camden. I am sure you are shocked, but trust me when I say that it was no-one of any significance, and he isn't sadly missed by anyone. Far more important is for you to solve Monique's murder. Yes, she was murdered. It was no accident. You know by now who killed her as well as I do, but you don't know the real reason why. You also don't know that she isn't the only woman whose death he has been involved in; nor is he the only one to be involved. Ask him where he lived before and after going to Hong Kong. I think that wife of his is a devil as well. I shall stop her too.' That's all it says, sir."

"Well done Catherine. Will you get forensics to go over the apartment, and get them to have a look at that letter whilst they're at it?"

Cooper then returned to the study.

"So can you confirm the timing of the events yesterday again for me, sir?"

292

"As I said to you, after breakfast my wife came down, dressed to go out. She left at about ten."

"You say your wife went out about ten in the morning. Did the constables see her go out?"

"I'm not sure." He paused. "No, I think they weren't there. I think they had gone by then. The next car arrived close to midday, as I remember."

"But they saw her first thing in the morning, when you gave them a cup of tea?"

"That's correct."

"And you were in the house the entire day?"

"Yes, I was."

"Did you speak to anyone at all, even on the telephone?"

"I spoke to my stockbroker at one point on the phone. That was late morning, at about eleven thirty. I didn't see anyone at all."

"Thank you Mister Edwards, I now need to return to the question of the death of Monique Bertrand. You are aware of the statement made by your wife?"

"Yes, I'm well aware of it."

"I will need you to come to the station and make your own statement sir, however that doesn't need to be today."

"Thank you inspector."

"Can you confirm your address at the time she died?"

"Of course. We lived in a tiny flat in Hampstead, inspector." He gave him the address.

"How long did you live there for?"

Edwards looked at him quizzically.

"Where is this leading to, inspector?"

"Just answer the question, please."

"We lived there for about a year in total."

"And after that?"

"After the incident with Monique we decided we didn't want to live there any longer. Or to be truthful, Isabelle said she couldn't stand being in that apartment any longer. For a while she returned to live with her family in France. I moved out of Hampstead and looked for another role. I found one in Hong Kong; I was there for several years. During that time my grandfather died and I inherited some money, which I used to buy this house when I came back from Hong Kong. Isabelle joined me in Hong Kong for part of the time I was there, the rest of the time she was with her family as she didn't enjoy living there. I loved it. Does that answer your question?"

"Partly, sir. Can you tell me where you lived when you moved out of Hampstead but before you went to Hong Kong, and where you lived when you returned from Hong Kong but before you moved in here?"

"On both occasions I lived in a house my family owned."

"Where was that, sir?"

"In West London, in Richmond."

"The address?"

Cooper noted it down.

"And when was that exactly?"

"Let me see. Monique died in March nineteen sixty nine, so it would have been from about June of that year."

"For how long, sir?"

"I was there for a little more than a year before I was able to go to Hong Kong. After I returned I lived in the house for another eighteen months or so."

"So you were living there until July or August nineteen seventy. And when did you return from Hong Kong?"

"In nineteen eighty. I lived there for eighteen months from February nineteen eighty."

* * * * *

It was late afternoon by the time Cooper and Catherine met at the station and were able to bring each other up to date.

"So he was living in Richmond when both Tina Marsh and Paulette Dijon disappeared. Paulette we know was in Richmond about that time. Is that a coincidence?" Catherine asked.

"Good question" he said. "This case gets more interesting by the minute. I wonder what Fox was implying when he said Edwards wasn't the only one involved. I need to talk to the chief. I think we should check to see if Edwards was involved in anything in Hong Kong we ought to know about."

"Or if any girls went missing there during that time" Catherine added.

"That too" he agreed.

They were sitting in Cooper's office; he looked at his watch. It was almost six o'clock in the evening.

"Good grief, I had no idea it was so late. You're supposed to be taking it easy. Get yourself home, and we'll carry on with this conversation tomorrow."

"I'm perfectly happy to stay, sir."

"No, get yourself home. This can wait until tomorrow."

"So what's our next step?"

"Apprehending Marcus Fox remains the priority, before he kills someone again. I've asked forensics to do more work to see if there's any help they can give us on where and when Isabelle Edwards was killed, but otherwise the rest is resolving old crimes, and one day more or less isn't going to matter. I'll be in late tomorrow; I'll go to see the chief to bring him up to date."

Cooper hesitated.

"Actually, you should be there too" he said. "Meet me at his office at nine thirty tomorrow morning."

"Of course, sir. One other thing before I go. I had a look through the contents of Isabelle Edwards handbag yesterday. Her address book was in there. It was clearly quite old, there were lots of address changes as people moved around, no doubt. There was one name scrubbed out completely. I dropped it off at the lab this morning and asked them to have a look. They called me on my way here this afternoon to tell me they could read the name. It was Monica Gascoigne."

He sat back in his chair.

"Well, well, well" he said. "So the girl who disappeared eighteen months ago, and whose blood was in Fox's boat, knew Isabelle Edwards. What do we make of that?"

Catherine left his office to go home. Cooper sat for an hour at his desk bringing his notes up to date. He had almost finished and was getting ready to leave when his desk phone rang.

"There's a French police officer on the phone for you, sir. A detective Delacroix."

"Thank you sergeant, put him through."

"Maurice here, Sam. I have just spoken to the police in Le Havre. They have arrested a young man this afternoon, and have now charged him with the murder of Bernadette Guillaume. He used to be her boyfriend. They tell me he has made a full confession, so it seems your man was not involved after all."

* * * * *

Cooper knocked on the chief's door, Catherine standing beside him. They walked in after a shout inviting them in.

"Good to see you Catherine. Sit down, both of you. So, Sam, where are we now?"

"The first thing to tell you, sir, is that I got a call from France last night to say they've charged a young boy with the murder in Le Havre. Seems he was a former boyfriend and he has confessed. That means Fox is off the hook for that one."

He glanced at Catherine as he spoke.

"Sorry Catherine, I didn't get chance to tell you that."

"So that leaves us with four girls who've disappeared" the chief said. "Monique Bertrand we know was killed and buried in Hampstead. We've found Monica Gascoigne's blood on Fox's boat, but no clue as to her whereabouts. One of the other two, Tina Marsh, disappeared from Hampstead about the same time as Monique, and one, Paulette Dijon, from Richmond, ten years later. We also have the murder of Isabelle Edwards."

"Correct, sir. Perhaps we should start with Monique Bertrand. It seems clear that Charles Edwards killed her. The question is whether it was an accident. He admits he knew Monique, she had followed him to England, he had told her he was now engaged to another woman, Isabelle, but he told us he never saw her again after that. His wife though contradicted that, claiming that, in fact, Monique went to their apartment, got in a fight and ended up being stabbed by Charles Edwards; she claims it was by accident. We have yet to ask Charles Edwards for his statement, sir."

"I know. Let's talk about that when we've gone through the evidence."

"Further to the statement by Mrs Edwards, we have a statement from Sophie Renard who knew Monique and Edwards when they were in Paris. She believes Edwards killed Monique because of money. Monique was threatening to tell the police that he had caused a car accident in France by driving whilst drunk, and someone had been killed. He would have lost his very substantial inheritance if that had come out, so he killed her."

"Do we have that in writing now?"

"I have spoken to my contact there, Delacroix, who has told me she has made it and he has sent it to me."

"Good."

"However, accident or no accident, Edwards buried Monique's body on Hampstead Heath. So we can charge him with illegal burial, at the very least."

"At this point I don't see enough evidence to convict him for murder, even with this French lady's statement. Do you think he will admit that he stabbed her, even if accidentally, as his wife said in her statement?"

"I'm not sure, sir. I look forward to hearing what he has to say."

"And the other three missing girls?"

"Tina Marsh went missing during the first time Edwards lived in Richmond, and Paulette Dijon during the second time. In addition Paulette Dijon lived in Richmond. We haven't found a link from Tina Marsh to Richmond as yet, but perhaps Catherine can talk to her mother once more, to see if there is a connection. We also have a connection from Edwards to Monica Gascoigne, who disappeared relatively recently, as her name was in his wife's address book."

"I see. This leads us to the death of his wife. What's your theory there?"

"She was strangled, as you know sir, but just who strangled her is open to doubt. If Charles Edwards was angry at her insistence on making a statement to us then perhaps they had a violent argument over that. During her interview I questioned some of her logic. She seemed quite shocked when I told her I knew her husband had been driving when that accident happened. It may well be that she confronted him on that, and this led to a confrontation and violence. Sophie Renard told me Edwards could be violent."

"How could he have strangled her with a police patrol outside?"

"There was a police car outside the door of his house for part of the day, but not all of it. We took the view that he was most at risk at night. The officers on duty were in fact called away to other things on several occasions; it's possible Edwards strangled her at home and then took her body down to Hampstead. However none of the officers noticed his car missing during the day."

"That part of the heath is usually busy. No-one could carry her down there in broad daylight and not be noticed."

"I agree, sir. The only way I see it as a possibility is if he killed her in the very early hours of the morning and took her body there and hid it before anyone else was around. I have checked with the patrol; they were called to a traffic accident at four in the morning, and didn't return to the Edwards until six. He told me that they'd been in for a cup of tea at about seven with him and his wife. They told me that they'd seen him but not her. He'd told them she was getting dressed."

"So it's possible, then. But we'll need more than that to convince a jury."

"Yes, sir, it's possible, but I agree. I also noted a muddy footprint on the stairs of his home when I went to talk to him after she'd been discovered. It's possible he came back in a hurry and went upstairs to change quickly. The next day the print had gone. It was only then I knew she had been murdered, and it would have been too late to get a warrant and inspect his shoes for mud; I'm sure they were all cleaned immediately."

"A pity. What about Marcus Fox? Where does he fit into this picture now? Are we eliminating him from the enquiry into Monique's death?"

"He's an enigma, sir. We still haven't tracked him down, so I can't talk to him. He did of course send a letter to me, which basically accused Edwards of murdering Monique Bertrand and several others, as well as being involved in some kind of a conspiracy with others unnamed. He also called Isabelle Edwards a devil."

"So could he have killed any of the girls?"

"We have the remains of a man, identity as yet unknown, in his apartment in Camden, and he has confessed to killing him in his letter, so we know he is capable of killing. As far as the death of Monique is concerned, unless Isabelle Edwards completely fabricated her story for reasons I don't understand, I rule him out for the moment. Could he have killed Isabelle Edwards? Well, in his letter he referred to her as a devil, so he clearly had no love for her. It is possible that he was watching the Edwards' house, saw her go out, strangled her and took her body to the heath, assuming he had access to a vehicle of course. We haven't found a car hired in any of the names he's used so far. He could have stolen one, but from what I've seen of him he is very careful; he doesn't take risks."

"And of course it could be someone else completely" the chief reminded him.

"That too is perfectly possible. As for Tina Marsh, in my book he is a suspect. He was living in an apartment where we know she had a friend, so he had the opportunity. I don't see a link to Paulette other than a newspaper article. Monica Gascoigne's blood in his boat makes him the prime suspect for that, despite the entry in Isabelle Edwards address book."

"So where do you go from here?"

"We need to find Marcus Fox, sir. That remains priority number one, because there are a lot of questions to put to him. The question is whether we arrest Charles Edwards for the illegal burial, or on suspicion of the murder of his wife, or on suspicion of the murder of Monique Bertrand."

"I want to be careful on Charles Edwards. Let's wait to see what else we can find out before we take any action."

Cooper glanced at Catherine.

"Can I at least ask him to come in and make a statement about the death of Monique Bertrand, sir?"

"No, not yet. Let's see if we can first pin down this Marcus Fox, then we can review the situation."

"Any particular reason why, sir?"

"There are a lot of senior people taking a close interest in this, Sam. Let's just be sure of our ground before we do anything."

"There is the question of his time in Hong Kong, sir. We need to ask if he was involved in any crimes, or investigated, during his time there" Catherine said.

"Leave that with me. I'll ask the question through the usual channels. I'll let you know what I find out."

When they left the chief's office Cooper suggested to Catherine that they go for a coffee; they walked across the busy London road to a cafe.

"There's something odd about this whole case" he said to her as he sipped his coffee. "I have a feeling there's a lot more to this than meets the eye. The fact that the original file on Monique Bertrand's disappearance is sitting with Special Branch makes me suspicious. And the chief is very touchy about Edwards. Somebody somewhere knows a lot more than they are saying."

"It would be interesting to know what else Fox has to say" Catherine answered.

"It would. It would indeed."

NINETEEN

It had been grey day, dark clouds blowing across the sky and by late afternoon it was raining as Catherine drove up the hill towards Hampstead Heath. Even in this weather she knew she would miss her cycle rides around Hampstead, and the familiar faces she had seen most days for the past couple of years. She would equally have to give some serious thought to joining a gym if she wasn't going to put on a huge amount of weight.

She parked outside a now familiar cottage and went to knock on the front door. At first Mrs Marsh didn't recognise Catherine.

"You aren't in your uniform, dear," she exclaimed.

"I won't be wearing that any more. I've been transferred to the plain clothes branch."

"So you're a detective now? Well that's nice. Do come in" Mrs Marsh said.

Catherine followed her into the living room once more where she was invited to sit.

"I'd like to ask a further question about Tina, if I may."

"Of course, dear. If you can help me to find her I'll help in any way I can."

"Did Tina know anyone who lived in Richmond, or did she ever go over there do you know?"

"I'm not particularly aware that Tina had any friends over there. I don't remember her ever talking about Richmond at all."

"I see. And the police investigating her disappearance never mentioned Richmond at all, or anyone from Richmond?"

"No, not that I recall."

"Does the name Paulette mean anything to you?"

"No dear, I don't know anyone of that name. That sounds like a French name; I don't have any French friends."

"And you don't recall Tina ever mentioning anyone called Paulette?"

"No, I don't. Did this girl live in Richmond?"

"Yes, she did."

Mrs Marsh seemed to be about to say something, but then changed her mind. Catherine waited for a moment, but she didn't seem to be about to say anything more so she stood up to go.

"Thank you, Mrs Marsh. You've been very helpful. I'm glad you're looking so well."

"I'm not sure I was much help, dear. I simply kept saying no."

She opened the door and Catherine started to go out when a thought occurred to her.

"Did your husband know anyone in Richmond at all, do you know?"

Mrs Marsh looked at her.

"Yes, he did. He used to go over to Richmond once a month when Tina was just a child. In fact he took Tina there once, I remember, but when she came home she cried a lot. I think she must have been bored silly. She never wanted to go again."

The hairs on the back of Catherine's neck stood on end. Her husband was probably a paedophile. Was Mrs Marsh shutting out the truth?

"What did Tina say? Did she never tell you why she got upset?"

Mrs Marsh looked away. She wouldn't look Catherine in the eye.

"I don't remember her saying anything."

"Do you know why your husband went there?"

"He used to play golf with a circle of friends. They then used to meet at one of the houses for dinner after which they used to play bridge. Sometimes he only arrived home very late."

"Do you know whose house they used to meet in?"

Catherine wrote down the name. It sounded familiar, but she couldn't place it.

"Can you remember the names of any of his friends who would have been there?"

"One of his friends you may have heard of, as he became an MP later. His name was Charles Edwards. I can't remember the names of the others I'm afraid."

* * * * *

Later that same evening Cooper was alone in his office. It was dark outside, the building was quiet and he could hear the rain blowing against the window. He had spoken to the chief; now he had a lot of work to catch up on and there was no real incentive to leave; however the image of Melanie had just popped into his head.

He stood up and walked to the window; he could see little outside, his own reflection staring back at him.

"What a plonker you are" he told his reflection. "She was the best thing that ever happened to you. Is this what you want, to be alone for the rest of your life? When you've got your next promotion, then what? Who do you tell?"

He turned back to his desk and sat down. Dispirited, he decided it was late enough to call it a day; he locked his files away, put on his coat and went down to his car. As he walked across the car park the security light picked out a small envelope on his windscreen. He picked it up, unlocked his car and climbed in. He then tore open the sodden envelope and held the note under the interior light of the car to be able to read it.

'Dear Inspector, I'll be waiting for you on Hampstead Heath at eight o'clock. Come alone if you want to find out the truth. Marcus.'

Cooper looked at his watch. It was seven forty. He might just make it. He started his engine and started to drive towards the Heath. He called Catherine Harper as he joined the road.

"Hello, listen carefully. I've got a note from Fox. He wants me to meet him on Hampstead Heath, alone, at eight. I'm on my way there now. I want you to get here with a couple of cars, but you need to be sure to stay well out of the way until I call."

"Are you sure that's a good idea, sir, seeing him alone?"

"I don't know. It's a risk, but we need to find him. If he wants to see me, then I think it's to tell me his side of the story. If he wanted to bump me off he could have found a way of doing that by now. I want to see him first and talk to him; then I'll call you. When you get here, position yourself so you can get onto the Heath as quickly as possible. But stay well out of sight."

Cooper drove on through the rain, which by now was coming down quite heavily. A few minutes after eight he arrived at the Heath, parking on a side street across the road. The note had given no clues where to meet, but he guessed Fox would be close by where Monique's body had been discovered. He quickly put on his heavy waterproof coat and cap and a pair of wellingtons he kept in his boot, before heading for the area.

He walked slowly along the path, his senses on high alert; the trees were creaking in the wind, the rain splashing onto the path so he could hear very little else. He was on the path close by the spot where the body had been found, but he could hear and see no-one. He stood, sheltering as best he could under the trees, wondering what to do next.

Then his mobile phone rang.

"Hello Inspector, it's Diana Freedman. I have a visitor here who wants to see you."

Cooper froze to the spot, his heart pounding.

"Is this an uninvited guest?"

"Yes, exactly" she said. "He says that you're to come here at once, alone and on foot."

"Tell him I'm alone, and I shall be outside of your house in five minutes."

There was a pause. He could hear another voice.

"Come in by the side entrance, which brings you into the garage. Once you're here, he says to take off your coat and shoes and leave them in the garage, and then wait."

"I understand. I'm on my way."

The line went dead. He called Catherine as he ran back past his car and on up the hill, his breathlessness immediately obvious to her.

"We're almost there, sir. Where exactly are you?"

"Hello Catherine. Change of plan. I'm running to Diana Freedman's house; Fox is holding her there, possibly as a kind of hostage. I'll be there in two minutes. I want you to go up the hill towards her house but make sure you keep well away. He mustn't see or hear a thing. No sirens, no lights."

"Ok, sir, understood."

He cautiously slowed to a walk as he made his way down the street towards Diana Freedman's house; he wasn't sure if Fox would stay inside the house or wait for him somewhere nearby.

He arrived at the entrance to the driveway. All was quiet; he could see no lights inside the house that were visible from the front. He stood surveying the scene, all the time wary of being taken by surprise by Fox All remained quiet; the garage was some twenty metres from where he stood.

He decided he had no option but to do as Fox demanded; he walked down to the garage, and entered by the side door, which was slightly open. It was dark inside the garage. He tried the light switch but it did not work; it seemed that Fox had switched the power off.

"I'm in the garage, Marcus" Cooper spoke out loudly, to make sure he could be heard. "I'm taking off my coat and shoes as you said."

He removed his coat, shivering as he was now cold and wet. He was reluctant to remove his wellington boots, but decided not to antagonise Fox any more than necessary.

"Ok, Marcus. What do you want me to do now?" he shouted again.

He could hear nothing. His eyes were slowly growing used to the dark, and he could make out a door, presumably leading to the house. As he looked a powerful torch suddenly shone directly at him and he was temporarily blinded; he put up one arm to shield his eyes.

"Turn and face the wall; put your hands up against it."

It was a man's voice.

Cooper turned and did as he was told.

"Now take a step back, keeping your hands on the wall. Keep your feet well apart."

He could hear someone approaching him from behind; he braced himself. A pair of hands patted his body and legs, feeling for any kind of weapon. He then felt the cold steel of a knife pressing hard against his neck.

"Stand up slowly. Don't do anything foolish. Now walk forwards, slowly."

The torch shone ahead of him, Fox staying close behind him, the knife pressed closely against his neck. They reached the door.

"Open it" Fox commanded.

Cooper did as he was told, and they entered a short corridor that led into the house. They entered the kitchen and in the torchlight he saw Diana sitting in a chair, her hands and legs tightly bound, a gag covering her mouth. She looked at him, her eyes wide open in alarm. She seemed to be unharmed; he felt a tingle of relief in his spine.

"Sit down" he was ordered.

He sat in another kitchen chair.

"You can let Mrs Freedman go now" Cooper told him "you have me where you want me. She has nothing to do with any of this."

"She'll go free later. She won't come to any harm as long as you co-operate."

"What do you want from me?"

Fox made no answer but gave him a piece of rope; it was the kind he had seen on his boat, he remembered.

"Tie your legs to the chair, quite firmly."

Cooper once again did as he was told.

"Now put your arms behind the chair."

Fox held out a canvas bag; Cooper put his arms behind and he quickly wrapped it around them, securing them tightly with more rope. Once he was satisfied, he stepped away from Cooper and walked towards Diana.

"I shall undo your gag now, to make you more comfortable" he said, "but you must understand that if you scream out then I shall kill both of you. Do you understand?"

Diana looked at him and nodded. He then undid her gag, laying it on the table. He then went to the sink, poured out a glass of water and walked back to Diana, offering a sip which she gratefully accepted.

That done, Fox then walked into the corridor leading to the garage; he heard a click and the lights came on in the kitchen, after which Fox came back in and sat at the table between the two of them.

Cooper looked at him for the first time. Fox looked a little younger than he had expected, tall but very thin, almost emaciated, with wispy dark hair, a little too long.

"I'm going to tell you a story" Fox said.

* * * * *

Catherine had moved as close as she dared to Diana's house. She was sitting in an unmarked police car, with three armed officers; another two cars were parked in different roads but within a short distance. She had already spoken to the chief several times. He was on his way now; she was to wait until he got there, he had said, but she was getting increasingly nervous. It had been almost half an hour since she had spoken to Cooper, after which she had heard nothing.

The roads near Diana's house were a maze of narrow streets and alleyways, reflecting the ancient village that it had once been, before being swallowed up as another district of London. Catherine had walked or cycled down most of them at sometime.

The streets were quiet; the rain had put off all but the hardiest of people although she saw one or two people out. As she waited an elderly man with a stick walked slowly towards her, with a small dog on a lead, his hat pulled well down on his head to keep off the worst of the rain. She watched him walk past, looking at her and the others in the car suspiciously, but then her phone bleeped once more. It was the chief, telling her he had arrived in Hampstead. She gave him directions and within minutes he was parking his car behind them. She stepped out and got into the front seat of the chief's car.

"How long has he been in there, now?" he asked.

"Just over half an hour, sir. I think we've waited long enough."

"What is the street like?"

"It's a narrow street, sir, as they tend to be around here. The house is set back from the road but with no front wall; it has a garage to the side and quite a lot of ground at the back. It's possible our man could escape through the back somehow. I've never been into the house at all, so I'm not sure."

"I see. Can we get in at the back of the house without being seen?"

"We can send a couple of men around the garage to see if they can get into the back garden. The danger is she has a dog which could give the game away; there may well be security lights at the back which we could trigger as well."

"Then if we are unsure, let's do a frontal approach, straight in through the front door, as quickly as possible."

"I agree, sir. I just hope they are ok."

"Well, sitting here isn't going to get us anywhere. Give the order to go."

Catherine returned to the police car and they set off quickly, but without sirens, pulling up slightly short of Diana's house. They then approached as silently as they could, forming a group by the front door. The lights were on in the house, but Catherine could hear and see no signs of life; she felt her heart sink as she gave the order for the officers to knock the door in and charge into the house, pistols ready. Against orders Catherine followed them in as they moved quickly through the ground floor rooms, the chief close behind her. A shout took her to the kitchen, where she could see both Cooper and Diana tied up and gagged. The chief told her to stay with them; he went off with the other officers to keep searching whilst she untied first Mrs Freedman then Cooper.

"He's gone" he said to her as soon as she removed his gag. "He went out about ten minutes ago. He took Diana's little dog with him."

Catherine started. "Then I saw him. An old man with a dog."

"He could be anywhere by now" he said.

One of the constables walked in.

"Get a call out quickly; we're looking for a little old man, with a stick and a dog" he told him.

"Not so little" Catherine added. "Tall and thin."

As Diana was very tearful, Catherine went to the sink and filled the kettle.

"I'm so worried about Buster" she sobbed. "He took him away."

Catherine made a large pot full of tea then sat by her and tried to comfort her; as she did so the chief came down from organising the continuing search and into the kitchen. He sat at the table with them.

"Thank God you're both unharmed" he said. "What did he want you both for? What was he hoping to achieve?"

"He wanted to tell his side of the story" Cooper answered. "He didn't think we'd give him a fair hearing, and he kept saying he was afraid that we'd send him back to the clinic."

"Which clinic?" the chief asked.

"I'm not sure, but it was important to him."

"He mentioned Switzerland at one point" Diana added.

"Yes, you're right he did." Cooper agreed.

"What kind of clinic, I wonder?"

"Possibly a psychiatric clinic, sir. He has been treated by a psychiatrist, of course."

"So what did he want to tell you that was so damn important?" the chief asked.

"I'll tell you, sir, but I think I need that tea first."

"Of course."

* * * * *

"He wanted to tell me his side of the story" Cooper began after he'd sipped tea for a minute.

"He started with his university days in Paris when he met Jean Paul. He says he fell in love with him the minute he saw him."

He saw Catherine open her eyes wide in astonishment, but continued.

"He says he fell in love with him early on. He tried to talk to him, but he just told him to go away. He became desperate, and decided to make friends with his girlfriend Sophie, as one way of staying close to him. He succeeded there for a little while, but then she started to avoid him as well. At first she thought him funny, he said, but then after a while she seemed scared; I think Fox took some pleasure from that. At the same time he got to know Monique, who was a good friend of Sophie's, and Charles Edwards. After that he used to follow them just to see what they were doing. Fox told me he avoided Edwards as he didn't like him or trust him. He witnessed a violent argument between Edwards and Monique when he grabbed her by the throat. He said he thought Edwards was going to kill her. When later he found out they'd been involved in a car accident, and that his beloved Jean Paul was dead, that really devastated him for months. He told me he went to attend the funeral, but was told in no uncertain terms by his family that it was a private affair. He had to watch from a distance. At that point he only knew there'd been an accident; he had no idea that Edwards had caused it. He left the university shortly after that; it was being closed down anyway, apparently, because of the unrest. He was told Monique and Edwards had gone back to London. He didn't see Sophie Renard again for a long time because she had gone back to her parents' home. Fox stayed in Paris for a while because he didn't know what else to do. He then went back to the UK, staying with his brother Richard, who insisted he see his doctor once more. I suspect his brother had already spoken to the doctor, because shortly afterwards Fox was sent to a clinic. As I said, he didn't tell us what type of clinic, but I think a psychiatric clinic may be right. After a period there, he came back to the UK."

"How long was he away?" the chief asked.

"He didn't say, and he wasn't in the mood for taking questions. I tried one question but he became angry so I just let him tell me the story. When Robinson spoke to the psychiatrist he told him he was away for about a year."

"I can call his brother tomorrow sir, and ask," suggested Catherine.

"Good idea" the chief replied. "Carry on," he said to Cooper.

"When he eventually got back to the UK from the clinic he wanted to talk to Monique. He felt he needed some sort of closure with Jean Paul, and needed to know why the accident had happened. Monique was nowhere to be found. He thought she'd returned to France but then after some time he discovered she'd gone missing altogether. He put two and two together and suspected that Edwards had something to do with her disappearance. Fox was keen to emphasise that he didn't think Charles Edward's wife was innocent in this, either. Fox then said that after some years he found out – he didn't say how – that Angus was related to Isabelle Edwards, and eventually befriended him by taking regular walks on the heath. He also knew that Angus occasionally met Elizabeth Marsh on the heath, Tina's mother."

"Oh, I know Mrs Marsh" commented Diana, who had been sitting quietly, listening. "Tina disappeared many years ago."

"Exactly" agreed Cooper. "Angus told Fox that Mrs Marsh had lost a daughter and that she was convinced her daughter was buried on the Heath. It was then that Angus told Fox he had seen Monique being carried out by Charles and Isabelle Edwards, and that he had later overheard them talking about burying her on the heath."

"So he had seen them" the chief said. "Presumably that's why he made his little drawings."

"Yes, Fox mentioned those. He said he had been keen to send those to us as he knew we might understand what they meant. Anyway, Fox and Angus between them

317

agreed to spend evenings searching the heath for signs of any burials."

"Why evenings, sir?" Catherine asked.

"Fox said they had once been chased by a gang of youths who had accused them of peeping at girls, so they'd decided it was safer to search through undergrowth in the dark."

"I remember thinking I had seen someone on that dreadful evening I discovered Monique" Diana said. "Perhaps it was one of them."

"I agree, it probably was one of them. Either way, ever since then Fox has been desperate to get Charles Edwards arrested for murder."

"But he carried out at least one murder himself, possibly two if he killed Monica Gascoigne; what about those?" the chief asked.

"He mentioned the man. He said he'd been told – although he didn't say by whom – to kill him as he was a beggar and a prostitute. His words. That's when I asked my question about Monica that nearly got my throat cut. I asked him how many more, and where they were. When he'd calmed down, he said there was only the one and it didn't matter anyway. What matters, as he put it, is that we do our job and get on and arrest Charles for the murder of Monique and the others."

"Others?" the chief asked.

"Fox told me he had asked Angus to talk to Mrs Marsh to see if her daughter had ever had contact with Charles Edwards. Eventually Angus told him she hadn't wanted to talk about Edwards, but there was something there. He suggested we should try. I then asked him if there was anyone else he thought had been murdered. He then got up and said yes, but it was time for him to leave.

He then walked straight out, taking the dog with him. It's funny, I had the impression he was actually quite scared of Edwards. His actual comment was 'If you think I'm mad, I'm nothing compared to Charles. He has done more than I've done.' What exactly he meant I don't know."

Cooper paused to take another drink. Suddenly they heard a dog barking.

Diana leapt to her feet and ran with a surprising turn of speed to open the front door. Buster was standing there, fairly wet but otherwise no worse for his little adventure.

Several biscuits and a dry towel later he was asleep in his basket as if nothing had happened at all.

TWENTY

Cooper had lain in bed, unable to sleep after his encounter with Marcus Fox, until the small hours of the morning. He woke briefly as the alarm went off but then fell asleep again for another hour. He leapt out of bed as soon as he was realised how late it was.

Catherine had spoken to Richard Clarke and left a report on his desk of the conversation by the time he was at his desk. When he had poured his first coffee of the day he asked her to come up. She came in and sat in the new chair straight away. He smiled as she did so but said nothing.

"How are you this morning, sir?"

"I've felt better; I was awake most of the night and then I slept longer than I intended. I see you've spoken to Richard Clarke. Why don't you tell me what he said to save me reading through the report?"

"He confirms that Fox went to Nanterre University in nineteen sixty eight, and that he returned to the UK in the early part of nineteen seventy. He says that when his brother returned from Paris he seemed depressed and confused, so he persuaded him to see his doctor. Fox told the doctor he had been hearing voices, so he recommended Fox stay in a care home where he could get the treatment he needed. Clarke says he found a clinic in Switzerland which had a good reputation."

"So when did Fox go to this clinic, and how long was he there for?"

"He went at the beginning of July nineteen seventy. He was there for just a year. His brother said he came home the following summer."

"That ties to what the doctor told Mike Robinson. I assume Fox was not able to come back to the UK whilst he was in this clinic? He didn't take the occasional break at all?" Cooper asked.

"Clarke told me his brother was angry with him for sending him there, because he wasn't allowed to leave, and it took some time to regain his trust."

"Interesting."

"Do you still think Fox could have killed either Tina Marsh or Paulette Dijon?"

"Tina Marsh disappeared a month before he went to this clinic, so in theory he could have killed her, if indeed she's dead. He could definitely have killed Paulette Dijon; we don't know when she disappeared in reality. We know when she left the Browns' in Richmond, but that doesn't mean she was killed then, if at all. Right now I'm keeping an open mind."

"Is it possible Fox is just pointing the finger at Edwards, someone he clearly loathes, because he blames him for the death of the man he fell in love with?"

"We need to know a lot more about Charles Edwards before we can answer that one."

"And what about Fox? Where do we go from here?"

"We'll have to see if the nationwide alert for him yields any results. He could have gone anywhere. Did his brother offer anything there?"

"No, he said he would let me know if he heard from him, but he wasn't expecting him to call."

"I'm going to talk to the chief to see if we can get hold of a missing file, and I need to persuade him to approve a search of Edwards' house despite his reluctance; we can use the suspicious death of his wife as a reason for a warrant, although I'd be interested to see what else turns up."

An hour later Catherine was updating her files at her desk, writing up her notes of yesterday's conversation with Mrs Marsh. She came to the name of the owner of the house in Richmond, where her husband had often gone. She tapped the name into her computer, looked carefully at the screen and picked up the phone to call Cooper.

* * * * *

By late afternoon they were both on the way to Charles Edwards' home, Catherine driving; they were followed by a marked police car with two constables inside. Cooper rang the bell. Edwards let them in.

"I've been expecting you" he said.

Cooper and Catherine went inside, followed by the two constables, Edwards leading the way into his study at the back of the house.

"What made you say you were expecting us?" Cooper asked as they walked into his study.

"Well, you haven't questioned me too closely as yet about my wife's death, nor have I heard any more from you about making a statement on Monique's death. I presume that's what you want to talk to me about."

"At the moment sir, we are questioning a number of people who called to say they witnessed something on the day your wife died; however I'd like to give you the opportunity to tell the story from your side if you have something to say."

Edwards smiled. "I'm not a fool, inspector. I have already told you what happened, and I have nothing to add to that."

He pulled a document from his pocket and handed it to Edwards.

"This is a search warrant, Mr Edwards. We intend to search your property fully for evidence in connection with the death of your wife."

"Are you arresting me as well?"

"I want to carry out the search first, sir. If you will please wait outside with one of the constables whilst we carry it out, then that would be for the best."

"Very well, as you wish."

"Right," Cooper said once he had gone out, "we need to start a thorough search of this place. You go upstairs and search there, I'll start down here."

Putting on thin plastic gloves, he decided to start in the study and began to search through the drawers of the desk and cupboards. He wasn't quite sure what he was looking for, but he was looking for anything unusual. He put Edwards' laptop computer into a bag to be taken back to the police station, before heading down to the kitchen. The kitchen cupboards didn't yield much. He once again went through the hallway and into the drawing room. This had a couple of large comfortable sofas, a large television and bookcases full of books. Cooper spent some time looking at the books, but nothing seemed out of place.

He was beginning to feel a little frustrated when he heard Catherine call out to him. He walked back into the hallway to see her standing at the top of the stairs.

"I think you should see this, sir."

He walked up the stairs and followed Catherine into one of the bedrooms. She pointed inside a wardrobe; at the back was a large wooden chest.

"Inside there" she said.

He pulled open the lid to reveal a range of rubber outfits for women, a couple of whips, leather belts, handcuffs and several lengths of rope.

Cooper looked at Catherine; she was blushing. He smiled.

"They used to play games, obviously."

Catherine looked around the bedroom.

"Seems quite ordinary, otherwise."

He told her to keep looking and went back downstairs. As he walked through the hallway he noticed a small door under the stairs; he opened it, expecting to see a cleaning cupboard. It revealed a set of stairs, leading down. He looked for a light switch and turned on the light. There seemed to be some kind of cellar. Cooper went down the steps and found himself in a storage room, with racks of wine bottles on one side, and tools on the other. There were a range of metal cupboards; he opened them and they contained various tins of paint and a few brushes. He could see something at the back of the top shelf. He carefully moved a couple of paint tins out of the way and lifted down an old biscuit tin. It contained several letters, brown at the edges, and an address book. Cooper looked at the first letter; it was in French. He looked at the signature; he couldn't quite make it out.

Then he realised; it was 'Paulette'. The letter began "Cher Isabelle".

* * * * *

Two days later Cooper was sitting in the chief's office in Scotland Yard.

"So you've found pornographic images of young girls on Edwards' computer?"

"Yes, sir. The lab called me this morning and I went straight over there. Quite disgusting."

"And what has the pathologist said about his wife's death?"

"His wife was suffocated, sir. The only clue at the moment is a minute fragment of cotton between her teeth. They suspect it's from a towel or pillow put over her face to suffocate her."

"What else do we have on him?"

"We found a number of sex toys in his house, so he clearly enjoyed dominating girls and women. Fox told me he'd seen Edwards getting very angry with Monique, and we know from the Special Branch file about his inclination for sadistic sex with prostitutes. Thank you for getting the file on Edwards from Special Branch, by the way. There was quite a lot in it of interest."

"I had to pull a lot of bloody strings to get that. He was seen as a security threat, and as a potential minister they were quite concerned about him at the time, hence the Special Branch investigation. Nonetheless they were extremely sensitive about the file."

"But Special Branch leaked the story to the press at the time?"

"Probably, to stop him getting into a position of real power where he could have caused a lot of embarrassment. What else do we know?"

"Well sir, we know Paulette Dijon was writing to his wife at the time they were living in Richmond, and we know she left the Brown's at short notice. My theory is she was invited to stay there with them, possibly by Isabelle. After that she disappeared. Perhaps she died in that house. Then we turn to Tina Marsh. Her father, who we suspect was a paedophile, used to go to Richmond on a regular basis; he had some so-called golf buddies there, and they used to meet up and then have dinner, often until late. At one time he took Tina with him, after which she was very upset and refused to go again. One of the regular attendees was Charles Edwards. He could well have been there when Tina was taken along; whether in fact she met Edwards we don't know. We do know she was a happy child who suddenly became withdrawn and distrusted her father. If her father involved her in some kind of sex games then she would have resented him for the rest of her life."

"But she didn't say anything to her mother?"

"I wouldn't have told my mother, if I was, say, thirteen or fourteen, which is about the age she became withdrawn. Whether she said anything as she became older we don't know. Catherine's view is that her mother is not telling us everything, because she's blocking that from her memory. She's refusing to even think about it."

"But Edwards would have been quite young at that point in time?"

"If he was in the house in Richmond at the same time as Tina then he would have been about eighteen or nineteen. He was twenty four when Tina disappeared. She was nineteen. He was about to go off to Hong Kong to train as a barrister."

"And the house they met in belonged to Sir William Garner, the civil servant who had to resign after the police found explicit photos of children on his computer?"

"That's the one."

"When was that?"

"Sir William resigned in nineteen ninety three, although Tina's father died in nineteen eighty."

"So I can see the possible link from Edwards to those two disappearances, but Monica Gascoigne's blood was in Fox's boat."

"That's true, sir, but her name was also in Isabelle Edwards address book. There's a link between Edwards and Fox somehow, although what it is I don't yet understand."

"Why do you think that?"

"They both say they hardly met, and yet Fox went to a lot of trouble to get us to investigate Edwards. That may have been triggered by his seeking revenge for the death of his boyfriend all those years ago, but my gut feeling is there's something else we don't know."

"Any ideas what that might be?"

"Just a hunch right now. If I can get hold of Fox I've a few questions for him."

"Any progress in finding Fox?"

"Not yet. He'll turn up, one day. We're keeping an eye on his boat. My hunch is that he'll try to use it at some point."

"So the next step?"

"We keep looking for Fox of course, but I also want permission now to bring Edwards in. I also want forensics to search Edwards' house and garden. I want them to see if they can match the fibre found in his wife's mouth, and to see whether there's any evidence that any of those girls have been there. I'd also like permission to have the house in Richmond searched, and the garden, if necessary."

"The house of Sir William Garner?"

"No, Edwards' family house. The one Garner lived in may be later, if necessary."

"Do what you need to do. I'll clear it with the powers above; I think we have enough now to push this further. Any further finds at Fox's flat in Camden?"

"No, nothing apart from the forensic evidence of the one male. When I saw Fox he spoke about a tramp, as he called him. We know he was around sixty years old, and we're assuming he was a homeless man. Beyond that we may never know who he was unless he was reported missing, or Fox gives us a name. We're working on it, but we have very few leads so far."

* * * * *

Cooper was leaving for the evening when the duty sergeant called to him.

"We've just been told of the theft of a small sailing boat from a Devon marina, sir, and that the image of a man behaving suspiciously shortly before the theft on CCTV matches the description of Marcus Fox."

"Make sure an alert with a description of the yacht goes out to all marinas and harbours along the South Coast, please. Ask that the same alert goes out to the French as well. Give me a call if he's spotted, at any time."

"Will do, sir. Goodnight."

After another night of disturbed sleep, waiting for a call, it came just as he got to the police station the next morning.

He called Catherine to his office straight away.

"The stolen boat's been spotted. A coastguard has reported seeing it moored to a buoy, just outside of Salcombe in Devon. The local police and coastguard are mounting an operation right now to board the yacht. We should hear back in the next fifteen to twenty minutes."

Catherine sat down opposite him, then she suddenly stood up again.

"You've just reminded me of something, sir. I'll be back shortly."

With that she rushed out.

After another nervous ten minutes the phone rang. Cooper picked it up. It was the Devon police.

"We've arrested the man on board the yacht, inspector. He has confirmed he is Marcus Fox. He didn't resist arrest at all, in fact I'd say he was relieved to be caught."

"That's excellent. Thank everyone involved from me, please. We'll get back to you regarding arrangements."

He suddenly felt as if a burden had been lifted from his shoulders.

Five minutes later Catherine reappeared in his office.

"They've boarded the yacht," he said. "Fox was on board. They've arrested him. He didn't put up any resistance, apparently. Perhaps he's had enough."

"That's excellent, sir. Sorry I decided to rush off before. I suddenly remembered as we were sitting here that whilst we were searching Edwards' home I noticed a few books about sailing on his desk. I've just checked on the Lloyds register. Edwards owns a boat; it's moored at a marina in Chichester. I've just spoken to them; it's there right now."

"That's interesting, well done. So he has a boat as well. As it'll be forty eight hours before we see Fox, why don't you get back onto that Marina at Chichester and tell them we'll go there tomorrow? If Edwards has a yacht of some kind down there, I'd like to have a look around it."

* * * * *

Cooper and Catherine arrived at the marina in Chichester by mid morning the next day, having driven down from London. They pulled up and then walked past a number of large, sleek yachts and motor boats before getting to the marina office. They entered and introduced themselves, after which a young man with a straggly beard and long hair, tied back into a pony tail, showed them to the boat, which was a large, expensive looking motor yacht. He unlocked the main hatch and stepped aside to let them go down the few steps inside. Cooper thanked him, and told him they would return the key to the office when they had finished. He took the hint and left them to it.

The yacht was very sleek and expensively finished, with leather seating and dark wood panelling everywhere. As he began to search the cupboards, Catherine went straight to the chart table and pulled out the charts. After looking through them for a moment, she opened one chart fully and spread it out on the table in the middle of the main cabin.

"Have a look at this, sir."

"What am I looking at?"

"It's a chart of Portsmouth harbour, and these pencil markings are the skipper's notes of the course taken."

She looked at him.

"So he's sailed down to Portsmouth."

"That's where Marcus Fox kept his yacht. I wonder if he ever met him down there."

"It was also where Monica Gascoigne lived" Catherine added.

She went back to the chart table and looked inside once more. She pulled out a note book.

"This is the log book."

She searched back through the pages.

"It goes back to two thousand and five. Probably when the boat was new."

"Does it tell you if he's been to Portsmouth? I'd also like to know where the boat was eighteen months ago."

Catherine read through the entries, turning the pages carefully.

"Yes, it's been down there several times. And here it tells me the boat went to Portsmouth just about eighteen months ago as well, September two thousand and eight. It stayed there for two nights and then went to the Isle of Wight, before returning here."

Cooper looked thoughtful.

"It doesn't mention who was on board, I don't suppose?"

"No, it just lists the journeys made, and the engine hours."

"Pity. So we know the boat happened to be in Portsmouth at around the time that Monica Gascoigne disappeared; we know there are traces of her blood on Fox's boat which may also have been in Portsmouth at the time. We also know that Monica's name was in Isabelle Edwards' address book. What we don't know is who was on this boat at the time. Let's ask at the marina office to see if they can help us."

They put the chart and the logbook into a bag, and tidied everything else away before locking the boat and walking back down to the marina office.

"Do you by any chance keep a log of people coming and going from the marina?" Cooper asked the manager.

"No sir, not a record of people who come and go from here. Why do you ask?"

"Well I see the yacht made a journey down to Portsmouth at one point. I wondered if there was any way of knowing who was on board."

"Most boats will tell the coastguard when they set out, telling them where they are headed for and how many on board. They do that for safety reasons. Sometimes they tell us as well. Would you like me to check?"

"Yes please."

The manager went to a cupboard in his small office and pulled out a handwritten ledger.

"When was this voyage?"

"In September two thousand and eight" Catherine responded.

The manager leafed through pages.

"Yes we have a voyage recorded here. The vessel sailed at eight o'clock in the morning of the twelfth of September, with six people on board, heading for Portsmouth."

"Do you have any names at all?" Cooper asked.

"Only one name, which is the owner, Charles Edwards."

"So he was definitely on board?"

"Yes, he was definitely on board."

They thanked him and were about to leave when Catherine reached into her bag. She pulled out a photograph and showed it to the manager.

"Have you ever seen this man here?"

The manager looked at the photograph of Marcus Fox.

"I haven't seen him for a long time. He used to keep a boat here as well, but he moved it some years ago."

"Did he know Charles Edwards at all, do you think?"

"We have a club here that holds races during the summer months. Mr Edwards used to have a racing yacht. That gentleman used to act as crew occasionally. I can't remember his name, to be honest. He and his brother used to sail here."

Catherine looked at Cooper.

"His brother? Can you remember what he looked like?" she asked.

"Yes he was a very nice gentleman, probably early forties, quite tall, as was his brother. Really old school. Lived in the North of England somewhere, but he liked to come down here to sail for a couple of months every summer."

Catherine put the photograph of Fox back in her bag. They thanked him and left to drive back to London.

TWENTY ONE

Twenty four hours later Cooper and Catherine walked into the interview room in Camden; Marcus Fox and his solicitor were already sitting in there. He noted that Fox seemed very relaxed, much more than that evening at Diana Freedman's.

He switched on the tape recorder, noting the time and date, after which Fox confirmed his name and his address in Camden.

"We have found evidence of body parts in your garden and, in the drains below the property where you have lived for a number of years. What can you tell me about that?" Cooper began.

"I put him there. It was a long time ago; in about nineteen seventy five I think."

"Can you tell me his name?"

"No. I don't remember if I even asked; if I did I can't remember it."

"How did he die?"

"I killed him, when he was asleep, or to be more precise in a drunken stupor. He was a tramp, he was a drunk. Disgusting man."

"Why did you kill him?"

Fox shrugged his shoulders.

"He didn't deserve to live."

"Why didn't he deserve to live?"

"He was a tramp. He was worthless. He had no life in front of him. He would have died soon anyway."

"Why would he have died soon?"

"He was an alcoholic. He had slept on the streets for years. He wouldn't have lasted much longer."

"How did you meet him?"

"He was begging for money. I found him revolting."

"But you didn't just walk away, you spoke to him. Did you invite him to your house?"

"Yes, I invited him."

"What made you invite him?"

Fox shrugged his shoulders again.

"Because he didn't deserve to live."

"So you decided to kill him, then you invited him to your house?"

"Something like that, yes."

"How did you kill him?"

"I put a pillow over his face while he slept. He struggled a bit but he soon stopped moving."

"Then what did you do after you killed him?"

"I put him in the bath, and cut off his legs and arms. Then I buried him in the garden. Some parts obviously washed down the drains."

"Who else did you kill?"

"No-one. He was the only one."

"I now want to talk to you about what you know of the death of Monique Bertrand."

"Charles Edwards killed her."

"How do you know he killed her?"

"Because he is a violent man, who enjoys dominating women. She was threatening to tell his family just what he was. So he killed her."

"But how do you know all this?"

"I just know. That's how he is. I know him well."

"How did you come to know Charles Edwards?"

"We were at school together."

"You first met Charles Edwards at school. Is that when you fell in love with him?" Cooper asked.

Catherine looked at him, trying not to show her surprise.

Fox looked at his solicitor before speaking.

"Yes, I did love him. I met him when we were both at Harrow. He was one year above me. I worshipped him. At first he strung me along, but then he invited me to one of his parties. I was so shocked I ran away. After that he started to make fun of me and the other boys mocked me as well. He made my life hell."

"Did he love you?"

"No, he wasn't gay at all."

"Tell me about these parties."

"He used to boast that he was invited to parties where young girls were available. No-one believed him at the time except me. I knew he was telling the truth."

"How did you know he was telling the truth?"

"He invited me once, as I said. We went to a big house. I went into one room, but then I ran away quickly."

"When was this?"

"He had just left school, I was eighteen. So it must have been nineteen sixty five."

"Where was this house?"

"In Richmond."

"What was happening in the room? What did you see?"

"I saw a group of men standing around. They were all naked. A girl was on her back on the floor, somebody on top of her."

"And this was a young girl?"

"I think so. I looked quickly but then ran away. I was frightened."

"How old was the girl?"

"I don't know. Younger than me. Probably fourteen or fifteen, maybe a bit older, maybe a bit younger. I told you before that he's committed worse acts than me."

"Charles Edwards?"

"Yes."

"Was he in that room? Was he one of the men?"

"He took me there, then he went in and I followed. I took one look and ran, as I said."

"Was he naked as well?"

"Not when he went in, but he was starting to take his clothes off."

"Were the people on the floor having sex?"

"It looked like it."

"What was the girl doing? Was she angry, or frightened?"

"She was lying still. I got the impression she was asleep because she didn't move at all. Maybe she'd been drugged. I didn't look any more. I ran away. I was frightened."

"What did Edwards say when you saw him again."

"He threatened me. He said if I ever told anyone he would kill me. I think he meant it, so I have never told anyone. I didn't speak to him for a long time after that, but as I said he made me out to be a fool and everyone laughed at me."

"So why did you follow him to Nanterre?"

Fox looked at Cooper.

"Haven't you ever been in love? You can't just pretend they don't exist any more. I started at Cambridge but when I saw him, so close all the time but pretending I wasn't there, it made me ill. I wanted to be accepted, so when I saw that everyone was taking drugs, I did as well. I wanted to seem as cool as he did at the time, and I thought it would help me to cope. Someone told the college I had drugs in my room so I got caught and thrown out, but he of course didn't."

"Who told the college?"

"I don't know, but I guess it was him. No-one else knew. He sold them to me, after all."

"He sold the drugs to you?"

"Yes."

"So you did speak to him?"

"I approached him and asked him if he would get some cannabis for me. He later handed me a pack in exchange for cash. It was a business transaction. He wasn't friendly."

"What happened after that?"

"When he went to university in Paris then I decided to follow him there. I couldn't help it."

Fox paused for a drink of water. It sounded to Cooper as if he was close to tears.

"And that's when you met Jean Paul?"

"Yes."

"And you fell in love with him?"

"Yes."

"Tell me what happened there."

"I saw Jean Paul in the first few days I was there. He had such a lovely smile. I spoke to him and he was so kind, so helpful. I guess it was love at first sight. It didn't last of course, it never does. He turned against me after Charles became friends with him. After that I befriended Sophie for a while but she took a dislike to me as well."

"What happened after Jean Paul died?"

"I was devastated. He had helped me to get over Charles, and now he was gone. I tried to go to the funeral but some of the family members wouldn't let me into the church. Family only, they said. They were quite determined, so I watched from a distance."

"What did you feel for Charles Edwards then?"

"At the time, nothing. I knew they had been in an accident, that's all. It was only when I found about Monique that I started to hate him for what he'd done. Yet again he'd got away with a crime, like the drugs in university, and the young girls at school."

Cooper paused. Fox looked at the floor. He wasn't going to add more.

"When did you next see Edwards after Jean Paul died?"

"I didn't see him again until several years later. I spent some time in Switzerland; when I returned he had gone to live in Hong Kong. When I discovered that Monique Bertrand had disappeared I knew he had killed her."

"What made you think that?"

"I had seen them shout and scream at each other. I remember he once told me if his family found out about his parties then he would lose millions. I knew she was definitely dead after Angus told me he'd seen them carrying her away. He'd been staying with them at the time; he'd been awoken be shouting and had crept out to see what was happening. After that I wanted to find a way to have him convicted for killing her. He had got away with too many crimes. I needed to find a way to get him put in prison. It was about ten years ago that I found out he sailed a boat. I have always liked to sail, so I bought a small boat and kept it at the same marina that Charles used, which is down on the south coast. I sailed there regularly. My brother was interested in sailing as well and came down with me from time to time. After a while we decided to buy a larger boat together, and we used to sail together quite regularly after that. During that time we got to know Charles; he and my brother got on well together. At first Charles didn't seem to remember

341

me, but then after one day's sailing we got slightly drunk and I told him who I was."

"This was in Chichester?"

Fox looked at him. "Well done," he said, "yes it was Chichester."

"Did your brother know Charles Edwards before they went sailing together?"

"No, not as far as I know."

"Did your brother not go to Harrow as well?"

"Yes, he did. But he would have been a couple of years older than Edwards. I don't think they were friends at all. My brother told me he didn't remember him from school at all."

So what happened when you reminded Edwards of who you were?"

"He just laughed. He said he had almost forgotten about me, although I knew he was lying. I decided to keep close to him by being friendly; I soon discovered he hadn't lost his weakness for good looking young girls. One day I saw him take a girl on board his boat. I walked past about an hour later and she was sitting by the side, crying. She'd been badly beaten, she had a black eye. She was only a teenager, probably sixteen or seventeen. She left shortly afterwards and I didn't see her again. A little while later my brother Richard told me he wanted to sell our boat; he needed the money for some project he was doing. He's always pouring money into that bloody manor house he's so fond of. When we sold the boat I still wanted to sail, so I found a smaller one to buy. By then however I wanted to distance myself from Edwards, so I decided to sail somewhere different. Eventually I found a mooring for it down in Portsmouth."

"Did you see Charles Edwards after that?"

"Not for a while. Then one day I saw this large motor boat arriving in Portsmouth, and I saw him walking around the marina. He was there with a couple of friends. He had his wife with him as well as a young blonde girl."

"His wife was on the boat as well?"

"Yes, she sailed sometimes too."

"So when was this?"

"It was about eighteen months ago."

"What happened after that?"

"I saw where they had moored, so I went across to them in my dinghy to say hello. I wanted to know what he was up to, and wanted to let him know I'd seen him. He invited me on board. After a while the others left, and he asked me if I could do him a favour."

"What was that?"

"He asked if he could use my boat to entertain the girl. I knew what he meant. He couldn't do what he wanted on his own boat, with the others there too. I was reluctant but he had a way of wrapping me around his little finger, just like at school, so I agreed. I left and went for a walk. As I left I saw him, with the girl and his wife, climbing aboard my boat."

"Are you sure his wife was there too?"

"Yes, absolutely positive. When I got back they were nowhere to be seen and his boat had been moved, but I could tell my boat had been cleaned. I later found blood stains on the floor under the rug that they hadn't managed to get rid of."

"Did you see him or the girl after that?"

"He came to see me briefly before he left and apologised for the mess; he said they had had a bit of a fight, that was all. I saw his wife; she was unharmed, not a mark on her. The girl was nowhere to be seen. I asked him where she was, but he said she had taken fright and gone off to make her own way home. He made it quite clear that I wasn't to say anything about the little incident, as he called it, if I knew what was good for me. Several weeks later I saw a television appeal for a girl who was missing; it was the same girl, no doubt about it."

Cooper took several photographs out of his folder and laid them on the table in front of Fox.

"Was the girl any one of these?"

Fox looked at each of them for a few seconds, frowning as if trying to remember, and then pointed to one.

"Yes" he said finally. "Yes, that's her."

It was the photograph of Monica Gascoigne.

"Did you speak to the girl at all, or did Edwards tell you her name?"

"No, I don't know what she was called."

Cooper turned to Catherine. "Could you pass me that logbook, please?"

He turned to the entry they had looked at before.

"Do you know the date this all took place?" Cooper asked him.

"Yes. It was the fourteenth of September, two thousand and eight."

"Can you be certain about that?"

"Yes, because I'd bought a new dinghy the same day and I used it for the first time when I went over to speak to Charles. I was looking at the receipt the last time I used the boat, which was late last year, because the dinghy had been stolen and I had to send a copy of the receipt to the insurers."

Cooper showed him the logbook. "Does this date coincide with the event you just described?"

"It says he left Chichester a day earlier heading for Portsmouth. That makes sense."

"Now I'd like to ask what you know about the death of Isabelle Edwards."

"I know she was a wicked woman, who drowned in Hampstead Pond. Good riddance."

"Did you kill her?"

Fox looked at him.

"I thought she'd committed suicide. If she was murdered you'd better ask her husband who killed her."

"I'm asking you. Did you kill her?"

"I didn't like her. That doesn't mean I killed her."

"Are you denying you killed her?"

"As I said, you should ask her husband. I didn't like her."

Cooper decided he would leave that one for the moment as he was getting nowhere.

"One other question for you." He took out from his folder the drawing and the newspaper cutting with the word 'Monica' written on it. "Have you seen this before?"

"Yes. Angus wrote that on the newspaper. He was going to write 'Monique' but then I asked him to write 'Monica' to see if it triggered an investigation into Monica Gascoigne's death."

$$* * * * *$$

The next morning Cooper and Catherine arrived at the house in Notting Hill where Edwards lived. The forensic pathologist saw them and waved.

"Hello Fred, how are you this morning?" he said.

"Hello Sam. Well my back would be better if I didn't have to keep doing all this digging, but otherwise fine."

"So what have you found?"

"We've had a good look around the house. You asked us to look for anything that might link the house to a murder. We've found no signs of any blood spots at all, so nothing to report there. We have however matched the fibre we found in Isabelle Edwards mouth with one of the pillowcases covering a pillow in the principal bedroom. My report will say that it is most likely that she was suffocated whilst she was asleep on the bed, by a pillow placed over her face. That might prove tricky to sustain in court however, as it could be argued that she may have bitten on a pillowcase whilst she was asleep. It's unlikely in my view, but you need to be aware of that."

"Nothing to prove who might have done it, I don't suppose?"

"We have seen fingerprints of both him and her all over the bedroom, but that doesn't prove a thing of course. No-one else at all."

"Anything in the garden?"

"Well we took some soil samples from a number of areas without any real evidence of anything buried. Then by chance one of my men spoke to a neighbour as he was taking a coffee and a cigarette at the front. She mentioned to him that the Edwards' patio was only repaired recently, so we decided to lift a few stones to see what we could find. We did find something. Come and see."

They walked down to the back of the property, and stepped inside a white tent that had been erected over part of the garden. Fred pointed down to a section of ground where several paving stones had been moved aside. There were the remains of a black plastic dustbin liner that had been cut open, to reveal what was mainly a skeleton, with some flesh and hair still visible. Catherine looked at it. She became visibly pale. She turned to walk outside of the tent.

"It's the body of a young girl" the pathologist said to him.

"How long do you think the body has been here?"

"It's been in the ground for a substantial number of years, possibly thirty years or so. But it's been moved recently, which explains why it was under the newly renovated section of the patio."

"Thirty years? So nineteen eighty, then. That would tie to the time Paulette Dijon disappeared. However they were living in Richmond at that time, so it may be the body was moved from there to here."

"We'll take a sample of the soil from that site, and see if it matches the soil inside the bag. If it was moved from there, we'll soon know."

"I wondered if you'd find evidence of a more recent burial, of a girl who disappeared eighteen months ago. I think you need to keep looking; there may be more remains here. Let me know if you find anything else. And thanks."

At this point Catherine reappeared, still pale.

"Sorry about that, sir. I felt quite nauseated for a moment."

"Will you talk to the French police as soon as we're through here?" he asked her. "I want to see if we can get a DNA sample from a relative of Paulette Dijon, to see if we can match it to the remains here."

MARCH 2010

It was almost two weeks after they had found Paulette's remains, but little else had turned up.

Cooper was at home. He was reading through his notes on the case. He read one note, put it on the desk, but then picked it up and reread it. He sat back in his chair, looking at the ceiling, deep in thought. Then he picked up the phone and dialled a number.

"Hello mum, how are you?"

"Hello Sam, I'm feeling a bit under the weather. It's been raining most of today though, that always makes my bones ache."

"I have someone to see in the north tomorrow, so I'll pop in and see you. I won't be able to spend more than an hour with you though."

"It'll be lovely to see you, Sam. Do you want lunch?"

"Well, alright then. But nothing too heavy, mum. I'm putting on too much weight."

Cooper ended the call and then called Catherine.

"Hello Catherine, sorry to bother you at home. I've just had a hunch about something. I'll be out all day tomorrow."

"Anything I can help with, sir?"

"It's just a hunch. It may be a wasted journey. I'll let you know when I get back."

* * * * *

Cooper drove up the motorway the next morning and arrived at his mother's just before midday. He stayed for almost two hours and, as he had suspected, was given an enormous meal.

He then left to drive to a more rural part of Lancashire, a forty minute drive away. His satellite navigation took him to the gateway to the drive of a house, and he drove down it to the parking area by the door.

The door was opened by a woman.

"Could I speak to Mr Richard Clarke, please?"

He showed her his ID card and she showed him into the library, telling him to sit whilst she found Clarke. He looked at the shelves; some of the books were old, but many were in poor condition. He heard the door open behind him; he turned to see a man standing there, who was obviously a relative of Marcus Fox, there was such a similarity between the two.

"Hello Inspector. I had no idea you were planning to call by. I hope you didn't come all this way just to see me" Richard Clarke said.

"Not really, sir. I came here to speak to Tina Marsh."

Clarke stared at him for a moment; he then came into the room, closing the door behind him as he did so, and sat on one of the armchairs.

"How did you know?" he asked, after sitting for a moment.

"When my constable called at your brother's apartment and was attacked, she was actually enquiring after your cousin, James Clarke. We were told he sold the apartment shortly before Tina disappeared, and he moved up here. She came up here to be with him, didn't she?"

Clarke smiled, a kind of grimace, and shrugged his shoulders.

"Yes. They moved up here together. She needed to get away from her mother, so my cousin sold his flat and moved here. She joined him shortly after that."

"But he was drug addicted. He died a few years after that, in nineteen seventy four, I believe. What happened to Tina?"

"Why don't you ask her yourself? I'll get her to come in."

Clarke went out. He could hear a murmured conversation outside. Then Clarke walked back in, followed by an elegantly dressed woman.

"This is my wife, Tina," Clarke said.

* * * * *

It was a week later. Cooper and Catherine were sitting in the chief's office, discussing the case to send to the Crown prosecution service.

"So the remains in the garden are confirmed as those of Paulette Dijon, according to forensics?" the chief asked him.

Catherine was sitting by his side, several files of reports in front of her.

"Yes sir" Cooper answered. "We have only recovered her remains, there is no trace of anyone else so far, but we haven't finished digging the garden in Richmond yet."

"This is a shocking case. What did Edwards say?"

"He denied knowing Paulette Dijon at all at first, until we showed him the letter to his wife. Then he decided to remember, saying his wife met Paulette through an English class she had taken at one time; Paulette had been in the same class, and they had then become friends. He said she had lost touch with her after the course finished."

"So how does he explain her body in the garden?"

"He doesn't. He just says he has no idea what happened. He is blaming his wife" Cooper said.

"I'm sure he is. So what about Monica Gascoigne? He denies knowing anything about her as well?"

"That's correct, sir," Cooper confirmed. "We have Fox's statement that Edwards and his wife were with Monica Gascoigne just before she disappeared, plus forensic evidence that her blood was found on a boat that he is alleged to have been on."

"That case is a little thin, without anything else."

"I agree, sir. We have evidence from his log book that he sailed to Portsmouth where the assault is alleged to have taken place, but the rest relies on the word of a man who is himself charged with murder."

"We do though have enough evidence that Edwards was involved in the death of Monique Bertrand. The statement his wife made before her death implicates him quite clearly. I'm going to recommend therefore that we prosecute him for the murder of Paulette Dijon and the murder and illegal burial of Monique Bertrand. We'll see what the prosecutors say, but my view is that a jury would convict him of both murders, even if part depends on a statement by Fox. The other case we'll have to leave on file, pending new evidence coming to light as we continue to dig."

Catherine spoke up. "What about the death of his wife, sir?"

"Well again we have little evidence apart from the fibre in her mouth. Clearly she was suffocated, and probably by Edwards using the pillow, but we have no witnesses that saw him taking her body to the Heath, or saw anything suspicious. It may well have been that Edwards killed his wife, but can we get a jury to convict him? I think we should send the case to the prosecutor anyway; I think they may prefer to go for a conviction on the two easier cases and leave that on file."

"Ok sir," Cooper replied, "we'll get the file drawn up and sent off today. The file on Fox is ready as well."

"That's more straightforward as we have a signed statement confessing the murder of the man found in his garden. I've already spoken to the DPP about him. They think he'll plead insanity, and be sectioned to a secure hospital, but we charge him anyway and see what happens. Send both files over to them at the same time.

Well done, both of you. Difficult cases these, when they go back years."

* * * * *

As they left Scotland Yard to make their way back to Camden, Catherine spoke to Cooper.

"I told Mrs Marsh that her daughter had been in contact with us, as you agreed I could, sir. She was extremely upset to know that she's been alive all these years, as you would expect. I don't really understand why her daughter left home like that."

"Tina was clearly very bitter about her mother, even after all these years. She told me she had finally plucked up the courage to tell her mother about her father when she was seventeen, after years of suffering through her childhood in silence. Her mother point blank refused to listen, or to discuss it at all. It was as if she was simply closing her mind to any possibility of what her husband had done. After that she told me that, as far as she was concerned, her mother was dead. She didn't have a mother. She spent as little time at home as possible after that until she met someone she could trust. And she was absolutely adamant that we didn't let her mother know where she was, although I did get her to agree that we could tell her she was still alive. We could also tell her why she had gone away, if her mother asked. Did she ask why Tina had never been in touch?"

"No sir, she didn't. She didn't ask at all."

"Then I suspect she's known in her heart all along that Tina walked out on her, and was never going back, whatever she told us."

"So Tina was in love with James Clarke, but then married his cousin after he died?"

"Yes. She says Richard took care of her after he died and has been her angel, as she called him, these past forty years. They seemed very happy together" Cooper said.

"So you've solved that mystery, and hopefully we'll get some satisfaction for Paulette and for Monique."

He suddenly smiled, despite himself.

"Edwards told me he had a nickname for Monique; he used to call her lemon, apparently."

Catherine looked at him. "Why lemon?"

"Because she was sweet to look at but left a bitter taste. I think he quite hated her in the end, you know."

* * * * *

Cooper was driving home. He felt weary; he felt he should have done better for Monica Gascoigne, but without a body or other substantial evidence it was unlikely to be solved to everyone's satisfaction, especially a jury. Perhaps they would find the body soon. He wasn't sure about Isabelle Edwards; perhaps Edwards would be tried for her murder after all.

As it was still light he decided at the last minute to drive up to the Heath to take a walk. Somehow he wanted to go back to where this had all started and tell Monique that they had got him in the end, so she could rest easy.

He parked his car in the late spring sunshine, and walked along, enjoying the weak but still pleasant feel of the sun on his face, to the spot where they had found her. He stood for a while, quietly.

He turned and walked back to his car. He was about to get in when his phone rang. He answered it without checking who was calling.

"Hello, how are you?"

It was Melanie.

He paused, not sure what to think.

"I'm fine, thanks" he said, finally.

"Can we meet? I need to talk to you, if you'll let me."

"Well, I'm still feeling a bit bruised."

"I know; I made a dreadful mistake. I was taken in by my former boyfriend. I left him originally because he has a short temper and I was afraid of him. But he persuaded me that he would reform, and like a stupid little girl I believed him. Well he has started again, and last night he hit me."

"He hit you?"

"Nothing too bad, just a punch in the stomach. It didn't even hurt really; it was just the shock of it. Sam I've been a fool. I was very impatient with you; I should have tried to understand more, but I didn't try at all. I should at least like to meet you and see you again, even if we don't get back together again and can just be friends. I miss you a lot."

"What do you want me to do about this guy?"

"You don't need to do anything. I've told him I want him out of my life, this time for good. He was annoyed, but more with himself. I don't think I'll see him again."

"So you want to meet?"

"I understand if you say no, but I need someone to talk to. Please."

"When would you like to meet?"

"Are you free this evening? I've asked mum, she's offered to look after Lilly."

Cooper hesitated. He missed her and wanted her, he knew that much. What the hell, he thought.

"Ok. I'll pick you up at seven thirty."

* * * * *

Cooper went home. Before getting changed to go out he decided to empty the contents of his briefcase onto his desk to sort through them so he could start wrapping up the case.

He found a piece of paper, on which was a handwritten poem. It had been amongst the drawings and other papers at Fox's house in Camden. He had forgotten about it.

His is the most wondrous face.

Deep, dark are the pools for eyes that would,

Were he to gaze upon you,

Draw you in until you drowned,

Held helpless by his gaze.

His is the most wondrous face.

Heavenly is the glimpse of a smile that would,

Were he to smile your way,

Blind the heart for ever and a day,

No other smile will do.

His is the most wondrous face.

THE END

The 1st Detective Sam Cooper book:

Available from Amazon as a paperback or ebook

"A great new book from a great new author"

"Once I got into this I could not put it down"

"The pace is relentless, never rushed but enough to keep you wanting more. A real page turner."

"I couldn't stop reading till the end."

Printed in Great Britain
by Amazon.co.uk, Ltd.,
Marston Gate.